ANGEL 4

Lock Down Publications and Ca$h
Presents
ANGEL 4
A Novel by *Anthony Fields*

Lock Down Publications
P.O. Box 944
Stockbridge, Ga 30281

Visit our website @
www.lockdownpublications.com

Copyright 2022 Anthony Fields
ANGEL 4

First Edition October 2022
Printed in the United States of America

This is a work of fiction. Names, characters, places, and incidents either are products of the author's imagination or are used fictitiously. Any similarity to actual events or locales or persons, living or dead, is entirely coincidental.

Lock Down Publications
Like our page on Facebook: Lock Down Publications @
www.facebook.com/lockdownpublications.ldp
Cover design and layout by: **Dynasty Cover Me**
Book interior design by: **Shawn Walker**
Editor: **Kiera Northington**

Stay Connected with Us!

Text **LOCKDOWN** to 22828 to stay up-to-date
with new releases, sneak peaks, contests and
more...
Thank you.

Submission Guideline.

Submit the first three chapters of your completed manuscript to ldpsubmissions@gmail.com, subject line: Your book's title. The manuscript must be in a .doc file and sent as an attachment. Document should be in Times New Roman, double spaced and in size 12 font. Also, provide your synopsis and full contact information. If sending multiple submissions, they must each be in a separate email.

Have a story but no way to send it electronically? You can still submit to LDP/Ca$h Presents. Send in the first three chapters, written or typed, of your completed manuscript to:

LDP: Submissions Dept
P.O. Box 944
Stockbridge, Ga 30281

DO NOT send original manuscript. Must be a duplicate.

Provide your synopsis and a cover letter containing your full contact information.

Thanks for considering LDP and Ca$h Presents.

Dedication

This book is dedicated to one of my biggest supporters, and probably the oldest. To Mr. David Tucker, this one is for you. Eighty years old must be the new sixty. Thank you for always loving and supporting my books.

Acknowledgements

Gotta first say that all praise is due to Allah. Without him, none of this would be possible. I sit in the cell, wondering all the time, "Why me?" Why did I have to be the one that dudes got jealous of and put the ATF on. I can think of a hundred good men in the streets, living their lives and getting money. Some have surpassed the things I was able to accomplish. And yet, they remain free. Maybe it was the company I kept. Maybe I wasn't nice enough to people. Maybe I didn't help enough people on the streets who said, "Slim, you doing too much, too fast. You making the rest of these niggas out here look like they standing still. You gotta be careful, Slim, these niggas out here gone put the people on you."

I can hear another good man tell me, "Bruh, your name is ringing too much. Tone it down. It was bad enough when you first came home and copped the Yukon and Lexus, but now you got a BMW 760 and a Range Rover. And you only have been home a year. You are getting ready to go back to jail." And I never listened.

Thought I was God's gift to the world. I couldn't hear sincere advice because my mind was on other stuff. Stupid stuff like Jimmy Choo sneakers, Margielas, Louboutin red bottoms, Balenciaga's, Giuseppe's, Gucci, Louis Vuitton, Versace, Fendi, Dior. My mind was on all the wrong stuff. What belt to rock with what jeans and shoes. My mind was on the money.

I remember thinking what I was doing was nothing, and there were dudes doing what I was doing times a hundred, and nobody had put the feds on them. I looked around at all the dudes I knew that had G-Wagons, Porsche Panamera's and SUVs, Jaguar trucks, Maybachs, Bentleys, Rolls Royces and all the big stuff. They owned land, houses, businesses, cars and such, but they were twelve feet deep in the streets and free. Nobody had put the people on them. I have been back in prison for years and all of those same people are still in the streets free.

Makes me wonder who they knew, or what they knew that I didn't. Some days I get mad at my situation. Some days I get mad at myself for being so dumb. But no matter how I feel from day to day, I never complain. Never. I made the choices I made, so I gotta live with the results. I accept that. I'ma do this number day for day, ten toes down, holding my head up. Knowing I can survive whatever, despite some people's whispers. (They better stay whispers, because if I hear any disrespect, I'ma come and address it.)

I never dishonored myself, never gave up, never broke under pressure. I remain who I have always been. A cold-blooded animal, half-man, half-amazing. And I challenge niggas to produce one scintilla of proof saying otherwise. With that being said, I gotta acknowledge the woman I love with all my heart, despite our missteps and tribulations, LeShawn Maria Wilson. As mad as I get at you, I can't deny what my heart and soul feels for you. I love you.

To my daughter, Aniyah Fields, you are the epitome of everything I hold dear. You mean the world to me. Always have, always will. Keeps up the good work in life and strive to be one hundred times better than me. Then again, with you being months aways from being a college graduate, you already are a hundred times better than me. You are my only daughter, but you're my best friend. I love you.

To my son, Kevin Grover, slim, I'm proud to call you my son. Real talk. To my sister Toi, I love you, baby. With all my heart. Nobody loves me like you. Thank you for always being my support. I love you. Give everybody my love. To Pretina "T T" Brown, sister girl, whoever thought that when we met in 2016, you and my brother Junior would still be together, and that you would be closer to me than ninety-five percent of my real family? Well, you are, I love you more than you can ever imagine.

To my brother, Junior. You are my brother, slim. Not any of them other jokers that share my blood. You're the one, slim. My respect and love knows no bounds. To Poochie, I love you. Gotta say what's up to Angie Scott, I love you, Angie, thanks for all your help, love and support. To my brother from another mother, Delmont player. Love you, slim.

To Dawn Bradley, Tina Grover, Tamara Coates, Eva Lee (Ft. Worth, Texas), Nene Capri, Tontieta Virgil, Anett Snyder, Ikea Jones, Nacheshia Foxx and Cheri Johnson, thank you. To Angelo

Daniels, Quise, DC Twin, Big Mac, Poochie, Pudgey, Dulee, Tap, Marco, K. D., Mummy, Rico Thomas, Rock, Ransom, K. Boogie, Hov, CB (Richmond, VA), Skip (Parkland), Leonte Mack, Pat, Trey, Face, Twan (Big Paradise) and others.

To Cash and LDP, good looking. Last but not least, to the Baltimore Homie, Gutta Almighty AKA Dante Bailey (MMP). Ain't no bloods in DC, Homie! If I didn't call your name, blame my head and not my heart.

P. S. Oh, my bad to Jason Poole, Nate Welch, Eyone Williams, Rex (from 21st), Poo Poo son, Lil Rico, and Rashad Hough aka Huff the Great. And I can't forget Kenneth Hoffman (Live fast, die young).

You know what it is, DC. Stand up, Buckey Fields.

Now, let's get back to the story…

Chapter 1

Detective Mitch Bell

Washington, DC

The patrolmen who had arrested Kareemah El-Amin, walked out through a door near the lobby entrance to Fifth District Police Department, on Bladensburg Road in Northeast. He walked up to me like he'd known me forever, with a half-hug, fist bump embrace.

"I'm Officer Daniel Thomas, Detective. Follow me to the evidence room so you can get a peek at that gun Ms. El-Amin was carrying. Sorry it took so long for us to be able to set up this little meeting, but shit has been hectic. There has been a record number of killings all over the city, and the mayor had an all 'hands on deck' initiative in place. So, I'm just getting back to the station."

"No worries, Officer Thomas," I replied as we started walking. "I appreciate you taking the time out to do this." I was thinking he looked awfully young to be an active police officer. The man looked no older than seventeen.

He led me through a door and down a flight of stairs, that let out to a long hallway.

"I'm sure the gun was a forty-caliber weapon. I remember that from all the reports I wrote. I believe it was a Glock model. Remembered thinking it was too big a gun for a woman that size to carry. Ms. El-Amin is only like five-three and maybe a hundred and thirty pounds. Have you seen her before?"

"Only in pictures," I replied.

"Beautiful woman, man! Beautiful. Beau–ti–ful! Too beautiful to be as dangerous as people around here say she is. I guess that's why she's still sitting in jail."

That tidbit of info was definitely a surprise to me." She's still in jail?"

Officer Thomas stopped in his tracks and looked at me." Yeah, over at the CTF. Prosecutor asked for a seven-day hold and the judge granted it."

"Granted a hold, why?"

"Beats me." He started walking again. "Never saw that before. She wasn't on supervision. No pending charges. No detainers. No warrants anywhere. Nothing. Prosecutor wanted her head. Judge thought it was a good idea." We stopped suddenly at a door marked, Evidence Room. "This is it. C'mon."

Inside the evidence room, we stopped behind a counter. A large white guy in uniform eyed me suspiciously. I pulled out my detective shield and flashed it at him.

"Hey, Wojinousky," Officer Thomas said before opening the green logbook on the counter. He flipped to the page he needed and signed in. Then I did the same.

We walked through the double doors. There were gray metal shelves lined with evidence of all kinds of things. Drugs, guns, knives, keys, bats, everything. I followed Officer Thomas until he stopped where he knew the gun to be.

"Here it is," he said. "It's a beauty, but not as beautiful as its owner." It was black, boxy and rustic. "Impressive." Then my mind rushed to something Chris Diggs, the assistant medical examiner told me the night of two murders. I'd pointed at the slight difference in the two entry wound sizes on both victims.

"It's barely centimeters, but it's there. The woman was probably shot with a nine-millimeter or a thirty-eight. The male's entry wounds appear to be slightly bigger. I'd say he was killed with a forty-caliber..."

"Who searched the car, Officer Thomas?" I asked.

"My partner, Dillan Words. Why?" Officer Thomas replied.

"Because I'm wondering if there were any other guns in that car. A nine-millimeter, maybe. Or a thirty-eight revolver that might have been overlooked."

Officer Thomas shrugged his shoulders. "Maybe. But I'd doubt it. Now that I think about it, the Glock was found in the front seat in her purse. After it was found, neither one of us continued the search. I pretty much just arrested the woman and took her in."

"The car...what did you do with the car?"

"Got it towed. Didn't want to just leave it where it was. Dope fiends and crack heads would have had a field day with that car. A new model BMW 760LI. It's over at the impound lot on 4th and New York Avenue."

"Was the key left in the vehicle?"

"Naw, I put in in her purse."

"And where would that purse be now?" I asked.

"I saw no reason to hold it as evidence, even though it's where the gun was found. Since she's still detained and therefore has not claimed her personal property, it's still at the property depot in Southeast, 603 Shannon Place. By the red brick building behind the 'Big Chair' on MLK Jr. Avenue."

I jotted down everything Officer Thomas said. "Thanks for all your help. I really appreciate this."

"Don't mention it, Detective. Anytime."

***

The building on Shannon Place was easy to find. The entire building was staffed by only one uniformed officer at the entrance lobby. My detective shield gained me admittance to the building. A lie got me to the crates where the property bags were held. I found the bins marked with the letter E, quickly found the clear plastic bag with Kareemah's purse and other personal effects in it. I could see the BMW key fob. I blew on the seal and gently peeled it off. I went inside the bag and got the key fob, then pocketed it. I put the bag back after replacing the seal and left the building. My next destination, the impound lot on New York Avenue.

***

At the impound lot, I showed the attendant my credentials and was led to the BMW. As I approached the car, two doors automatically unlocked. It sensed the key fob in my pocket. The inside of the BMW was luxurious and spacious.

"Sure wish I could afford one of these babies," I said to myself. I started my search in the front of the car. Looked under the seats and checked the seat cushions. Then I made my way to the back. Checked every crack and crevice of the back seats but found nothing. The key fob had a button that opened the trunk, so I hit it next. There wasn't much inside the trunk, but a few articles of clothing and some shoes, a jacket and an umbrella.

I lifted the carpet in the trunk to reveal the spare tire and the tools to change the tires, there was nothing there. I closed the trunk and went back to the front of the BMW. The center console revealed nothing. Neither did the glove box or visors. I checked under the floor mats. Then just as I declared my search fruitless, I saw something. A white piece of paper was wedged in the driver's seat cushion and the tight space near the console. I pulled it out and unfolded it. It was a handwritten letter. I read it.

Dear Angel,

How does it feel to come home and find your mother dead? Not too good, huh? Well, now you know how I felt. I thought by killing your mother, we'd be even. Then I remembered you killed my father too. You were always one up on me. But not today. You killed my father and my mother. I killed your mother and took your daughter. Now we're even.

Honesty

My heart stopped. I couldn't believe what I was reading. Honesty Phillips and Kareemah El-Amin were engaged in a deadly game of tit for tat murder. Just as I had originally suspected, Honesty Phillips had made up the "intruder" story the night her mother was killed, she covered up the truth. The truth being she came home and found her mother dead, with Angel somewhere nearby. She'd pulled a gun and tried to kill Angel, but Angel had escaped. Almost a year later, Honesty went to Angel's mother's house and killed her.

After killing Naimah El-Amin, she took Angel's daughter and left the letter behind for Angel to find. Angel had been looking for

Honesty and her daughter when she'd run the red light, thereby getting herself arrested. Quickly, I pulled my notepad and thumbed through two pages. I found the address I needed, then raced back to my car. I got on the radio and called dispatch.

"Dispatch, send a car to 12114 Benedict Court in Kettering. Be on the lookout for a possible kidnapped child. Approximately nine or ten years of age. Child's name is unknown at this time. I'm on my way there now."

***

"What did you find at the house?" Sgt. Able Voss asked.

"Nothing," I replied, leaning back in the chair, rubbing my head. "Nobody was there. If Honesty Phillips really has the kid, she is smart enough to not keep her at her home."

"Thought about an Amber Alert?"

"Naw. I can't put out an alert for a child nobody said was missing. All I have is that confession."

Sgt. Voss read over the letter in his hand again. "I wouldn't exactly call this a confession, per se, but it is incriminating. That is, if you can prove Honesty Phillips wrote it. The night we interviewed her at her house, or the other time we talked to her, did you get her to sign anything?"

"Don't think I did. No."

"You gotta get something to compare this writing to." Sgt. Voss passed the letter back to me.

"Second thing, it would be hard to prove Kareemah El-Amin actually killed Tina Brown. We didn't find anything that linked her to that murder. Or anybody for that matter. We already knew she was thought to have killed Anthony Phillips, but she was never formally charged..."

"Only because the witness who accused her of the murder was poisoned."

"Either way, she was never charged. Remember Sean Jones?"

I nodded my head. "Of course, I remember Captain Jones."

"Well, Sean was the investigating detective on the Anthony Phillips murder case. He had no proof other than the confession of that poisoned witness—Fatima Muhammad. She confessed Kareemah El-Amin had killed Anthony Phillips, told her about it, and gave her some of the money taken from the apartments that night. I went back through the case files last year after I realized that Honesty Phillips, and Tina Brown the murder victim, were in fact, the same Tina Brown and her daughter Honesty Phillips from Sean's case. It's there in the file that Tina Brown was convinced that Kareemah El-Amin had killed Anthony Phillips and robbed him. After Muhammad was killed, the DA's office never pursued the case. That letter is good evidence but not strong enough to get a judge to sign a warrant to arrest. Maybe a search, but definitely not to arrest either one."

"I think you're right, but I still got to meet with Assistant District Attorney Dominique Oliver. Let's see what she says," I told Sgt. Voss.

Able Voss smiled a wicked smile. "Don't you mean *he*, buddy?"

***

ADA Oliver read the letter. "Where did you get this letter, Detective?"

"Out of the BMW Kareemah El-Amin was driving when she got arrested in DC. The vehicle was impounded."

"And your probable cause to search that vehicle was?"

I had no answer to the question, so I kept quiet.

"No answer, huh? Okay. Since you gave me a heads-up about what you had and what you want to do, I got proactive and did a little research. Kareemah El-Amin is at the Central Detention fac—no—excuse me, the Central Treatment Facility at 1901 E. Street in Southeast DC on a CPWL charge. She's being represented by Jarvis Alexander Williams. Ever heard of him, Detective?"

"Can't say that I have," I replied.

"Let me help you out then. Jarvis Alexander Williams happens to be one of the best criminal defense attorneys in the county. Hands down. He's the Johnny Cochran of our era. He'd have a field day in court with that letter. And especially how you obtained it. You're investigating a double murder that occurred at Kareemah El-Amin's mother's house in Clinton. One of the victims being her mother, Naimah El-Amin. The other is her uncle, Samir Nadir. You have DNA evidence that puts a daughter in her mother's house either before or after the murders. Said DNA evidence leads you to the District of Columbia, where Kareemah has been arrested for an illegal firearm. Without a warrant or any probable cause, you go to Fifth District's evidence room and inspect the firearm. You decide it might be one of the murder weapons used in your double murder in Maryland. Emphasis on Maryland. I'm on point, so far?"

"Spot on."

"Okay. You then leave the evidence room and travel to Shannon Place in Southeast DC, where you illegally unseal a sealed property bag and extract a key fob for Kareemah El-Amin impounded vehicle. You, a Prince George's County homicide detective, then travel to an impound lot in Northeast DC, for further investigation on a Maryland homicide…double homicide case. You illegally search a vehicle belonging to Kareemah El-Amin. There you find a letter, allegedly written by Honesty Phillips, who wrote to someone named 'Angel.'"

"Angel is the nickname in our system for Kareemah El-Amin."

"Irregardless of that fact, in said letter, Honesty Phillips admits to killing Angel's mother, who you believe is Naimah El-Amin, one of the victims in your case here in Maryland. She also admits to kidnapping a child, a felony offense…but nobody's reported a kidnapped child. For all you know, this child could be with relatives. The letter goes on to state that Honesty Phillips committed said crimes because she believes that Kareemah El-Amin—no—Angel, killed her mother, Tina Brown and her father, Anthony Phillips. And you expect a circuit judge here in the affluent, mostly white Prince George's County, to sign off on a warrant to either search the premises belonging to Kareemah El-Amin and Honesty Phillips, or arrest one or both of them?"

"Yeah, something like that," I admitted.

"Well, Detective, not only does all this sound a bit contrived, if you think that a judge will sign off on an arrest warrant with only what you have now, that makes you retarded. And borderline a criminal. Keep climbing this tree and you might find yourself getting arrested. If you come up with anything more concrete, come back. If not, stay away. You asked for an audience this late in the day and I gave you one. Now, if you'll excuse me, I gotta get home."

***

I sat in my car and thought about something. The letter from Honesty said nothing about her killing Angel's uncle. If Honesty had killed Samir Nadir, wouldn't she have said something about it in the letter? Whether she knew who he was or not, it would have been further bragging rights to mention him. As I pulled away from the district attorney's office, my cell phone vibrated, and a question came to mind. If Honesty hadn't killed Angel's uncle, that meant Angel must have. *Why would she do that?*

The caller on my cell phone was Sgt. Able Voss. "She didn't go for it, huh?" he asked.

"Naw, not even a little bit. Called me a criminal and retarded."

Able Voss laughed out loud. "Thought that might be the case–the criminal part, not the retard part. Just didn't say that to you. But nevertheless, I got some news you can use."

"News I can use? Definitely need that. What is it?"

"Something I forgot all about until after you left. That fucking letter made me think about it. I checked my desk and found something I meant to give you a long time ago, but you were knee deep in that Walker Mills Road massacre investigation."

"The Dante Stevenson case. Please don't remind me about that."

"There's a DVD I got. Video from a security camera across the street from Tina Brown's home, from the day of the murder."

My spirits lifted instantly. "Have you looked at the DVD?"

"Never got the chance to. James Haskett and Special Agent Sam Chaney both got ambushed and killed on Marlboro Pike. An agent and a P. G. cop getting killed always trumps everything else. Come back to the station and we'll check it out together. See what's on it."

"I'm on my way, Sarge. I'm on my way."

***

"Van is parked here. Across the street. Tina Brown pulls into her driveway at 6:09 pm. She exits the Mercedes Benz SUV, briefcase in hand. Purse slung across her body, straps on her shoulders. She enters the house a minute later and enters the front door. The driver of the van gets out at 6:14 p.m. Balloons in hand and approaches the front door though the front gate. Can't see a face at all. Balloons in the way. The person with the balloons either knocks or rings a doorbell. Minutes later, the front door opens and the person with the balloons enter the house. then nothing. The person never comes out again."

"The person holding the balloons never left," Sgt. Voss said. "Until..."

"Fast forward to thirty minutes later. A dark colored SUV pulled into the driveway behind the Lexus sedan, next to the Mercedes SUV. A woman gets out...that would be Honesty Phillips. She looks at the side of the house it appears, then goes back to her vehicle. She goes to the Benz SUV and looks into the window. Then she walks back to her vehicle...Appears to be the Cadillac truck that was there when we arrived. Honesty gets back inside the Caddy truck..."

"She's getting the gun."

"Maybe. Maybe not. Honesty gets out of the Caddy truck and walks to the back of the house. Out of the view of the camera. But if you look closely, minutes later, a light comes on in the back of the house, then…"

"You see what appears to be flashes of light. Gun fired," Sgt. Able Voss surmised.

"Guess that's the shootout Honesty told us about. We saw the bullet holes in the wall. Look at what happens next. The person who delivered the balloons exits the house," I said.

"And is still holding the balloons."

"But why? Why not leave the balloons? Just exits through the front door and walks across the street. Then starts to run a little eventually."

"He or she must've heard the police sirens."

I leaned forward in my seat and stared at the TV monitor. "And if the person had just killed Tina Brown and shot it out with Honesty, why doesn't Honesty pursue the killer? The person holding the balloons couldn't have engaged in a shootout with the balloons in hand. So, he or she must've picked them up on the way out the door. And again, where was Honesty then?"

"Good questions, no answers. The person with the balloon just gets in the car and pulls off. And at no time is that person's face visible."

"The only person who knows who that person was is Honesty Phillips. If we question her again, she's not going to admit Kareemah El-Amin was there in that house. Let alone killed her mother."

"She only admits that in her letter to Angel," Sgt. Able Voss said and sighed. "From here, I can think of two things that need to be done. You interview Honesty Phillips again and confront her with this DVD. Maybe she breaks and tells us everything."

"She won't. She wants to kill Kareemah herself."

"Interview her anyway but leave out the letter. And second, we need to find out who owns Cheek 2 Cheek Balloons, the name printed on the side of that van. The license plates appear to be DC plates."

"I see that. I'll get in touch with someone at the DC Department of Consumer and Regulatory Affairs to find out who owns

Cheek 2 Cheek Balloons.   Then I'll set up an interview with Honesty Phillips and at the very least get her to write something, so I can see if her handwriting matches the writing in the letter."

"Sounds good to me, Mitch.   I love it," Sgt.   Voss said dismissively.

I gathered the DVD and the letter from Honesty and left the room.

Chapter 2

Keith "Killa" Dunn

East Orange, NJ

The two 30-mg Percocet I took had my body in a relaxed state. I laid my head back on the headrest and reclined my seat. The windows on the Audi R8 were tinted triple black, even the star light pole and the night sky couldn't penetrate the car. With my eyes closed, I thought about the two bags of money in the backseat. The second bag filled with the fifty-thousand dollars Najee had made me, Rah Rah, Tye, Goo and Shottie split after he killed BeBe, who the fifty racks had belonged to.

I replayed the moment my partner Brian "BeBe" Bullock had died and it bother me to no end. Images of him going back and forth with Najee, then Najee shooting him wouldn't leave my head. His mutilated corpse that I helped to move from the house later haunted me without pause. I thought about the people I helped to kill as they either walked to or left the masjids. Innocent people that had not wronged me.

Again, I thought about the money in the bag. The blood money I had accepted. The most money I had ever had at one time in my life. As bad as I felt about BeBe, I felt even worse about the fact that I never told Najee he was wrong. No matter what BeBe had said wrong, nothing said out of his mouth warranted what happened to him. I allowed a lone tear to escape my eye. I felt bad for the life that was taken from me. I felt bad about the lives I had taken. I felt bad about the secrets I held.

Once the lone tear rolled down my cheek, I wiped at the wet residual of that one tear. It was gone. Just like BeBe. Just like the innocent Muslim lives I'd taken. Gone like parts of my sanity. I felt cold. I felt alone. I felt like a coward. Suddenly, headlights got my attention. I watched India's gold Mercedes Benz CLS 330 park in a space not far from me. My phone rang next. I never answered the call. I didn't have to. Instead, I exited the Audi and walked to the motel room, but not before taking a blow of dope.

***

"Is it bad that/ I never made love/ no, I never did it/ but I sure know how to fuck/ I'll be a bad girl/ I'll prove it to you/ I can't promise that I'll be good to you/ cause I had some issues/ I won't admit/ I'm not hiding it/ but at least I can admit that I be bad to you/ I'll be good in bed/ but I'll be bad to you/ baby, I never made love/ I never did it/ but, I sure know how to fuck/ Is it bad that I never made love/ I never did it, but I sure know how to fuck—"

India sang the Wale and Tiara Thomas song, "Bad," in my ear as she kissed my neck. India's lips were soft on my skin. Her hand was inside my pants, gripping my erection. I laid back and let her take my mind off all the things that wouldn't leave my mind.

My eyes focused on India's pretty face. Her glossy lips, her chinky green eyes that locked on mine as she moved down my body and freed my dick from the confines of my Rockstar jeans. The next thing I felt was her warm mouth on me. Her tongue had me enthralled. I wanted to close my eyes and let India's head go, take me away like Calgon, but watching her do her thing turned me on more. It was more intense. I watch India's hands move, her nails painted red with glitter adorning the thumb, her neck rotated as if on a swivel, her lips and tongue in sync, leaving me coated with saliva.

My toes curled in my Timberland field boots. I couldn't think of a better feeling. India's head was exactly what I needed to excise my demons. Her hair was layered and dyed red. It whipped around like the tail of the horse it used to belong to. She twisted, stroked, spit, deep throated, swiped, kissed, licked and sucked me into submission. My hands tapped the bed. My moans filled the silence loudly. Seconds later, I erupted. India never stopped sucking.

***

I walked back into the room with one of the duffles of money. I opened the bag to reveal bundles of bills.

"Where the fuck you get all that money from, Keith?" India asked, eyes as large as cupcakes.

"None of your fucking business," I said as I counted out twenty thousand in cash. "That's your problem now, you ask too many fucking questions."

India smacked her lips. "I'm getting sick and tired of your funky ass attitude, nigga. Whoever ruffled your feathers—"

"Shut the fuck up, India. That's why I keep my dick in your mouth. Because you are always talking!"

"I asked you two questions earlier. What was all that burgundy-looking shit on your jeans? 'Cause the shit looks like blood. What did you do all day that got you copping an attitude with me? I ain't done shit to your ass. And as far as you keeping your dick in my mouth—"

I tossed the twenty thousand dollars to India, which quieted her mouth instantly.

"I thought that would shut you the fuck up. That's the money you need to have surgery—"

"The reassignment surgery is twenty grand, Keith—"

"That's twenty grand. I promised you I'd pay for the surgery. There's the money."

"Oh, my gawd—-thank you, baby," India cooed. Then she found her purse and put the money in it. "But I still need money to get to the Philippines—"

"The Philippines? Fuck you tryna go there for?" I asked.

"That's where they do the surgery. They are the best at it," India replied.

"I thought it was Brazil."

"Brazil is where I went and got my ass done at. And my titties. When I schedule the surgery, it's gonna take about a week to receive it. From what I hear, it's cheap to stay over there for a week, but I'ma need money for room, food, you know—expenses."

I went back into the bag and counted out ten more thousand dollars. Then passed that to India. "Here. That's ten more. That should cover all that shit. Air fare there and back, and all that other shit. When you gon schedule the surgery?"

"For as soon as possible. In the next coming weeks, if I can."

"After the surgery, how long it's gone be before I can fuck you?"

"In my ass…as soon as I get back. In the new pussy, I don't know. But it should be fun. You breakin me in and all that. Can't wait, boo."

I zipped the duffle back up and slung it over my shoulder. "Yeah, me too. I'm about to hit the candlelight joint for all my friends. I'll get up with you when I leave there or either tomorrow."

"Okay, boo." India put her coat on. "Hit me up."

***

As the trunk slammed shut, I felt something being pressed into the back of my head. I closed my eyes thinking my time had come, and all my past sins and come back to finish me. I knew what I felt was the barrel of a gun. I knew I'd hear a brief explosion and then nothing. In a strange way, I welcomed it. Then as sudden as it touched me, the gun barrel was removed.

"Don't turn around, Killa," a familiar voice said.

"I thought men talked face-to-face," I said.

"Whoever said you were a man? If you were a man, you wouldn't be fucking a tranny. Or is that what men do now? Huh? Is that what men do?"

"Fuck you, Amir!" I said through clenched teeth. "Who are you to judge me?"

"I'm a man who's not fucking with a chick with a dick. That's who I am. And don't ask me later how I know what that monster is. Because I know everything about you, Killa. Everything."

"You don't know shit about me, Amir."

"Oh, is that so?" Amir hissed. "I know you are a piece of shit. I know you are a traitor. And that you've been betraying your friends for months. I know you are fucked up mentally, thinking you're still a man when you're fuckin' another man, no matter how much like a woman he looks. And most importantly, I know where you are at all times. Times like now. Think about that, booty lover. How do you think I knew where you were tonight?"

I had no response for Amir's tirade. He was my uncle, who just happened to have a gun to my head.

"I know all about you, Killa. More than you'll ever know. But here's a question fo you. Do you want Najee to know what I know? What would Najee do if he knew you told us everything? What would Gunz do if he knew you are the one that gave us all the addresses where their families lived? That it was you who told us when and where to get Yasir? And how he was the one who'd know where Salimah was? Answer that, Killa? What would they do? Najee and Gunz?"

"They'd kill me," I admitted with conviction.

"Do you want them to find that out, plus your other secrets?"

"No."

"I can't hear you, Killa. Say that again," Amir said.

"I said, no."

"That's what I thought. Now, we're getting somewhere. You're on your way to the candlelight vigil at Brick Towers, right?"

"Yeah."

"Najee's gonna be there, right?"

"I think so, yeah."

"All I need you to do is call me and tell me what he's wearing and where he is at any one moment. I'll do the rest. Can you do that for me, Killa?" Amir asked me.

"Yeah," I replied.

"I can't hear you. What?"

"You heard what the fuck I said, yo."

"Say it anyway, muthafucka! Can you do it?"

"I'll do it, yo! What the fuck? I'll do it."

"You talk real tough for a gay guy. One more question before you leave. Was that Najee and your friends who killed the Muslims earlier today? I guessed it was, but I wanna be sure."

"It was us. Me, Najee, Gunz, Tye—"

"When all of this is done, you gone have a to atone for your sins, nephew."

After saying that, the night got quiet. I looked behind me and Amir was gone.

***

The towers looked like a Summer Jam concert. There were cars parked everywhere. People all over the place. I parked my car on Springhill and got out. I zipped my Canadian Goose bubble all the way up to my chin to ward off the chill. Dudes from all over Newark had showed up to remember Hasan, Yasir, Salimah and all the other people that had died. I shook hands and gave out a pound all the way to the entrance of building 715. As soon as I walked in the building, I saw Gunz, Tye, and Rah Rah. I embraced them all.

"Where Najee at, yo?" I asked Gunz.

"He's around here somewhere, son," Gunz replied and went back to talking to Ikea Jones, Wayne Foo Foo's daughter.

"Who got the loud?" Rah Rah asked me.

I shrugged my shoulders. "You tell me. I need an eighth."

"Come on, let's go and find Shotgun. I knew he was holding, yo."

I left with Rah Rah in search of Shotgun. But who I really needed to find was Najee.

Chapter 3

Najee

Brick Towers Projects

Leaving one of the apartments in 715, I bumped into a woman as I left.

"Excuse me, baby girl," I apologized.

"Don't trip. Hey, Najee," the woman said.   It was Aminah.

"Aminah, what's good, yo?"

"I'm good, Najee, but I'm sick about Salimah.   I'm sorry this happened to her.   That was my girl right there."

I didn't want the mood to be too somber between us, so I steered the conversation elsewhere.   "You look good, Aminah.   Real good."

Aminah gave herself the once-over and smiled.   "Boy, these Drena jeans are old as shit.   My shirt you can't see and I'm glad you can't.   And my coat is cool.   This is a Moncler my cousin Angel brought me the last time she was here.   You still talk to her, right?"

"Let me see your shirt?" I said.

"Why do you wanna see my shirt?"

"Because of what you just said about it."

"It's an old shirt.   A little too tight—but it's cool," Aminah said.

"Let me see it," I said forcefully.

Aminah unzipped her coat.   She had on a button-up shirt that was snug around her ample breasts.

"I like your shirt," I told Aminah, then reached out and touched it.   While her eyes followed my finger, I circled on her nipples. She made no move to stop me.   I stopped circling and pushed on the nipple.   "I *really* like this shirt."

Aminah's eyes met mine, I grabbed her hand and led her away.

***

"Damn! Oh...my...gawd...Najee! Shit!"

"Your pussy good as shit!"

"Fuck this pussy, Najee!"

I gripped Aminah's waist and pounded into her like a man possessed. Her apple-bottom ass turned me on as I looked down at it and watched it jiggle with every collision of my body and hers. The bottom of the stairwell smelled like straight piss, but I was somewhat immune to it. I hoped Aminah was as well. At our feet, trash littered the ground. Aminah's hands were wrapped around her ankles, her boots were untied. Her jeans were gathered at her calves, her panties black cotton with white hearts all over them. Aminah's coat and shirt rose over the small of her back and I rubbed her there as I thrusted inside her, assaulting her wetness.

"A-a-aw–shit—a-a-aw-w–da-m-m-n!"

"You like this dick, Aminah?" I asked.

"Y-e-e-s-s-s! Ye-s-s-s-!" she stammered.

"Can I cum in this wet pussy?"

"Y-e-s-s-s, p-pl-e-e-a-a-s-s-e!"

"You gon tell Angel you gave me this pussy?"

"N-n-o-o-o-no...I'm-m-m not!"

I believed Aminah when she said she wouldn't tell Angel. There was no way Angel could ever know. I wouldn't tell, either. So, I kept fucking her cousin. But thoughts of Angel took over my head as I pounded Aminah. In my mind, she became Angel. We were fucking. Just as I had Aminah bent over, I had done Angel the same way on too many occasions to count.

Images of us outside on the playground, in the woods, on the beach, at the car, on balconies, in my studio near the control boards, in the stores, in our offices, everywhere came to mind. Up until now, I hadn't even thought about fucking. My grief had disguised my need for pussy. Maybe it was the weed. Maybe it was the two cups of Gray Goose I'd had. I looked down and saw Aminah's pussy juices covering my dick as it went in and out of her.

"I'ma—I'ma—I'ma bout to cum! I'm about to cum!" Aminah moaned.

"Cum on this dick! Cum on me!"

Aminah's pussy tightened and clinched me in its embrace. She moved herself back onto me and held herself there. She grinded herself on the length of me while moaning the entire time. By the time I moved out of her again, thick, white nut formed at the base of my dick and coated my pubic hair. After seeing that, it didn't take long for me to follow suit. I came hard and heavy inside Aminah.

***

I pulled the New Jersey Nets throwback cap down low over my unruly curls. I promised myself a haircut when things calmed down. My eyes found Aminah as she mingled into the crowd. The Mango OG filled my lungs after inhaling the blunt. I almost coughed up a lung. Gunz eyed me and nodded his head. I nodded back. People were spread out all over the back area behind 715. Candles were being lit suddenly, Music blasted from speakers strategically placed in and around the back courtyard.

Hundreds of doves were released from boxes. The doves flew straight in the sky, away from the grief and heartache that blanketed the project buildings. I strained my eyes to follow just one of the doves' flight trajectory as it ascended, but the weed and liquor prevented it. Then the birds were gone. Just like the friends and family we'd all just lost. A song came on and changed the mood of the large crowd. The women all went crazy. It was my sister's favorite song....

"Y'all haters corny with all that illuminati mess/paparazzi catch my fly and my cocky fresh/ I'm so reckless when I rock my Givenchy dress/ I'm so possessive, so I rock his Roc necklace/my daddy Alabama, my ma Louisiana/you mix that Negro with that Creole/make a Texas bamma...."

Under the lights attached to the buildings and all the street lights, the neighborhood women lined up and danced if they were on stage with Beyoncé. They mouthed the lyrics, word for word.

I allowed myself a brief moment to smile.   I remembered Salimah, Capri and Aminah in her living room doing the same thing.

"Okay ladies, let's get in formation/okay ladies, now let's get in formation/prove to me you got some coordination/I slay/ slay trick or you'll get eliminated/when he fuck me good, I take his ass to Red Lobster/I slay/if he hit it right I might take him for a ride on my chopper/drop him off at the mall, let him buy some J's, let him shop up/ I might get your song played on the radio station/I might get your song played on the radio station/just might be a black Bill Gates in the making—"

"Cause I slay," I repeated after Beyonce and suddenly felt gay as shit, I hit the weed again and laughed at myself.

"Ayo, Najee!" a voice called out, getting my attention.   I turned and saw three men approaching me.   One of them was my man Tye, but still I unzipped my coat to reveal the brand-new FN 57 handgun that shot 223 AK bullets.

"Fam," Tye said and pointed at the two dudes with him.   "This is my man Brazo I was telling you about, from Grafton Avenue. And this is his young pup, Red Hot." I eyed both men suspiciously and simply nodded my head.

Brazo was equal to me in height.   His skin was the color of coffee.   He had a razor cut that crossed his nose and headed down to his lip.   Two red tattooed teardrops stained his face.   A red Gucci skully was pulled down on his head.   "What's good, blood?"

"I'm good, son. How you?" I replied.

"I'm hurtin' bad, yo.   My man getting Peter rolled like that has me fucked up.   Has my whole hood fucked up, and we gon do what we gotta do to make his name live forever.   I heard a lot of good things about you out here in these streets, so it's a pleasure to meet you, blood.   Just sorry we had to meet under these circumstances."

"Likewise, yo.   Likewise."

"I didn't know your sister that good, but big bruh fucked with her tough.   He brought her through on a couple of occasions.   She was *brazy*, but *bool*. Because of Drama, that made her blood sacred to Brim.   We been riding and we gon keep riding for both of them,

blood.   That's on the set.   Just wanted you to hear that from me.
Because my word is iron."

"Respect, yo…. did Tye fill y'all in on who it was that killed
Limah, Yasir and Drama?" I asked Brazo.

"He did and I'm glad that he pulled our coats to that.   Never
suspected Muslims did that.   Didn't even know the Ocks get down
like that.   Thought their shit was all about peace and prayer.   But
now I know different.   And I'm about to light a fire under the Ocks.
We thought that either them 'Sex, Money, Murder' niggas did that
shit or the Grape Street Crip crabs did that. We thought Drama was
the target.   Fucked us up when we heard Salimah was the target
the whole time.

I still can't believe that shit, blood.   We done hit both gangs
on every front since we found out Drama was touched.   We at them
niggas tops in all the prisons across the state.   Top Max, Trenton,
Rahway, Northern State.   We been fucking all the county jails up.
Shit been hectic for a nigga, yo.   In Irvington, Patterson, Camden,
Elizabeth, Hillside—the Brims been rippin' shit up.   Hours ago, I
had to redirect niggas.   Put niggas down with the fact that the Ocks
are food on the plate now.   That nigga Muhammad Shadeen—"

"Muhammad Shahid is his name," I interjected.   "But he's
mine, yo.   I'ma kill everybody he loves *and* him.   I put that on
Limah's soul. . .   I never met Drama, but I heard son was *live*. If
Limah fucked with him, then so did I.   Give your men my condolences on his loss."

"They already know.   But listen, I did some research before
coming this way and I found out the Ocks got a deli on Orange
Street and North 7th called Coney Island.   They got another spot
over on Avon near 20th Street.   And a halal sandwich spot on 18th
and Columbia.   We on their ass first thing tomorrow.   I promise
you the—"

Gunshots rang out suddenly.   Automatic assault rifle gunfire
could be heard over the sound of music.   People ran in all directions
to get away.   I pulled my gun and scanned the area in search of the
people firing the shots.

"Naj…get low!" Tye screamed.   "Get low!"

Ignoring Tye completely, I spotted three men dressed in dark clothes firing indiscriminately into the crowds that were running away. I became furious. The weed and drink took over me.

I took off running, but not away from the gun men. I ran at them. Firing the FN as I went. Screams left my mouth and were drowned by the music that still played. I was on a mission, I felt possessed. The three gunmen started to recede. As I watched, one of the three men fell. I kept running and firing my gun. I could hear other guns blazing near me. Handgun and semi-auto gunfire. Then I was close. I slowed my gait and walked over to the man who had fallen. I stood over him and looked into his eyes. He was hit bad. Blood soaked through the jacket he wore over a jellabiya. A thin line of blood escaped his mouth. That told me his wounds were fatal. His time on earth almost at an end.

"Assalamu Alaikum," I said to the fallen man.

"Walaikum As Salaam," he said feebly.

"Dying out here in the cold alone is a horrible death, Ock. But I can help you. Save your life. I just need to know two things. Did Muhammad Shahid send you?"

The man shook his head. "It was Aziz."

"Aziz?" I repeated.

The doomed man nodded.

"Next question. Who told you I'd be here? Who's the leak in my squad?"

The man tried to speak but his words came out gargled. . He was choking on his own blood. His eyes grew large. He was starting to panic. I pointed to the ground and fired. His suffering was over.

***

"For those of you who have just tuned in, let me recap. We are live at the scene of a candlelight vigil that turned into a massacre. Here at the Brick Towers housing project, hundreds of people were celebrating the lives of several people killed in the city over the last few days, when gunmen opened fire on the crowds. The images you are seeing on your TV screen does not give life to the horrific reality of what we at *Action News Nine* have witnessed. Newark Police are all over the place here, along with EMS personnel. Sources close to the scene here, tell us at *Action News* that the death toll is at ten dead and rising. There are scenes of people injured as well..."

I watched the news inside my homie Jayquan's apartment. But I didn't need to see the broadcast to know what had happened in my hood that night. I was a couple of feet away from a window where I could see the carnage and mayhem left in the courtyard behind 715. If my eyes deceived me, my ears couldn't. The screams that pierced the thin walls emanating from next door chilled me to the bone. One of the families next door had lost a loved one in the Brick Towers massacre, as it was being called. The female cries and screams told the story of pain and hurt. I leaned against the wall and prayed for quiet and serenity. But there was none to be found.

Gunz sat across the room on a broken radiator. The look on his face spoke words our silence couldn't say. Tye laid on the ragged carpet near the couch. His attention on his phone. Rah Rah and Jayquan rounded up our band of misfits.

The FN handgun in my waist got heavy, despite its empty clip. "Tye, did you holla at your man Brazo? See if they are good?"

"Yeah, I did," Tye replied without looking at me." When the shooting started, they got low, but eventually tried to return fire at the niggas that were shooting. I still can't believe them niggas...the shooters, got away. Niggas never come in the towers and make hits like that and escape. Never."

"You preachin' to the choir on that one."

"Yo," Jayquan added, "when you ran at them niggas blazin your hammer, son, I thought about that nigga Kurt Russell in that movie *Tombstone* where he played Wyatt Earp. In that scene where he started screaming and ran at the niggas he was beefin with. That shit was wild, yo. Your shit bugged out, Naj."

Before I could respond, my phone vibrated in my coat pocket. I pulled the phone out. The caller was Carlos Trinidad. "Yo what's good, Pops?

"Pops, huh? I can get used to the sound of that. Listen, I got some info for you. I just got it. Are you ready for it?" Carlos asked.

"Am I ready for it? Does a bear shit in the woods? Them niggas came for my head, yo. About an hour ago. Killed a rack of people in my hood on some reckless shit. As a matter of fact, I need you to check on something for me. See if Shahid has someone in his organization named Aziz. I'm checking—"

"Whoa...Najee! Slow down. Let me give you what I have and let's go from there. Muhammad Shahid wasn't always Muhammad. He was born fifty-two years ago and named Melvin Proctor. He was born and raised in Newburgh, New York. He still has family there. And property. I'ma text you all that info in a minute—"

"I need that. I need that."

"Well, everything I got, you'll have in minutes, but let me finish. I have to answer what you just asked me.... about a guy named Aziz.

Muhammad Farid Shahid is the boss of his organization, but the man who takes care of everything, the everyday running of it, is named Aziz Navid. Aziz Navid is the strength behind the organization. He's a few years younger than Muhammad Shahid, but they both hail from Newburgh—"

"Newburgh?"

"Yeah. Piece of shit small city. Nothing's there but crime, gangs, a community college and a high murder rate. Aziz Navid's family still lives in Newburgh too. If Muhammad Shahid sent men to kill Salimah, best believe Aziz either handled it personally or he orchestrated the hit. Navid is the person that absolutely has to die once you kill Shahid. You can't leave him at your back."

"I need everything you have on both of them, yo. As soon as—"

"I'm texting it now. And as soon as I got a line on Shahid and Aziz directly, I'm sending you that, too."

"I appreciate you, Pops. Word is bond," I told Carlos.

"I already know. Just do me a favor and stay safe, would ya?"

"You got my word on that."

"And one more thing, kid. I told you the story of what happened with me and your mother. She left me, not the other way around. If I could have found you sooner, I'd have been in your life. And like you say, that's facts. But that's neither here nor there. What I'm trying to say is, you are my son. My blood. We're practically twins and that means something to me.

"I know what it's like to face off against your enemies. Wanting to and needing to vanquish them. So, I'ma stay on the sideline and let you handle your business as a man, I have to, although, I don't like it. But if you should need me anyway, Najee please don't hesitate to swallow your pride and call for me. I'll be by your side in a New York minute."

"That's good to know and believe me, I appreciate you saying it, but I'm good. Trust me. I'm good. All I need you to do is keep feeding me that info. Does what you just sent include info on Shahid's properties?"

"The ones in Newburgh, yeah. I'm still looking for everything else."

"Again, thanks a lot, yo. You a real nigga...I gotta respect you on a lot of levels. And you're my father. So, my love for you is without question. Let me go, before I get mushy, yo. Shahid's men just got at me...I need to respond. I'm holla back when I come back from Newburgh."

"Aight, son. Ditto on the love. Later."

The call ended and I felt a lot better. The text messages from Carlos came through. I opened them and read them. I smiled.

"Baby boy," Gunz called out. "Tell me, what's good. So that I can smile too. And what's in Newburgh?"

"Muhammad Shahid's family is in Newburgh. That's why I'm smiling. Get a couple whips gassed up. It looks like we're going to Newburgh. I'll fill you in on everything once we get there."

"Newburgh?" Tye said, befuddled, "Fuck is Newburgh at?"
"Google it," I told him. "Stupid ass, nigga. Google it."

***

"Ayo, Gunz, you remember that time we went on that move and got bricks from Joe Dirt and Tobias Mitchell?"
Gunz thought for a minute. "The house on Chancellor Avenue?"
I nodded.
"You remember how we got into the house?"
Gunz smiled. "I remember exactly how we got in. We were dressed up like ATF agents."
"Still got the jackets, hats and fake badges?"
"Of course, I do. You never get rid of shit like that."
"What about the lights we put on our dashboards?" I asked.
"In the garage somewhere, but I'm sure I got em," Gunz replied.
"Good. Go and get that shit. We gon need it in Newburgh."

Chapter 4

Benito

Our Lady Queen of Peace

Washington, DC

The rain started to come down pretty good, despite the sun being out. It was after ten in the morning and the skies were light blue, despite the one dark cloud that spawned rain on one section of the city. Stepping out of the car, I pulled my jacket over my head to ward off the rain and ran up the steps that led to the church entrance.

Inside the Catholic church, I removed my jacket completely and shook it out. Organs played softly as I could hear the priest at the front of the church give the benediction for Little Manuel Vasquez. The teenager had been killed weeks ago, inside the cafe on 14th Street. Killed by Najee Bashir and his friend Gunz. I walked slowly down the aisle towards the casket that held the fifteen-year-old lifeless shell, thinking of Carlos and the man that had put Little Manuel in the casket. Carlos' son.

Little Manuel's father had been a good and loyal soldier of the Trinidad organization, up until he'd lost his life in the war with Armand Rueles Jr. several years ago. A war that proved costly and deadly, but had to be fought because Armand Rueles Jr. could not forget Carlos and I had killed his father, mother and siblings almost thirty years earlier. Before Emmanuel Vasquez's death, I had promised him if anything had happened to him, we would always take care of his son, Manuel. A promise I had failed to keep.

I had given Manuel the job at Mamacita's to keep him close to the organization. I never knew the decision I'd made a few years before would lead to his demise. On the way down the long aisle, I locked eyes with other men in the pews attending the funeral. Men who were a part of our organization. Men with accusing eyes, questioning eyes. They hadn't been told the man responsible for Manuel, and other associates and friends' deaths, was now off limits to them. I couldn't bring myself to tell them that. To tell them their enemy was discovered to be their leader's long-lost son. I don't believe they would accept that reality.

It could only stir up anarchy and civil war in the organization and there was no time for that now. I shuffled past Manuel's casket, stared down at the body devoid of life and let a tear fall. He was a good kid. One who didn't deserve the fate life had dealt him. Although his remaining family would be well taken care of, to me it still wouldn't be enough. The diminutive teenager who had been small in height, had been large in life and I would see to it he'd never be forgotten. I pulled a single rose from a bouquet near the casket and placed it on Little Manuel's chest, then I kissed his fore-head. It was hard, cold.

Not far from the casket, Little Manuel's family sat in the front pew. Every one of them was crying. I walked down to his mother, Lucinda, and embraced her. In her ear, I whispered, "Your son did not die in vain. His killers will be dealt with. You have my word on that." With a simple nod of her head, Lucinda Vasquez accepted my words. I then turned and walked back down the aisle.

At the exit doors, I stopped and turned around one last time be-fore leaving. I thought about the other funerals I had been to in the last few weeks. Funerals for Robert Aguilar, Javier Mijores, Ortego Fuentes and Marth Pealto-Ruiz. Four good men who'd also lost their lives inside Mamacita's Cafe. I thought about all the people associated with our organization, who'd died in the last three weeks, the organization I helped to build, piece by piece.

From the very beginning, images of Mama Caesar, the old woman who ran Salazar's restaurant came to mind. I thought about Mareya Garcia. Beautiful, young Mareya. Blown to bits inside Salazar's restaurant with scores of other people. I'd flown to Mex-ico to attend a memorial for the young woman.

What was left of Mareya had to be shipped to the family in a small pine box. Her memorial at a tiny church in Guadalajara was a sad affair. I thought about the bag of money I'd given her family. But no amount of money would ever suffice to take away the look of pure grief in her mother's eyes. A mother who had toiled all of her life to send her youngest daughter to an American college, in hopes of building a better life for herself and her family.   It was her dream to bring her family to America.   A dream now deferred forever.

Other dead people came to mind then.   Vito Margues, Jesus Lazaedo, Diego Campos, Dario Morales and Ivan Castro, Phillipe Guzman and Pepe Suares.   All killed on a drive-by shooting. Thoughts of the dead brought back thoughts of the living.   The two men responsible for all the faces of dead people I'd seen, were still alive.   Those two men were supposed to be dead.   Could have been dead.   Both have been in my clutches.   Both spared.   I couldn't believe the hand of cards life had dealt me.

I couldn't believe the twisted humor of it all.   I could see the celestial being in the heavens laughing at us.   At me.   Therein lies the dilemma I faced.   How could I mete out the justice the blood of the dead called out for, without going against my closest and oldest friend?   How could Carlos not understand, after all we've been through together, son or no son, Najee Bashir had to die? How could there be no reprisal or the many lives he'd unjustly taken? If it was my son who'd committed such acts, his life would be Carlos' to take.   No questions asked.

I turned and left the church through the double doors I'd entered through.   The first thing I noticed was the rain had stopped. Maybe that was a sign of good things to come.   I walked casually to the Jaguar as an old tune popped in my head.   One from my youth.   I started to whistle.   Enrique opened the back door of the Jaguar for me.   His eyes met mine and said things his mouth didn't, couldn't.   I nodded while whistling to signal I understood and climbed into the backseat.   As the car pulled away from the curb on Ridge Road, I vowed to myself the next funeral I went to would be for either Najee or Gunz.

As soon as the Jaguar entered the gates, I saw cars lined the driveway of the big house. All of them except one looked familiar. At the entrance to the house, I was met by one of the housekeepers, Hilda, a European beauty. I handed her my jacket. "Send the jacket out to the dry cleaners, Hilda.   Where is Carlos?"

"Mr. Trinidad is his study, Mr. Alvarez, with his guest," Hilda replied, her accent thick with foreign ancestry.

I climbed the stairs and entered the study unannounced.   All eyes upon me.

"Benito, I'm glad you're here. I need you to record this or write it down.   Your choice," Carlos said.   "Latesha, you remember Benito, right?"

"How could I ever forget Benito?" Latesha Garrison stated.

I smiled at that, then pulled out my phone to record whatever was said.

"Okay, good.   Start over for me, so Benito can get everything you just said."

"Honesty Shanee Phillips was born in 1991. She's twenty-three years old, with a birthday coming up in May. Her mother, Tina Brown, was killed last May inside her home.   That case remains unsolved.   Her father, Anthony Phillips, is also deceased. Honesty is a graduate of Howard University but has no job on file.   Her address is listed as 12114 Benedict Court in Kettering, Maryland. Checked the Maryland DMV computers, she was listed as the owner of a black 2002 Cadillac Escalade."

"The Caddy truck she was driving the day she shot Angel," Carlos said almost to himself.   "It belonged to her father, Tony."

"Relatives on both sides of the family," Latesha continued, "but only a few who live here in DC.   Her father's mother is Portia Phillips.   Sixty-five years old.   Works at a school on 20th Place in Northeast. Charles Young Elementary.   She lives nearby on 16th and Gale Street, 1521 Gale. Red brick, two-story house.   Drives a late model, Lincoln Continental. Tina Brown's mother is Desiree Brown.   No job that I could find.   Lives in a house that's paid for on 3317 Fort Davis Drive in Southeast, DC. Three-story, brown brick, colonial-style house.

"There's one aunt.   Wanda Marie Brown.   Wanda has five children, age three to fifteen. Lives in a project apartment on Chesapeake Street in Southeast.   724 Chesapeake.   Works at a Family Dollar store in Eastover Shopping Center.   I also found out some more stuff on Mr. Muhammad Shahid, aka Melvin Proctor—"

"Excuse me, Latesha," Carlos interjected and turned to face me. "Benito, you remember Tony Bills, right?"

I nodded my head.

"Honesty Phillips is Tony's daughter. She knows Angel killed her father and her mother. Recently, she went to Angel's mother's house in Clinton, Maryland and killed her…"

"She killed Angel's mother? Honesty?" I asked, perplexed.

"Yeah, she killed Angel's mother and took off with Angel's daughter, my daughter. I have never met this little girl, my daughter and I would like to, as soon as possible. I need you to get her back from Honesty for me. That is, if she still lives. In which case if she's dead, I will kill every person Latesha just named—including Honesty—personally. But if my daughter lives…and I think she does, I need her with me now. Send men to every address Latesha has for Honesty and her family.

"Make sure the entire family understands their lives are in the balance and if I don't have my daughter in the next twenty-four to forty-eight hours, a person will die every day until my daughter is returned unharmed. Do whatever you must to make them understand how serious I am. Once you've located Honesty, and / or my daughter, call me immediately."

No other words needed to be said. With all the info recorded on my cell phone, I left the study. Then the house.

Anthony Fields

Chapter 5

Detective Mitch Bell

Records from the DC Department of Consumers and Regulatory Affairs revealed Cheek 2 Cheek Balloons was owned and operated by a thirty-eight-year-old woman named Jenelle Kearney, who ran the business from her home in Southeast, Washington DC, 1417 Howard Road. The black Ford Econoline van with the Cheek 2 Cheek logo on it was parked across from the house on Howard Road.

In front of the house, a burgundy Kia Sorrento and a forest green Honda Accord were parked outside. I pulled behind the Kia SUV and parked. Inside the front yard was an off-road dirt bike chained to the fence that surrounded the property. I walked up to the front door, opened the screen door and knocked.

The door was answered by a teenage male dressed in a Nike jogger suit and Nike flip flops. His dreads hung loosely down his back. He eyed me suspiciously. "What's up?"

"I need to speak to Jenelle Kearney, if I can," I told the teen.

"And you are?"

I pulled my credentials and showed them to the teen. "Detective Mitch Bell."

The teen eyed me from head to toe, then sneered and said, "Aye, Cheeks, twelve at the door. '' Then he turned and walked away. I could hear him say, "Fucking hate cops."

"Twelve?" a female voice said in the distance. "Fuck is that?" Seconds later, a beautiful, voluptuous and light-complexioned woman, with blonde dreads and hazel eyes appeared at the door. She gave me the suspicious head to toe look, just like the teen had moments ago. I could see the resemblance in them. The teen was her brother. "Yes, can I help you?"

"Jenelle Kearney?"

The woman nodded her head.

I flashed my badge again. "Ms. Kearney, I'm investigating a crime in the state of Maryland and unfortunately, your van may have been involved in that crime. I—"

"My van? My work van? How the fuck was my work van involved?"

"If you give me a chance, I'll explain that to you. Can I come in for a few minutes or do we do this right here?" When the woman hesitated, I added, "Or, I can get a subpoena to confiscate the van, and a warrant that will force you to talk to me. The choice is completely up to you. I'm not saying you committed a crime. Just that your van may have been used while a crime was being committed."

Jenelle Kearney reluctantly stepped aside. "You might as well come in and get this over, without subpoenas and warrants, I'd like to do that. Come in."

The smell of marijuana hit me as soon as I walked into the house, the smell of chicken cooking overpowered it, but not much. The living room was lavish, but untidy.

"You gotta excuse my house," Jenelle Kearney said. "Wasn't expecting any company today. Please sit."

I sat down on a leather loveseat but remained quiet as the woman walked around, picking things up from the floor and off the furniture.

"Lil man, come get all this shit outta my living room!" Jenelle screamed suddenly.

The teenaged dude that answered the door appeared immediately and grabbed all the clothes, bags and other items from Jenelle. Then he disappeared just as quick. "Whatever it was, I didn't do it!" he called out from another part of the house.

Jenelle Kearney was dressed in a Juicy Couture suit that hugged her curves. Her small feet were bare, her pretty toes polished a light orange color. She sat on the couch across from me, her eyes bore into mine.

"According to the DC DCRA records, you've owned and operated Cheek 2 Cheek Balloons for about five years now, right?"

"Yeah. I also own an online boutique, and event planner business and I promote parties all over the DMV. I'm an influencer of the culture. Everything I do is completely legit."

"Whoa…my investigation does not involve any of your businesses, Ms. Kearney. Just the van parked outside. How many employees does your balloon business have?"

"None. I subcontract work when it's available, to family members and friends. The balloon business isn't profitable to retain a full-time employee. The van is used for all of my business!"

"Have you ever loaned the van out?"

"Don't think so, why?"

"Was it ever stolen last year?"

"Stolen? No, never stolen."

"Ms. Kearney, there is only one Cheek 2 Cheek Balloons registered to do business in the DMV area—"

"There better be only one,'' Jenelle Kearney replied smugly.

"Your business is registered as an LLC, with sole proprietorship. And according to the DC Department of Motor Vehicles, that black 2010 Ford Econoline cargo van outside, with the Cheek 2 Cheek logo emblazoned across it belongs to you, Jenelle Kearney."

"Okay, so?"

"So?" I pulled out my laptop and powered it up. The DVD footage was already queued up. I turned the laptop around for Jenelle to see. She got up off the couch and got closer to my laptop screen. She watched the footage in silence. "Does the van in that video look familiar to you?"

"It looks like my van. It has my logo on it— yeah, that's my van—but when…?

"The video you've watching was taken from a home security system on a house across the street from the one in the video. The footage is from May of last year. The twenty-third. I can see the person driving the car enough to know it's not you making that delivery."

"Yeah, that's definitely not me.I would remember that day. Is this the crime you've been talking about?" Jenelle asked me.

"Yes. A woman was killed in that house, either before or after that balloon delivery was made and I need to identify who that person is in the video. I need to talk to him or her as soon as possible. So, again, I ask, did you lend the van out, was it stolen, or can you tell me who that person is who made that delivery on the twenty-third of May?"

Confusion crossed Jenelle Kearney's face, then that expression was replaced by one of trepidation and fear. I thought about Angel's reputation for cold blooded murder and wondered if that was the source of Jenelle Kearney's fear.

"I-um-um...I'm not sure who that is."

It was time to step up my assault on the woman's mental. "Jenelle—I hope you don't mind me calling you by your first name, but listen to me. When I tell you that I don't want you or your business caught up in any of this, I mean that. You are a business-woman. A young, black entrepreneur. I applaud that. Encourage it. Love to see beautiful, black sisters doing their thing in small business. And from what I can see, it appears you've been doing well for yourself. Don't throw everything away trying to protect someone. Someone who, if my hunch is correct, was involved in the murder...they obviously care nothing for you to do something so evil while using your van. You are not testifying against anyone. I'm not implicating you..."

"You can't implicate me in shit!" Jenelle exclaimed. "I don't know nothing about no murder or had anything to do with no mur-der!"

"Never said you did, Jenelle. But I need to know who you let drive your van and delivered those balloons on May twenty-third of last year. If you refuse to tell me, then you'll be forcing my hand. I'll have to assume you know something about this crime and start interfering with your life. I don't want to do that. So, just tell me who that is in the video driving your van, delivering your company balloons."

Jenelle appeared deep in thought. "You said a woman was killed in that house the balloons were delivered to?"

I nodded. "Tina Brown. A forty-year-old mother of one. Do you know her?"

"No, don't think I do"

"Who did you give the van to that day, Jenelle?".

"I let a friend of mine use the van," Jenelle answered meekly.

"Was that friend a male or female, Jenelle?" I pressed.

"Female."

"What's your friend's name? Who was it?"

"Angel. I gave the van to my girlfriend, Angel."

"Kareemah El-Amin?"

Jenelle Kearney nodded her head, then closed her eyes.

***

Outside in the car, I couldn't suppress my smile. I had that old chilly feeling I always got when my luck was about to change. The first person I called was D. A. Dominique Oliver.

"Detective Bell—"

"Please, can you call me Mitch?"

"Mitch, you do know today is Saturday, right?" Oliver asked.

"I do and I'm sorry to bother you, but…"

"Some of us public servants cherish our days off."

"I'm sorry, Dom, really I am, but I got a lot I need for you to know, to see. I have a DVD that contains video footage from a house across—"

"Detective…Mitch, I don't care if you have a DVD with footage of Michael Jackson rising from the dead in a real-life *Thriller* video. It's the weekend. My office is closed. I'm at home."

"Enjoy the rest of your weekend. I'll call you on Monday."

"Thank you, Mitch. Goodbye." The call ended.

A little disheartened, I called Sgt. Voss and told him about my meeting with Jenelle Kearney.

"Way to go, Mitch. I knew you could do great things. Keep up the good work and close the case. You might have my job by next year," Able Voss said.

"If I close both of these cases soon, I might have your job this year, Sarge."

"And I'd gladly give it to you, Mitch. Keep me posted."

My next call went to Christopher Diggs, the AME for Prince George's County. "Chris, I already know it's the weekend. Did I disturb you?"

"Actually no, Mitch. I'm working, but not busy. What do you need?"

"Did you do that postmortem on the male vic from the house in Clinton?"

"Samir Nadir? Yes. Did it yesterday. Why?" Chris asked.

"The bullet. I need info on the bullets. Was it in fact a forty cal?"

"My bad, Mitch. Meant to call you yesterday and confirm that. Yes, it was a forty-caliber bullet, Hydra-Shok, deformed but recognizable. The female victim, Naimah El-Amin was killed with a nine-millimeter bullet, not a .38 or .380 like we first suspected."

"I'ma need that forty bullet, Chris. Got a possible suspect detained in DC. Caught with a Glock .40 the night of the murders. I need to see if the ballistics match."

"No problem, Mitch. The bullets are in my office. You can pick them up at any time."

"Is now too soon?"

"Not at all. You're in luck. I said I was working. I'm at the office now. I'll be here until about five p.m., stop by."

"I'm on my way now, Chris. Thanks, buddy."

"Don't mention it. See you soon."

***

I sat outside the medical examiner's office and fingered the bag with the forty-caliber bullet fragments inside it. If the bullets in the bag matched ballistics with the gun Angel was caught with, the murder case against her would grow exponentially. It wasn't a slam dunk by any stretch of the imagination, but worse prosecutors than Dom Oliver had secured convictions with weaker evidence at trial. Thinking about Angel, the .40 caliber gun and the bullet fragments in my hand, brought my mind back to two things. Honesty Phillips herself and the letter that I had, which I believe she'd written. I pulled the letter out and read it again. Still couldn't believe the implications of what it meant. I decided then it was time to talk to Honesty again. And to get a handwriting sample from her.

I wanted to see if I could poke holes in her story about the evening her mother was killed. Once confronted with the video footage from that event, I needed to see if she'd break and admit Angel was indeed the person delivering the balloons and death. Wanted to see if she'd confess to killing Angel's mother. On my phone were text messages from Sgt. Able Voss. He had succeeded where I'd failed. He was able to get a phone number for Honesty Phillips. I found the number and dialed it.

A woman answered the third ring. "Hello?"

"Honesty Phillips?"

"Speaking."

"Honesty, hi. This is Detective Mitchell Bell. Remember me?" I asked.

"I remember you, Detective. You're the black one," Honesty replied.

"Right. Well, Honesty, I'm gonna need to talk to you again. I need to show you something we just discovered in your mother's case. I know it's the weekend, so I won't bother you now, but do you think you can come to the station early this week? Preferably Monday?"

"In like two days, Monday?"

"Yep. This Monday coming up."

"I guess so. It's important, right?"

"Very."

"Well, I'll be there, Detective. What time?"

"One o'clock, Honesty. Is that good for you?"

"One o'clock is fine."

"Thank you, Honesty. Goodbye." I ended the call and smiled. That chilly feeling washed over me again.

Chapter 6

Angel

"Take that shit up, Bay. Ain't no such word as 'COXA.' Get that shit up."

"Angel, are you challenging it? If so, go to the dictionary right there. If not, gimme my forty-two points."

"Forty-two? How is that forty-two points?"

"It's forty-two points because the 'X' is on the double-letter square, so that's sixteen right here. The 'C' is three points. That's nineteen. The *O* is one and the *A* is one. That's twenty-one right there…"

"Aight, I get that part, but…"

"And the word is on a double-word square too—that doubles the twenty-one. Forty-two points. Gimme my money or challenge the word. "What are you going to do?"

I looked at the score of the Scrabble game and saw she was close. If I gave Bay One forty-two points, that would put her in the lead by thirty points. "How many tiles are left in the bag?" I said and felt the bag.

"Fuck all that, Angel. What are you gon do? You challenging COXA or what?" There were only three tiles left in the bag. If I let the word go and Bay One pulled the last three tiles, she'd have six left. But she already has the last blank and the last "S." I couldn't let her beat me because I was scared to challenge a word I didn't like. I picked up the *Fifth Edition Scrabble Dictionary.*

"You know once you open the book, you gotta challenge the word," Bay One reminded.

"I know the rules," I assured her and said, "fuck it." I opened the book and looked up COXA. And to my dismay, there it was. Right under the word COX. It means a small dagger. "Fuck!" I exclaimed.

Bay One burst out laughing. "Gimme my fucking money! Got her ass, y'all! Tricked the shit outta her smart ass." To me, she said, "I had COAX, I needed you to challenge something, so I put COXA.

Knew it was good. Put my money on the score sheet and it's my go again. She dropped all six tiles onto the board to spell the word BEAUTS. "I get that plus visions and that's all of em'. Scrabble, baby!"

All I could do was smile. Out of ten games, Bay One had finally won a game. "It's about time you won," I told her.

"El-Amin,'' the C.O. called out. "El-Amin!"

"Yeah? What's up?" I said and stood up from the table. "That's me."

"You got two places to go. Come and get your passes."

"Damn, bitch. Two places to go."

"I know, right," I replied and went to the C.O.'s office.

"Here," the pretty young C.O. named Hossiter gave me two hall passes. "Go to the medical and the chapel. They called at the same time almost, so go to whichever one you want to first. Are you ready now?"

I stared down at the passes. Chapel and medical. What the fuck? "Naw, let me go and freshen up, then I'll be ready," I said and went to my cell. Bay One met me in the cell.

"Where you gotta go at?" she asked me.

"Chapel and medical," I replied as I put toothpaste on my toothbrush.

"Medical can be anything, but that chapel joint is scary. It's always bad news when they call you to the chapel out of the blue. You gon be aight?"

"Yeah, I'm good, Bay. Thanks for asking. Whatever it is, I'm built for this shit," I said outwardly, but inwardly I was deathly afraid. Silently I prayed this wasn't bad news about Aniyah. If it was, I was going to need medical assistance, maybe Allah planned the second call out for that reason.

"Aight. Just holla at me when you get back," Bay One said and left the cell.

***

The chapel at CTF was a small area no bigger than the average house's living room. All denominations worshiped in the same room, depending on what day. A full-time Christian chaplain was always on call in-house.

"Kareemah El-Amin?" the white lady asked.

"That's me, ma'am," I replied respectfully.

"Hello, I'm Chaplain McDonough. I hope I haven't alarmed you. Most inmates tell me when the chaplain calls for them it's usually not good news. Anyhow…in your case, I guess it's a little bit of bad news and good news. Do you have an uncle by the name of Hasan?"

"Yes, ma'am. Hasan Nadir. My mother's brother."

"Correct. We get so many calls to the chaplain where people attempt to get in touch with inmates and they are not really relatives. In your case, I'm satisfied Mr. Nadir is who he says he is. The good news, Kareemah, is your mother… well, the bad news is obviously you know your mother has passed away. Rather tragically, I'm told. My condolences. But the good news is, her body was released to your uncle yesterday evening. He was elated about it because he wants to follow the Islamic practice of burying the dead in seventy-two hours. Although it's past that time, your uncle feels God will be forgiving about the family not being able to adhere all the way to the time restraint.

"The reasons for calling, though is not only to tell you your mother's body was released by Prince George's County authorities. He says you were named executor of your mother's estate in her will and therefore, he needs your consent on how to proceed with laying your mother to rest."

"Chaplain McDonough, thank you very much for bringing me here and relaying the messages. But in the interest of time, can I please make two phone calls?"

"Two?"

"Yes, ma'am. One will be to the person who manages my financial affairs. I'm gonna need him to allocate funds to my family for my mother's burial. I am sort of the primary bread winner in the family…"

"I see. And the second call?"

"To my Uncle Hasan, of course."

"The phones here are unmonitored and unrecorded. I will have to sit here and listen to what you say on those calls. Is that a problem?" the chaplain asked.

"No, ma'am," I replied.

"Well, you may make the calls."

I picked up the landline phone on the chaplain's desk and dialed a familiar number.

James answered on the second ring. "Hello?"

"James, it's me, Angel. I don't have much time—"

"Why in the hell are you calling me from a detention facility?"

"I'll explain it to you later…but listen. I need you to withdraw fifty thousand dollars from my business account at Navy Federal. Get a cashier's check, a blank one. Then I need you to get that check to my uncle Hasan. His phone number is 202-555-1703. I need you to do that today, James."

"Angel, it's Saturday…"

"The Navy Federal branch off of Forestville Road and Walker Mill is open. This is important. Get that check to my uncle."

***

"Do you have a pass, young lady?" the older C. O. lady asked.

I handed her my medical pass.

She reads it. "Okay go on in. Dr. Manchin is in there."

When I walked into the doctor's office, a white, male doctor that resembled Joe Theismann, the famed Redskins former quarterback, sat at a desk writing something. He looked at me as I entered.

"Please sit down," he said and went back to writing.

The only chair other than his was seated next to the wall on the side of his desk. I sat down in the chair.

After about five minutes of silence while he wrote, the doctor dropped his ink pen and faced me. "Kareemah El-Amin, correct?"

I nodded my head, trying to read his demeanor. I couldn't.

"On—well, during your intake medical screening process, you gave a urine sample and blood was taken from you. We do that to test for STD's, certain cancers, viruses, and other issues a person entering this facility might have, whether they know about it or not. I was going through your lab results and saw you are pregnant. How long, we won't—"

"Pregnant?" I repeated.

"Yes. By the look on your face, I take it you didn't know you were pregnant until I just told you, is that correct?"

Pregnant? How the fuck could I be pregnant? "Uh…correct. I had no clue. Are you sure about that, Doctor? About me being pregnant?"

"Positive. The urinalysis and the blood work matched the conclusion. They confirm each other. You are definitely pregnant. I don't know how long—"

***

The unit was loud when I returned. That was welcoming because I was unable to hear my own thoughts in my head. I walked to my cell in a daze. I sat on Bay One's bottom bunk and stared at the wall. Minutes later, Bay One walked in.

"Angel, what happened? Is everything okay?"

I looked up at Bay One and said, "I'm pregnant, Bay. Fucking pregnant."

Chapter 7

Najee

Newburgh, NY

LaQuinta Inn

"We're going to leave the Maxima and the Expedition here at the motel. They both got Virginia paper tags and make us stick out too much. I saw a rental car place down the street as we pulled in here. We rent four different cars. That way, we can all switch up cars throughout the day tomorrow. The second thing on the agenda after getting the rentals is Tye...You need to put together a couple of joints you made in DC that you used on the restaurant. Muhammad Shahid owns three properties here that I know about. A communications store on Gidney Avenue, a warehouse in the industrial area near the George Washington Bridge and an apartment building on Broadway and Dubois.

"Tye, you go and get all the materials you need to hit the warehouse and the communications spot. Them shits you put together ain't gon bring down no building. It takes dynamite to do that. So, we'll just hit the warehouse with a couple and the cellphone spots, or whatever. We are doing this tonight. The killing, we save for tomorrow."

"Tomorrow? Why put off for tomorrow—" Rah Rah said.

"We not from here, yo. We gotta get familiar with the terrain. The police station, precincts, the area. A lot of what we do and get away with is gonna be about timing. I got some info on all of the targets, but not a lot. So, we gotta do our homework. Figure out escape routes and all that shit. Which streets lead to a dead end and which ones lead to the highway. Feel me? Aight yo, now pay attention to what I'm about to say.

Muhammad Shahid's mother and father are still alive. Mom's name is Viola Proctor. She's seventy-five years old. Church going real heavy. On Sundays, the daughter — Shahid's younger sister, Evelyn, takes Viola to church and stays there with her.   I can't think of a better place to body their asses.   And that—hitting them there—allow me time to go into the house and body Muhammad's father, Melvin Sr., and whoever else is in there.   I can do that while Tye handles the mother and sister and vice versa, it don't matter.

"Muhammad has a daughter, Marissa…his only child, who works at St.   Luke's Hospital. She's a registered nurse.   If she is at St.   Luke's tomorrow, I'm on her ass.   If not, I'm not leaving until I kill her.   Point blank, period.   Aight now, here's where Gunz and Rah get to have a little fun.   Muhammad Shahid has a right-hand man, Aziz Navid, formerly known as Anthony Jones. He doesn't live in Newburgh no more, but his family does.

"According to my info I got, this dude Aziz Navid is the strength of the organization.   Him and his crew do all the dirty work.   Like, kill our folks.   So now, we get to kill his. His father is deceased, but his mother is alive. Married to a nigga named Douglas Norwood. They live in a house on Chambers Street.   Just them two.

"Aziz has a sister named Angelina, who lives in a housing complex near the community college. It's called Chadwick Gardens. She has one son and a teenage daughter, Andre and Maya.   They live with her, so they die with her.   He has another sister named Kayla Jones.   Works at the McDonald's on Broadway.   If we can get her, we get her.   If not, fuck it.   But again, I ain't leaving Newburgh with Muhammad Shahid's daughter still alive.   I wanna get all of this done in one day.

"There's four of us and a lot of shit to do, but we can handle it. We just gotta do our homework, be smart and hope for a lot of luck. The best weapon we have is the element of surprise.   Let's show Muhammad Shahid and his men that they fucked up when they decided to war with us.   Let's show them niggas how we get down in the Brick.   No pity, no remorse.   No survivors."

***

"Goo, listen to me, yo. You, Killa, and Shottie gotta put some work in while we're gone. Give the streets the illusion we are still there in Newark.   Feel me? I'll text you some info on some ops and where they can be found. Go get 'em, son.   Leave the ground vibrating when y'all leave.   Just make sure to be extra careful. The pigs in the city are on high alert.   No extra shit, yo.   Get in, get out. Watch each other's backs. Evidently, Muhammad Shahid don't know about y'all and that's how I wanna keep it."

"I got you, yo," Goo replied.   "I got you."

"And remember, no survivors."

"Text me the info."

***

I left the room where everybody was and walked around the motel grounds until I saw the gold Acura SUV Aminah told me she'd be driving.   I smiled.   As if reading my mind, my cell phone vibrated.   The caller was Aminah.

"What room are you in?" I asked.

"I'm in 1410."

***

"Thank you for coming."

"I had to.   They haven't created an app where a bitch can get bomb dick over the phone."

"Damn, man." I feigned being hurt. "Now my feelings are hurt. I thought this was about me as a person.   Now you made me feel like a piece of meat."

"Well, join the club.   I have been tryna get your attention for years, but to you I never existed.   My cousin shows up from DC, and you end up leaving town with her.   Pussy must've been a torch. I'm just tryna show you good pussy runs in the family.   After all, that's what this is about, right? This thing between you and me. You fucking me because she ain't here?"

"Aminah, you're overthinking this shit. Making shit difficult when it ain't. What we did yesterday ain't got shit to do with Angel. If I wanted to, I could still be in DC fucking her. She didn't curb me. I left her. And that was before this shit happened with my sister. Listen, you know how I get down with women. You said you've known me for almost thirty years, right? Okay. This shit is simple. I'm going through a rack of shit right now. Mentally. I saw you yesterday and for the first time really noticed how fucking sexy you are. I got turned on. You responded. We did it. It was great for me.

"Then, last night happened. That one dude the police say was doing the shooting...I killed his ass. Me. I'm fucked up about all the people in the hood that died last night. Those bullets were for me. For my men. We survived. You survived. They died. Because of me. And that shit has been fucking with my mental. Salimah's death has been fucking with my mental. My grand-mother, Gunz' mother and grandmother, Yasir, his peoples, Hasan and his peoples, all this shit has been fucking with me.

I haven't even been thinking about Angel since I been back in the Brick. All I've been thinking about is killing shit. To avenge my friends. When I called you, I just wanted to make sure you were okay, that you didn't get shot, or hurt or worse. Then I thought about what we did in the hallway—"

"That stinking ass hallway," Aminah said, "smelled just like piss and ass."

I laughed. "I thought about you and how great that pussy was. Decided to see if you'd help me get my mind off of all the other shit. So, I asked you to come to me. And you came—"

"All the way to fucking Newburgh. What the fuck is New-burgh? I ain't never heard of this shit in my life."

"It's New York. What do you mean?" I asked.

"This ain't New York. New York is the five boroughs. New York is upstate, Rochester, Buffalo and all that shit. Newburgh is some other shit. This shit is...Delaware."

I couldn't help but to laugh.   The look on Aminah's face and the bougie tone she used when she said Newburgh was Delaware cracked me up.

"I done came all the way to fucking Delaware for some dick.   I must be coo-coo for Cocoa Puffs.   But it's all good, yo.   Maybe I was overthinking shit, forgive me for that.   I'm a Cancer, we tend to do that sometimes.   It's just that I have wanted your ass for so long..."

"Stop thinking about all that, ma.   You gotta learn to live in the moment.   Not the past.   Not the future." I grabbed Aminah's hand and pulled her close.   "The moment.   Live in the moment." Then, I kissed her lips.

"Wait for you to say—" Aminah said and gave in to seduction. We undressed and got to it.

"O-o-o-w, Najee! Shit! You in my stomach! You in my stomach! You in me too deep! Take some out! Please!"

I laid on Aminah with both of her feet near her ears.   I pressed down on her ankles and that elevated her pelvic area, which gave me deeper access to her middle.   I wasn't trying to hurt her purposely.   I was just relieving stress.   Her pussy was so wet and good that I couldn't help ravaging her, time and time again.

***

"How are you today? Can I help you?"

"Yes, you can.   I need a rental."

"Any particular make or model?"

"No."

"And how long will you need the car for?"

"Until tomorrow evening, Monday morning the latest."

The lady behind the counter at Budget Rental Cars typed on her keyboard then looked at her computer screen.   "All we have left is a Dodge Durango SUV and a Mitsubishi Gallant sedan.   Which would you prefer?"

"Gimme the Durango.   And I'll be paying cash."

Chapter 8

Killa

Newark, NJ

The Lincoln Navigator was old. It smelled of car air fresheners and gasoline. I sat in the back seat and stared out the window at the Al-Hajj Resource Center. The building that housed it was sand-wiched between a boarded-up, abandoned property and a shoe re-pair shop that was closed.

"You sure this is the place?" I asked Goo, who sat in the front seat.

"This is the address I got on my phone," Goo replied. "Najee sent me the text. I double checked it. This the place."

I pulled out a small glassine bag and opened it. Then I spilled the bag's contents out onto my palm. The powder was beige, its texture a little grainy. With a deep inhale, I snorted the powder into my nose, then coughed.

Shotgun looked into the backseat at me, just as I poured out another blast. "Look at your big nose ass."

"That's niggas problems now. Always worried about the next nigga."

"*Worried about the next nigga?* I accept that, son. You got that. But with all the wild shit these niggas putting in their blow, you should be worried about yourself. Cause if you go out back there bullshittin, nigga, you gon die," Shotgun said and laughed. "I ain't bringing you back. I ain't putting no ice on your nuts. Not none of that shit, so go ahead and do you. Stupid ass, dopefiend ass nigga."

"I got your dopefiend, nigga. Ten inches long."

"Well, take that big motherfucker and bend it, then stretch it and stick it in your own ass, nigga. How about that?"

"You gone make me fuck you up, Shottie. Keep it up, yo."

"Fuck who up, Killa? Nigga, you already know not to play with—"

"Yo, y'all niggas chill with that shit," Goo cut in. "Neither one of y'all niggas can fight a lick. On some real shit, though, Killmonger, Shotgun is right, yo. These niggas out here wildin' out with the blow nowadays, son. They mixing all types of wild shit with the dope...fentanyl, meth, synthetic opioids, rat poison...all kinds of shit. Niggas just tryna have your best interest at heart."

Goo was the only person that called me Killmonger, someone he'd gotten out of a comic book. He knew I hated that shit. "Yeah, right. The same way y'all niggas had BeBe's best interest at heart."

"Ayo, son, fuck you tryna say?" Shotgun exploded.

"Chill, yo" Goo said to calm Shotgun. "Yo Killa, that was foul, son. You was outta line back there, yo. Facts. I'ma chalk that shit up to that shit you back there blowing, but don't let me hear you say that shit again. Real spit. You act like we took part in that..."

"Ain't saying you took part. But ain't nobody stop the shit either. Or said anything about it after it was done. That nigga BeBe was our man, yo. Our motherfuckin right-hand and ain't nobody say shit when Naj did that shit."

"Did you say anything? Huh, nigga?" Shotgun exploded again.

"Yo, chill—" Goo started.

"Naw, Goo, fuck that! This nigga gon sit in this whip and talk shit to a nigga like he a muthafucka gangsta. Talking bout we ain't say shit. Bitch nigga, neither did you. And BeBe been with your ass all day, every day, nigga! He was my day-one, but he was your man, nigga. Fuck you talking bout? Popping that slick shit to a nigga—"

"I ain't gonna be too many bitches, yo!"

"What do you wanna do? We can get it poppin—"

"We can do whatever nigga!" I exploded back. "What's good, Shottie?"

Goo twisted his body to put himself between me and Shotgun. His frame filled the entire space between the two front seats." I just told y'all niggas to chill. On some real G-shit, I ain't gon say it again! You'll gon fuck around and make me dome check both of y'all asses. We are a family, yo. And just like all families, we goin through some rough times right now. We lost some family members—BeBe, Yasir, Lil Haleem, Salimah, and we are all hurting, yo. All of us. Look at what the fuck happened yesterday, yo. "Muthafuckers came in our hood and tried to end the homies. But they couldn't, yet they killed a lot of people. Ten motherfuckers died outside last night. Ten of our peoples, yo! Five niggas, three chicks and two kids. We can't fall apart. Can't start beefing amongst ourselves. Killing each other and shit. We didn't start all this wild shit the hood is in, that Naj and nem is in, but we gon finish it. Just like we always do. Together. We gotta stick together, yo. Losing BeBe was a bad blow. a hard, sad blow, but BeBe knew the rules. BeBe was smart. He should have assessed the whole situation and shut the fuck up. He could've—"

"Kinda sounds like you are blaming the man for his own death," I interjected.

"Listen, say whatever the fuck you want to, but BeBe's mouth was always the cause of his undoing, yo. That was my man, but like I always told him, he talked too fucking much and never listened. I ain't saying he deserved to die because of that and I'm definitely not tryna take sides, but come on, yo. The man had just lost his sister and was going through some heavy shit. And BeBe couldn't leave well enough alone.

"Had a mutherfucker killed my sister or my daughter, I would've been on the same shit. Big facts. And I would've bodied anybody standing in my way of full retribution. Anybody, yo! That's why I ain't say shit after Naj did that shit. Not because of fear, but because I felt that man's pain. Limah was the closest person in the world to that man and muthafuckas killed her because Naj bodied Mu's bitch ass. Fuck that. I would be on the same shit. That's all I'm saying. And you two niggas going at each other ain't gon change shit or bring BeBe back. You feel me?"

"Yeah, I feel you, big homie," I whispered.

"You feel me?" Goo said as he looked at Shotgun.

"Yeah, I feel you one hundred percent, but I'ma still tell Gunz and Naj that Killa back there feeling some kinda way about BeBe…"

"Tell 'em, nigga! I don't give a fuck."

"Yeah, aight. Talk that tough shit now, nigga. But I wanna see you say that shit to Najee and Gunz, nigga. Tough ass nigga, and I'm telling them you snorting that shit too," Shotgun laughed and said.

"Tell them whatever you wanna tell them, yo. Naj ain't my P.O. and Gunz ain't my father, yo. Fuck I care if you tell them niggas I'm getting high? I'm a grown ass man, son. I'ma do me regardless of who don't like that shit."

"Aight, tough guy, we gone see. We gon see," Shotgun stated. Goo turned around and sat down in his seat.

"Fuck that. It's time to go in here and put this work in. We walk through the front door and give it to anybody on the spot! Y'all got that?"

"I'm ready, yo." Shotgun said and racked his weapon.

"Let's do this," I replied and got out of the truck.

Me, Shotgun, and Goo walked into the Al-Hajj Resource Center and climbed the stairs. At the top of the landing was a door. Goo peeped inside.

"There's like seven niggas in a halakha on the musala. And one nigga on the mumbah. That's eight muthafuckas. Are y'all ready?" Without waiting for an answer, Goo threw the door open and raced inside the room. Me and Shotgun, followed.

All the men turned their heads toward us as we came in.

"Assalamu Alaikum," the man behind the podium called out.

"Walalum Assaleem," Goo said and upped his weapon.

The next thing I knew, we all fired our weapons, killing the men instantly.

The next stop on our list was Medina Oils Scents. The man who owned the oil shop was allegedly a part of Muhammad Farid Shahid's organization. Israel Abu Sufyan was the only person in-side the shop when we walked in. There was no one left in the shop when we departed because Israel Abu Sufyan was dead. Two shots to the head by an Afghanistan ARP .50 made sure of that. There were two more destinations on the list Najee had supplied. City Trendz, a local, urban outfit store on South Street and Haria-bugani's, a small Halal grocery market on 7th Avenue, owned by Arike Islam and both addresses met the same fate as the next. We walked in and killed everybody we saw.

***

"The death toll in Newark has reached an all-time high. Thank you for joining us tonight on *NBC Nightly News* and I'm Jade Copeland. Law enforcement officials and the Newark Police Departments are baffled and outraged tonight. The recent increase in violent crime and murder is at the forefront of every discussion at City Hall. The recent attacks of Muslims throughout the city have forced local authorities to call in the Federal Bureau of Investigation. Mayor Abdul Sallam Rasheed has a news conference scheduled for tomorrow morning at nine a.m., outside of El-Hajj Malik El-Shabazz Center in downtown Newark—"

"Keith, you ain't gon cum like this," India urged. "You need to fuck me in my ass if you tryna cum."

"Bitch, shut the fuck up and do what I paid you to do. Suck this dick," I replied, then grabbed India's head and forced her back onto the dick. But I knew she was right. When I had liquor and dope in me, it was always hard for me to nut. I clicked the news off the TV and decided to find a porn channel. Seconds later, I did. A strong ass, black dude with a bald head was punishing a Latin bitch who spoke no English. I half-watched the porn and half-watched India eat my dick. It was a good way to relieve stress.

Chapter 9

Benito

Washington, DC

"I checked the house. There's no alarm on it," Marco Cherro said.

"I need to speak to the woman in the house, Marco. Get inside, but make sure no harm comes to anyone inside. Do I make myself clear?"

"Very clear, Mr. Alvarez."

"Go. Be careful and be discreet. Call me when you're inside."

I watched Marco and Pedro walk down the dark alley adjacent to Fort Davis Drive in Southeast.

"Benito," Enrique Suarez called out from the front seat of the Jaguar. "Is it that we are trying to find Carlos's daughter? A little girl?"

"It's true, Enrique. How did you know?"

"I hear things. That's all. It turns out Carlos was a rolling stone. Wherever he laid his head was home."

"Ain't that the truth," I agreed.

"I couldn't imagine being his age and finding out in a matter of days I have not one, but two children."

I thought about what Enrique said. I had felt the same way. "Carlos just found out about the daughter, but he already knew about the son. He just didn't know his name was *Najee* and he didn't know where Najee was."

Enrique turned to face me. "I hope I'm not out of line, mi amigo, but given the chance, I know exactly where Najee will be after I'm finished with him."

Smiling, I asked, "And where is that, Enrique?"

"In a shallow grave somewhere."

The phone in my hand vibrated. "Hello."

"We're in. The woman is safe. Afraid, but safe."

"Was she alone?"

"Si. She is the only person here."

"Okay. You did good. You and Pedro sit tight. I'll be in touch."

***

The Jaguar rode down Gale Street in Northeast. I could see the dark-colored Toyota Avalon sitting nearby. The faces of Pascal Escovedo and Raul Torres stared at the tinted windows of the Jaguar as we passed by. I picked up the phone and dialed Pascal.

"Hola?"

In Spanish, I told Pascal there should only be an old woman inside the house. I told them to check the hours for alarms, then to call me back. Enrique parked the car on 17th Street near the Rosedale Recreation Center. I leaned back into the heated seat and waited.

Several minutes later, Pascal called me back. He saw no alarms on the way. He had tapped a back window, and nothing happened.

"Give it ten minutes, Pascal," I told him. "The alarm could be a silent one. If no one shows up at the house, we know for sure there's no alarm. Did you check for an entry point?"

Pascal relayed to me in Spanish that the locks on the rear door were antiques and he could pick them easily.

"Good, Pascal. If no police slow up in ten minutes, get inside the house. Take whoever is inside the house as hostage. Call me when it's done," I told him and ended the call.

Twenty minutes later, Pascal called to say they were inside the house on Gale Street and there was only one person inside. Portia Phillips, and she was under their control.

"Good job, Pascal, but when it's time to communicate, make sure you let Raul do the talking, his English is better. Stay put. I'll be in touch."

***

On Chesapeake Street in Southeast, things were a little different, but the same result was reached. There were seven people inside the project tenement. After my men were inside the house, I got out of my car and went inside.

The lone grown male was separated from the women and children. The woman, Wanda Brown, sat huddled on a small couch with all five of her children.

"Wanda Brown, my name is Benito Alvarez. Your niece, Honesty, has done something she should not have done. I'm gonna need you to call her for me. If you call her and we talk, you'll live. If I don't talk to Honesty in the next few hours, you and…" I pointed at the man by the wall. "What is his name? And who is he to you?"

"He's my…my…boyfriend, Dave," Wanda Brown stammered.

"Well, if I don't talk to Honesty soon, you, Dave and your children will all die. What's it gonna be?"

"I need my cell phone. It's in the kitchen."

"Juan, please get Wanda her cell phone so she can call Honesty."

Anthony Fields

Chapter 10

Aziz

Lawnside, NJ

Bistro Aracosia

Bahraini music flowed through the restaurant. There were painted portraits of prophets and kings on the wall.   The smell of garlic yogurt stew and beef tenderloins assaulted my nostrils from the table where we sat.

"You haven't touched your lamb steak moghul or the appetizers," Nadia said to me.

"The lamb smells great, but for some reason, I can only smell your stew and beef.   The appetizers, what are they?"

"Leek and scallion dumplings.   In Bahrain, they are known as aushaki.   They are really good, Aziz.   Please try them.   My grandmother made them every Sunday for us back home."

Using my fingers, I picked up one of the dumplings and bit it. It was rich in flavor, tasted good like Nadia had said.   "You were right.   They are really good."

"I knew you'd like them, Aziz.   The food here reminds me of home.   The taste of Bahrain is in the spices.   Turmeric, cumin, sumac.   All the meats are marinated for a long time to achieve such good flavors."

"The name of the place—Aracosia.   What does it mean?"

"It is spelling of the Hellenic name of a province near Kandalor. In a time before Alexander the Great conquered the region."

"Dinner and a history lesson.   A perfect way to spend an evening with one's wife." The cellphone in my pocket vibrated.   I pulled it out.   The caller was Muhammad Shahid.   I looked across the table at Nadia.

She smiled.   "If only a wife would enjoy a dinner with a husband without interruption.

"I won't answer it."

"It's Muhammad, isn't it?"

I nodded.

"I swear, that man has a sixth sense about him. He seems to call you whenever we are together and enjoying ourselves. Answer the phone, Aziz."

I answered the call. "Hello? Assalamu Alaikum. I can come to you, but not tonight, I am at dinner…"

"You don't have to come here. I can talk over the phone. Sorry to interrupt your dinner. Give my apologies to Nadia.

"Muhammad says he apologizes for the interruption," I told Nadia.

Nadia waved me off.

"What is the problem, Ocki?" I asked.

"First, I need to know what happened last night. I was told that we lost Minister Rico."

"Yeah, unfortunately, that's true. I sent men to the projects at Brick Towers to find Najee and his friends. My instructions were to send a message."

"And what a message you sent, Aziz. Several people killed and several other injured. And we lost a good soldier in Rico."

"Collateral damage, ain't that what you called it, Muhammad?"

"Messy. Things are getting way too messy."

"I felt that way when you instructed me to kill Hafizah at the hospital."

"Quiet. It's what I told you to do. The massacre in the projects there has been all over the national news."

"I apologize for that, Ocki, but it's either we're in this thing or not. Quiet or loud. You can't have it both ways," I expressed fervently.

"Okay, Aziz, I get what you're saying, but how can it be this hard to kill one group of street trash?"

"Najee is a formidable opponent. The streets protect him."

"I don't want to hear Najee's accolades, Aziz. I want to read his obituary," Muhammad Shahid spat venomously.

"And so you shall, Ocki. So, you shall."

"Do you happen to know where Najee and his gang are at this moment?"

"Somewhere in Newark, I presume. Why?"

"Why? Because my warehouse in Newburgh was blown up hours ago and the telecommunication depot I own was set to flame."

"In Newburgh?"

"Yes."

"And you think Najee is responsible?"

"I don't know what to think, Aziz."

"How would Najee even know about Newburgh? Nobody knows about Newburgh."

"Somebody has to know about our ties to Newburgh. Losing two businesses in the same day is not coincidental, something is going on here, Aziz. Something…"

"Muhammad, I think you're just being paranoid."

"Paranoid? The Al-Hajj Resource Center was attacked today. Everybody inside was killed. Medina Oils, City Trendz and Hariabugani's was all hit one after another. Casualties a plenty. Israel and Arike were both killed, too. And you think I'm just being paranoid?"

Was it possible that another organization was at war with us? Because there was absolutely no way possible for Najee and his crew to know the affiliation of Muhammad Farid Shahid. The implications were unfathomable.

"Are you still there, Aziz? Muhammad asked.

"I'm here, Ocki. Just thinking about what you just said."

"Good. Think about it, Aziz. Then try to make me understand how all the businesses I own or am associated with, getting attacked in Newburgh and Newark, and there's no explanation for it. Think about it long and hard and then call me back," Muhammad Shahid ended the call.

Slowly, I pulled the phone away from my ear and laid it on the table.

Nadia nibbled her food while looking directly at me. "Is everything okay, Aziz?"

"I don't know, sweetheart," I told her. "I really don't know."

Anthony Fields

Chapter 11

Honesty

Suitland, MD

"Have you ever noticed that all we do is fuck?" Trigger asked me out of the blue.

I looked at him like he was crazy. "What else do you wanna do, Trigger? Travel? Run a marathon? Go see the Ice Capades at the Capital One Arena?"

"You tryna be funny.   But you know what the fuck I mean, True."

"Naw, I don't.   I don't know what else you want from me.   I'm in the middle of a war disguised as a chess match with a bitch that's determined to exterminate my whole family.   I can't do shit else until that bitch is dead.   I got money in the bank, my mother's house that reverts to me, cars, trucks, and good credit.   And everything I have is yours.   We ain't hurtin for nothing.   I don't have to work and neither do you.   So, outside of babysitting that little girl in there until I can find and kill her mother, what's wrong with fucking all day?"

My cellphone on the floor vibrated loudly, I ignored it.

"Somebody has been blowing your phone up for hours and you ain't even looked to see who it is.   I'm starting to think you're cheating on me."

"Cheating on you?" I replied and rolled over to get the phone."

"When would I have the chance? You just said you and me fuck too much.   I know my pussy torch and all that, but that would be too much fucking." I looked at the home screen on my phone.   I had eleven missed calls.   After unlocking the phone, I saw I had calls from every person in my immediate family.   "That's weird."

"What?" Trigger asked. "What's weird?"

"Everybody in my family has called me in the last couple of hours.   Both grandmothers, Aunt Wanda, my little cousin…" I sat up on the couch. "Something's wrong. Something's wrong." I saw who started calling me first and pressed send on that number.

My grandmother Portia's cell phone rang once, and she answered. "Honesty?"

"Yeah, Grandma, what's wrong?" I asked, alarmed.

"Some men are here looking for you…what in the hell have you done?"

"Did you just say that some men are there?"

A man's voice came over the phone suddenly. "Is this Honesty Phillips?"

I shot straight up off the couch. A foreboding came over me as my mind raced a mile a minute. Who could these men be at Grandma's? "This is her."

"True, what the fuck is up? Who is that on the phone?" Trigger asked.

I put my finger to my lips to quiet him. "Who is this?"

"Honesty, who I am is not important, but why I am here in your grandmother's house is. You have a personal vendetta against a woman named Angel. You killed her mother and left her a note telling her you took her daughter and that now the two of you are even. Does that sound familiar?"

"It does, but who are you? The police?" I already knew the man on the other end of the phone was no police officer.

The man laughed a long, wicked laugh that chilled me to the bone.

"Honesty," the man said, "do me a favor and call your aunt Wanda."

"My aunt Wanda? How do you know my aunt?"

"We know all your living relatives. Call Wanda. Right now." The line went dead.

"Shit!" I muttered and paced the floor. I was visibly shaken.

"What the fuck is up, True? Tell me something about who was on the phone?"

I stopped pacing right in front of Trigger. "I'm not sure who he is, but he knows my whole name and he says he knows all of my relatives. When I called Grandma, she spoke for a second and then he got on the phone. He knows about the letter I left Angel."

"I told your ass not to leave that stupid ass letter," Trigger exploded.

Ignoring Trigger, I said, "And he knows what the letter said. Word for word."

"So, what did he say when you asked if he was twelve?"

"He laughed at me. Then told me to call my aunt Wanda."

"What the fuck? Call Wanda. Call her, True. Right now."

My hands shook and I had to steady my nerves. I pressed send on Aunt Wanda's cell phone number.

The phone was answered immediately. "Hello, Honesty," a different man said, but the accent was the same as the first man. "Glad you could call."

"Who is this? What's going on and where is my aunt Wanda?"

"I'll answer the last questions first. Your aunt Wanda is here. Across the room holding onto her five children for dear life. Her boyfriend Dave is here, too. Listen closely," the man said. "Aunt Wanda, say something to your lovely niece, Honesty."

"Bitch…what the fuck you done got us into?" Aunt Wanda shouted.

The man laughed again. "As you can see, I mean hear, Aunt Wanda is very much alive and so are the kids. But whether they stay that way is up to you. I've been sitting here in the projects, in dusty ass Southeast, waiting hours for you to pick up the phone call. I'm pissed off about that, Honesty. And I also want you to understand the severity of your precarious situation. So, someone here has to die."

I heard a gunshot, then screams. My heart stopped for a minute.

"Everybody shut the fuck up!" the man bellowed.

"Aunt Wanda! Ciera!" I screamed.

"True, stop screaming in here. You're gonna wake up the kid," Trigger said. The man on the phone laughed again. "Aunt Wanda and Ciera are okay. But not for long. Sorry, but I can't say the same thing about her boyfriend, Dave. His brains are all over the wall behind him.   It's gonna leave a stain.   I guess that answers your questions about us being the police, huh?"

My body started to tremble. "What—what do you want?"

"I'll tell you in a minute but first, why don't you call your grandmother?   Call Desiree Brown, Honesty.   Leave me on the phone while you do that.   Merge the calls."

I did as I was instructed, then merged the calls. The line on Grandmother's end was answered by a man, with the same accent. "Hello?"

"Grandma…are you okay?"

"She's okay, Honesty," the man at Wanda's house said.   "For now.   Depends on you if she stays okay."

"Depends on me how? Who are you and what do you want from me?" I asked frantically.

"The little girl you've taken from her family. We know you killed the little girl's grandmother.   We care nothing about that. What you've done by taking the girl is bigger than your issue with Angel.   The little girl has a father.   A very important father.   A very dangerous father who wants his daughter back.   Have you ever heard of Carlos Trinidad, Honesty?"

My blood suddenly ran cold.   Who hasn't heard of the notorious drug kingpin? He was rumored to be responsible for hundreds of murders over the years.   "I have."

"Well, you have his daughter and if you don't return her at once, everybody you love will die.   Tonight.   Then eventually we'll find you and kill you, too.   It's only a matter of time.   There is nowhere for you to hide. This situation is simple, Honesty.   Give us the little girl immediately or your entire family dies.   What's it gonna be?"

"If I give you the girl, then you leave everybody alone? Everybody lives? Even me?"

"You have my word.   All we want is the little girl."

The decision I was forced to make was a no-brainer. I never meant things to get this far out of hand.   I never meant to involve my extended family, in my beef with Angel.   "You win.   Spare my family and I'll give you the girl."

"Good decision, Honesty.   Smart girl."

"How do I return her? Where do I bring her?" I asked the man.

"Stay off the phone. I'll call you back in five minutes," the man said and ended the call.

I dropped the cell phone. The look on my face must've told the story.

"You're giving the little girl back. I heard that part," Trigger said.

I nodded. "I have to. They have people at all my family's houses."

"Who are they?"

"Carlos Trinidad's people. Turns out the little girl in there, is his daughter."

"Get the fuck outta here. Aniyah is Carlos Trinidad's daughter?"

I nodded my head. "Crazy, right?"

"Beyond crazy," Trigger said and sat down.

"Out of all the people in the city to have a baby by, this bitch bags the most dangerous muthafucka in the country. Like I've said a hundred times already, that's one lucky bitch."

"Fuck lucky because is there enough to go around to you, to us. Because if what you said is true about Carlos Trinidad's people having the letter or at least having *read* the letter, then that means that Angel must've told them about it or gave it to them. Which also means that she's in cahoots with them and…"

"That she could possibly be there when we arrive. So, I could be walking into an ambush?" I finished Trigger's sentence and looked into his eyes. He nodded his head. "I thought about that already. But what choice do I really have?"

Chapter 12

Benito

The terrified faces of Honesty Phillips' aunt and her children stared back at me. I look over at the dead man by the wall. "I apologize for my savagery. And that your children had to witness that. Dave was probably a good man, but judging by the condition of your home and its location, you could do better. Your niece took a little girl from her grandmother…well, I'm quite sure you heard our conversation, so no need to repeat myself.

"But let me say this, killing is easy for me. I've been doing it for almost thirty-five years. I will not hesitate to come back here to kill you and each one of your children if you talk to the police about what happened here tonight. Tell them someone broke through the window and killed Dave. I don't care what you tell them. Just make them believe you. The man I mentioned on the phone…Carlos Trinidad, he's a very powerful man. The police cannot save you or your family from him or us. Witness protection is a joke. We'll find you…we found you once, we'll find you again. Do we understand each other?"

The terrified woman with tears in her eyes nodded her head.

"I want to hear you say it, Wanda. Tell me you understand me."

"I-I-I-understand you. I won't…say a word," Wanda stammered. "I-I-I promise. You…you…won't have to come back and kill us."

"What happened here?" I asked the woman.

"Some…Someone climbed through the window and killed Dave. He owed some people money for drugs."

I rose from my seat. "Sounds good to me, Wanda. Good night."

***

Sitting in the back of the Jaguar, I made the two calls. The first one to Carlos.

"Benito, tell me something good."

"I just spoke with Honesty.   She's returning your daughter tonight."

"Good news, comrade. Good news."

"Question, mi amigo.   Do I kill Honesty?"

"No, Benito.   Just get my daughter."

"I will.   Should have her within the hour."

"Good.   Call me when you do."

I ended the call with Carlos and called Honesty's phone back. "Hello, Honesty?"

"I'm here."

"There's an America's Best Wings on Alabama Avenue, in Southeast…"

"Right next door to the Subway Sandwich shop and the Pizza Hut. I know exactly where it is."

"Great.   I'll be there in ten minutes.   Bring the girl to me. After I have her in my possession, I will instruct my men to leave your relatives' homes.   Is that clear?"

"Crystal.   I'll be there in twenty minutes."

"Wonderful.   Goodbye."

***

The strip mall on Alabama Avenue was small.   Six businesses total.   All of which were closed except for the America's Best Wings shop.   The parking lot was deserted, but for a few vehicles that probably belonged to a handful of patrons inside the wing place shop, or its employees.

"Benito," Enrique called out.   "There's a black Cadillac Escalade about to turn into a parking lot. A black man is driving, but a black female is in the passenger seat.   Didn't you say Honesty Phillips had a black Escalade?"

"That should be her, Enrique," I replied.

I watched the Escalade pull into the parking lot and park.   I pulled out my phone and called Honesty.

"Hello, I'm here," Honesty said.

"I see you. I'm in the silver Jaguar parked to the left of you."

"I see it."

"Get out of the truck—just you—and bring the girl to me."

"I'm coming out alone.   The girl is in the back seat."

"Good.   Come to me."

The passenger door opened and out stepped Honesty Phillips. A beautiful young lady who resembled her father.   Tony Bills. The woman had been about ten when I had last seen her.

"Time flies," I muttered to myself.

At the rear of the Escalade, the door was opened, and Honesty helped a little girl exit the big SUV.   She grabbed the girl's hand and walked towards the car. I exited the Jaguar.   In seconds, both woman and girl stood directly in front of me.   The girl was also beautiful.   She looked like a mirror image of Carlos as a child.   It was uncanny.

"Hello, Aniyah."

"Hi," the little girl said.

"My name is Benito.   I am a good friend of your father. Would you like to meet him?"

"My father?" the little girl repeated, a puzzled look on her face.

I nodded.   "Yes, your father.   He's waiting to meet you.   Your mommy asked him to take care of you until she comes back."

"Come back from where? She hasn't been answering my calls."

"Uh…you know what? I don't know where.   But your father does.   She's been talking to him.   You can ask him when you see him.   I want to take you to him.   Can I?"

"You want to take me to Puerto Rico?" the little girl asked. "Because Mommy said my daddy lives in Puerto Rico and one day, she'd take me there to see him."

"Well, guess what, Aniyah? Good news.   You don't have to fly all the way to Puerto Rico, because your daddy is here, and he can't wait to see you."

Aniyah smiled.   Her smile was her father's smile.   "I can't wait to see him, too."

"Come with me then.   "I reached out my hand and the little girl took it.   I led her to the rear of the Jaguar, helped her settle into her seat and fasten her seatbelt. "I need to talk to Honesty for a minute—"

"Honesty? Who's Honesty?" Aniyah asked.

"The woman right here," I pointed at Honesty.

"Oh…I call her Michelle." Then to Honesty, Aniyah said,"Bye, Ms. Michelle."

"Bye, Aniyah," Honesty replied, but her attention was elsewhere.

Once the car door was shut, I turned back to Honesty. "I see your furtive glances around the area. No need to be worried. No one here is going to hurt you. You can relax. Carlos knew your father and so did I. He was a good man. Loyal to us. That's why we won't take your life. Not because you gave the girl back. Because of your father, Tony."

"Thank you, I guess. Is my family safe? All my relatives?"

"The men at all the homes will be gone in minutes."

"Can I ask you a question?"

"Of course. You're already asked several and I answered."

Honesty looked around the parking lot again. "Where is Angel? Is she here?"

I laughed. Honesty's fear became clear to me. "No. Angel is not here. She is in jail. At the CTF. She was arrested a few days ago during a traffic stop. The police found a gun in her car. She was looking for you."

"Damn, that's why I haven't heard from her. On the phone, you said that…or one of your men said Carlos Trinidad didn't care about my beef with the girl's mother. Angel. You know that she killed my father and my mother. And that I killed her mother and took the girl. Well, I've returned the girl. I took good care of her while I had her. Me and Angel have unfinished business. If I kill her, will you and Carlos Trinidad get involved? I need to know that."

I laughed again as I often did. "We have nothing to do with your feud with Angel. As long as that feud doesn't include the little girl again. Does that answer your questions?"

"I guess it does.   Thank you. Tell Mr. Trinidad that I didn't know the girl was—"

"He already knows that, Honesty."

"I'm just making sure," Honesty said and turned to leave.

I called out to her.   She stopped and turned around.   "I respect you, Honesty.   Really, I do.   What man can't respect a daughter's quest to avenge her slain father? Especially when he was killed unjustly? Angel may be Carlos Trinidad's daughter's mother, but she is no friend of mine.   Never has been.   I believe she should have been killed for what she did to your father.   But the decision was not mine to make.   Angel is being held in custody for a seven-day period.   She'll be released on Wednesday.   A little more than three days from now.   I suggest you get to the Superior Courthouse and surprise her as she leaves the building or somewhere near there. It's what I would do.   Take care, Honesty, and have a good night."

***

As the Jaguar passed through the iron gates that surrounded the property of Carlos' home, the little girl turned to me.

"Mr. Benito?"

"Yes, Aniyah?"

"Mommy said my daddy's name is Carlos.   Is that true?"

I nodded my head.   "Yes, Aniyah.   His name is Carlos Trinidad."

"Carlos Trinidad? I like that name."

"It's a good name, Aniyah."

"Is my daddy Muslim?" Aniyah asked.

"Muslim? Why, no.   Why do you ask that?" I asked her, curiously.

"I don't know.   Just asked. Maybe because my mommy is Muslim.   I am Muslim.   My entire family on my mommy's side is Muslim."

"Is that so?"

Aniyah nodded.   "Thought maybe my daddy was too."

Carlos awaited the car at the front door. The expression on his face was unreadable.

"We're here, Aniyah, and here's your father."

The Jaguar stopped at the entrance to the house. Right in front of Carlos. Aniyah unfastened her seatbelt and got out of the car. I did the same.

Without a word, Aniyah and Carlos met in the middle of the short distance to one another. He reached down and lifted her to him. They embraced. I saw a tear escaping Carlo's face.

As I watched the scene unfold, I stood by deep in thought. How could a man go from being completely childless, to having not one, but two children in a week or so? It was a hard pill to swallow for any man. But Carlos Trinidad wasn't just any man. I'd watched him grow from a sniveling child to one of the most revered, feared and powerful men to come out of my era.

I watched him hold onto his child. No words had passed between them, but that made me think of another child. A teenager, but someone's child, nonetheless. Little Manuel Vasquez. I thought about the fact that his family would never get to hug him or hug his children the way Carlos held Aniyah. I thought about the fact that Little Manuel was killed by Aniyah's brother, Najee. Carlos' son. Then I thought about how truly unjust life was. How unfair it was. I thought about the scales of life and how sometimes, they were completely unbalanced.

In life, I'd learned that man couldn't wait for an unseen higher power to balance out his life's scales. Sometimes men had to do that themselves. Mortal men had to help God out sometimes. Help to balance the scales.

Chapter 13

Najee

Sunday morning, Newburgh, NY

"What can I get for you gentlemen this morning?"

The waitress looked like a shorter version of Alicia Keys, micro braids and all. She was sexy in her uniform and in any other situations, I would have shot my shot at her.

"Gimme the Belgian waffle, scrambled eggs with mozzarella cheese and turkey sausage links. And a side order of grits," I told her.

"I'll have the southwestern omelet with the works," Gunz ordered.

"Southwestern omelet?" Tye joked. "Fuck you is, part Mexican?" Everybody laughed. "Can't eat no chili and chives early in the morning. Gimme the hash brown fried hard, fried eggs with the yolk still runny, French toast and turkey bacon."

The waitress wrote down the orders and then looked at Rah Rah. "And you sir?"

"Anybody ever told you that you look like Alicia Keys?" Rah Rah asked.

"I get that a lot, yes."

"Oh, aight. Just saying…gimme the ribeye steak and egg breakfast. Eggs scrambled hard with onions and no cheese. And a couple of them homemade biscuits with butter and jelly."

"Fuck you looking at the woman for like that, yo?" Tye asked.

"Cause nigga, I'm tryna be her Swizz Beatz," Rah Rah replied.

Me, Tye and Gunz laughed.

"I don't know 'bout that, but I just hope you can tip like Swizz Beatz," the waitress said and smiled. "What y'all drinking?"

"Orange juice for the table," I told her.

The waitress turned and left.

The diner was small and quaint. Reminded me of a place I'd seen on TV. There were pictures of famous black people all over the walls.   Michelle and Barack Obama, Stevie Wonder, Martin Lawrence.   Will Smith, Jasmine Guy, Maya Angelou.   Sidney Poitier and others.   Our booth was by the window, but at the rear of the diner.   The tables near us were empty.

"I bet they got a whole pig on the grill back there," Rah Rah commented.

"This whole shit smells like pork bacon.   Thought I was buggin," Tye added.   "Shit smells good as hell, though."

We all laughed at that.

Gunz sipped water from a glass in front of him.   "Fuck it.   We are already going to hell anyway.   Might as well add swine grease to our list of sins."

My cell phone pinged, alerting me to an incoming text message. I read it.

"Just got the word. Donell Dyson died this morning from his gunshot wounds. That brings the total of people killed yesterday to eleven. With a lot of people still fighting for their lives in hospitals," I announced.

"Damn, yo," Rah Rah replied, "Don Juan was my man.   Never even knew he was outside last night.   I never saw him."

Gunz shook his head. "I saw him out there.   In a crowd with his sister."

"That's fucked up, fam," Tye said. "I used to fuck his sister, Deidra. She told me once their mother moved them out of the towers to keep both of her sons from getting killed.   They came back to the hood for the candlelight vigil and one of her sons ended up getting killed anyway.   Shit fucked up."

"Seems like this is all we've been saying for a week now," Gunz said.   "I'm tired of feeling sorry for everybody.   I'm ready to kill muthafuckas, yo."

"So, you shall, big boy. So, you shall.   Listen, change of plans. All I said yesterday is gone with yesterday.   Ain't gon be no solo missions.   We are in a city that ain't ours and anything can happen. We gotta look out for each other.   It doesn't matter if we ride in separate whips.   We can still pair off and get busy.   Here's what I want to do…"

Chapter 14

Najee And Gunz

St. Luke's Hospital

Good morning, ma'am. I'm investigating a crime that was committed against a woman named Rochelle Patterson a few days ago. She was brought here by an ambulance and treated. She spoke to a nurse that works here. I need to speak to that nurse about what Rachelle Patterson might have said to her. It's pretty important."

"So, what do you need from me, Officer?"

"I need to know if Marissa Proctor is working today and how I might find her?'

The woman that sat behind the counter of the information booth, dressed in hospital scrubs, typed quickly on her computer in front of her. "You're in luck, Officer. Marissa is here today. She's in the OB/GYN department on the fourth floor. Just catch the elevator over there to the fourth floor and someone at the desk, well…nurse's station, will call her for you."

"Thank you very much." I read the woman's name tag. "Ms. Burrell. You've been a big help."

"Anytime, Officer," Tonya Burrell answered. "Anytime."

I walked over to the elevator and pressed the button. A minute later the door opened. Instead of pressing the four, I pressed one. On the first floor, I exited the elevator and found the stairs. I descended the stairs quickly and walked out of the lobby. In the parking lot, I hopped into the Chevy Impala with Tye.

"Was she in there?" he asked as soon as the passenger door was shut.

"Yeah," I replied and smiled. "She's there. Drop me off at the Durango, then follow me to Shahid's parents' house. Hopefully, we can catch his mother and sister before they leave for church."

***

Chadwick Gardens Housing Complex

Knock. Knock. Knock. Knock.

"Who is that?" a voice from inside Apartment 36-B hollered out.

"Police! Open up! Need to speak to Angelina Jones!" I replied.

The door opened and a woman with a polka dot bonnet on her head stood there. The look on her face was one of annoyance. She was brown-skinned, with pretty eyes and lips. Her robe came open a little at the chest area and she moved to close it. "I'm Angelina Jones."

I pushed her immediately, catching her off guard. She fell to the floor.

"Hey! What the fuck are…?"

I stepped into the apartment with Rah Rah on my heels. He closed the door and locked it. I pulled the silenced nine-millimeter.

"Shut the fuck up!" I told the woman. "Where is Andre and Maya?"

The woman's expression changed from annoyance to terror. When the woman didn't respond, I told Rah Rah, who had his silenced gun in hand. "Go and search the spot."

Minutes later, I could hear the faint cough of Rah Rah's weapon. Then, he was back at my side. "No Andre, yo. But the girl was in her bedroom in bed. On her phone."

"And?"

"You already know."

The terrified woman heard the exchange between Rah Rah and me and opened her mouth to scream. But before a sound left her mouth, I silenced her. Two shots to her face knocked her brains out.

"Do you wanna wait for the son? See if he comes home?" Rah Rah asked.

I shook my head. "Ain't no telling when that will be. Let's bounce."

***

The old woman walked with the assistance of a cane.   Her daughter walked beside her.   The duo eventually got into a Mercedes S 550 sedan.

I put my cell phone in my pocket and turned to face Tye.   "That was Gunz.   They crushed Aziz's sister and her daughter.   The son wasn't home, so they left."

"That's what's up," Tye responded, watching the Mercedes.

"Go ahead and bounce.   Follow them to the church.   If you can, hit them before they go in.   If not, wait until they come out."

Tye hopped out of the Dodge Durango and jogged back to the Impala.   Seconds after the Mercedes pulled off, Tye was right behind it.

I glanced across the street at the house the two women had just exited.   The house at 103 Landers Street was three stories and not connected to either house on its side.   The lawn was well kept, and several luxury vehicles lined its driveway.   The house was painted with dark gray wooden shutters.   Black metal bars were on all of the first-level windows.   The front door was black.

I got out of the truck and walked across the street.   The navy windbreaker I wore over my sweatshirt had the word POLICE emblazoned across the back of it.   The baseball cap, I wore had the letters ATF on it.   A ball link chain hung from my neck.   A leather case held a fake badge that identified me as a federal agent.   I walked through the gate that surrounded the house, up the steps and knocked on the front door.

Seconds later, the door was answered by a woman in medical scrubs and Crocs.   She looked at me up and down. I flashed my fake badge on her.   "Can I help you?"   The woman had an African accent.

I pulled the silenced gun from my waist and pointed it at the woman.   "You sure can.   Back up and don't make a sound."

"Who are you?" I asked once the door was shut behind me.   We were in a foyer, the room beyond the foyer was empty.

"I-I-I'm a nurse," the woman replied. "A home health care nurse. For…for…for…Mr. Proctor."

"How many people are in this house right now?"

"Three—M-Mr. Proctor, his daughter Paula, and m…m…me."

"Where are the other two?" I asked.

"Ms. Paula…is…is…in her room on the second floor. Mr. Proctor's bedroom is on the third floor. He's there …in the room."

"Wrong place, wrong time, ma," I said and then shot the woman in the face. Her body dropped. I stood over her and shot her once more.

I walked around the dead nurse and climbed the stairs. On the second level of the house, I could hear gospel music coming from one of the bedrooms. "He saw the best in me/When everyone else around could only see the worst in me. They saw the best in me…"

"Rebecca, who was that at the door?" a woman's voice called out. I followed the sound of the music and the voice. It led me to the room at the end of the hall. The door was ajar. I peeked inside and saw a middle-aged woman with short hair, sitting on a bed with a laptop in her lap. She was wearing pajamas.

"Becca? The door. Who was at the door?"

I walked into the room then. "I was at the door. Hello, Paula."

"Hi," the woman said. Her face registered surprise and confusion.

"Do you have a brother named Muhammad Farid Shahid?"

Paula Proctor nodded her head.

"Too bad," I said and produced the gun from behind my back. I shot the woman named Paula repeatedly in the head and body. Then I walked over and unloaded my gun into her swollen head.

I turned and left the room. Ejecting the empty clip from the Ruger, I pocketed it, then slammed home a fresh, full clip into the gun. I moved through the house with authority. Up the stairs, then down a hall. I found the old man's room with ease. His door was ajar as well.

Using the elongated attachment on the gun barrel, I pushed the door open. The room smelled of Pine Sol, medicine and waste. It was a large room, painted a greenish color. An empty recliner sat next to a hospital style bed.   In the bed lay Melvin Proctor Sr., Muhammad Shahid's father.   He appeared to be asleep.   I walked over to the bed.   His eyes were closed.   I upped the gun and shot the old man repeatedly until he was no longer recognizable.   I pocketed the gun and calmly left the house.

***

Rah Rah's car was parked a block away from 244 Liberty Street. I sat in the car with him and watched the neighborhood that had come alive with activity in the last hour.

"The house sits next door to a bodega, yo.   With all the foot traffic, I know two things," I explained to Rah Rah.   "There's cameras everywhere…on the bodega and probably the lampposts and all the houses.   And there's people everywhere, who probably know the Joneses.   Even though we dressed like cops, we'd draw too much unwanted attention.   We can't walk up to the front of the house.   It's niggas panhandling by the bodega, they gotta bird's eye view of the both of us and we don't want that.   Plus, they see your vehicle.   Don't want that, either.   So, we gon have to ditch the police shit and blend in.   Make our way to the back of the house and do our thing from there.   Come on."

We did as I said and ended up in an alley directly behind 244. In the back yard, Rah Rah said, "Big homie, I got an idea." He picked up a green plastic recycling bin and walked up to the back door.   He knocked on the door.

Minutes later, a woman answered the door.   "Yes?"

"We're here to pick up the recyclable items, but your bin is empty.   Do you have…"

"The recycled stuff was already picked up two days ago.   They do it every Friday at noon…"

In a flash, Rah Rah produced his silenced weapons and shot the lady in the face.   Her body fell backwards as I walked up the back porch steps and entered the house behind Rah Rah.   I tapped him on the shoulder.

"Ease up, cowboy. You did good, but now the stepfather is mine," I told Rah Rah. From there I led the way through the house in search of Aziz Navid's stepfather. We found him in the living room watching TV. He looked down as we appeared and jumped to his feet.

"Who the hell…" was all he got the chance to say

I pulled the gun out and shot the man in the chest. Once he fell back on the couch, I walked up and put two in his forehead.

"Ayo, Gunz?" Rah Rah called out from behind me.

"Yo?" I responded and turned around.

"Son, I gotta shit. That breakfast I ordered from that diner got my stomach fucked up. My shit bubbling like a muthafucka. And I can't hold it."

Rah Rah looked like Martin Lawrence holding his stomach. I laughed.

"Go find a bathroom, nigga. Hurry up and shit, then come on. And don't touch anything and leave no prints."

Rah Rah farted as he left and all I could do was laugh.

***

"Tell me what happened," I told Tye as we leaned on the Durango in the parking lot of the Walmart.

"I can do better than that," Tye said and pulled out his cellphone. He pulled something up on the phone and passed it to me. "The news people can tell you."

"About an hour ago, on this busy intersection at First and Dubois, a new model Mercedes Benz carrying two females pulled into a parking lot here at the Ebenezer Baptist Church. and according to witnesses at the scene, as the two women exited the vehicle a lone man approached them. He helped the elderly woman in the passenger seat out of the car. As the woman grabbed a cane from the vehicle, the man pulled a gun and shot the elderly woman. Then he turned his gun on the second woman. Both women have been pronounced dead at the scene behind us here. Local authorities…"

"Good job. But please tell me you didn't wear the police jacket."

Tye gave me a crazy look. "Of course, I didn't. But I need to get rid of the clothes I have on now."

"Okay. Hop in and…then again, we're at Walmart, they got clothes in your size…"

"Naj," Tye protested, "I ain't wearing no clothes that come out of no…"

"Would you rather wear the clothes the jail gives you?" I asked.

"On that note, Walmart clothes it is. Come on."

"After that, we turn in your rental and go to the hospital. I think…Wait a minute, I just thought about something. If Shahid's daughter keeps up with the news, she'll know the two women in the new model Mercedes killed at Ebenezer Baptist were her aunt and grandmother. She'll leave to go home…"

"So, what are you saying? Fuck the clothes?"

"Yeah. Leave your car here. Let's get to the hospital and catch Marissa before…"

"I already know. Let's go."

***

"What's good, baby boy? Where are you at?" I asked Najee over the phone.

"At the hospital, about to go and holla at Shahid's daughter."

"You by yourself?"

"Naw. Me and Tye together. You?"

"Me and Rah inside the McDonald's eating a meal. This nigga Rah, yo, tha nigga shitted on hisself about an hour ago…"

"Don't believe that shit, Naj," Rah Rah hollered out.

"Wait a minute, yo. What McDonald's are y'all at?" Najee asked.

"The one where baby girl works. But she ain't here," I told him.

"So, y'all niggas decided to have a couple burgers?"

"Naw, yo — you know me. I ain't fuckin' with them burgers. I ordered the fish…"

"You know what the fuck I mean, son. Did you check and see—"

"Come on, son. You think you're the only muthafucka with a brain? Of course, I asked about ole girl. She comes in at three p.m."

"Y'all gon sit there and wait for her?"

"Baby boy, you acting crazy, yo. That bitch you creeping with fuckin with your head. Let me handle this over here and you handle that over there. Am I gon sit here and wait? I'm out. Holla back." I ended the call with Najee and looked at Rah Rah who was stuffing French fries in his mouth four at a time. "That nigga buggin', yo."

"Who, Naj?" Rah Rah asked.

I nodded. "Asking me a rack of dumb shit."

"Big bruh shit stressed out. He lost his bitch…"

"Who, Angel?"

"Yeah, Limah, his grandmother, Anessa…"

"Anessa? Hassan's sister?"

"Yeah. You know Najee always had a thing for Anessa. But Ha said she was off limits."

"I forgot about that." I told Rah Rah. "But.we all done lost somebody close. I lost Moms and Grandma. It don't get no worse than that. Losing them, Yasir, all of our friends…but we gotta keep pushin'."

"And killing," Rah Rah added.

"Most definitely. Kayla Jones is scheduled to come to work at 3:00 today. She's going to die at 2:59." I grabbed my Filet-o-Fish sandwich and my soda and stood up. "I'll be in the parking lot if you need me."

***

St.   Luke's Hospital

The OB/GYN department on the fourth floor of St. Luke's was active. Women with their children by their sides moved up and down the hallways. I found the nurses' station easy enough. There was a male nurse sitting at the desk writing something on a note pad. He was light-complexioned, mixed with hair obviously dyed pink. His hospital scrubs were multicolored. As I approached the station, his eyes found me.

The male nurse smiled. "Can I help you, sir?"

"You can. I'm looking for a nurse that works here."

"And her name is?"

"Marissa Proctor."

The man looked around for a moment, then pointed. "You're in luck then, because there's Marissa right over there by room 403."

"Thank you," I said.

"You're welcome," male nurse replied.

Marissa Proctor was young looking but put together nicely. Her hair was perfectly coiffed, her nails showed a French manicure, her skin was golden brown and flawless. She was petite and sexy. Her scrubs and Crocs were a solid pink color. I walked in line with her. "Marissa Proctor?"

The women eyed me suspiciously. "I'm she."

"My name is Special Agent Mike Thomas. Is there somewhere private that we can speak? It won't take long and it's very important."

Her look of suspicion changed to one of concern. "Of course, offi...Special Agent. There's a break room this way." Marissa Proctor led me to a room with a microwave oven, a small refrigerator and several chairs.

Once in the room, I didn't waste time. "Is your father named Muhammad Farid Shahid, formerly known as Melvin Proctor, Jr.?"

Marissa nodded her head.

"Sit down for a minute, please," I said.

When Marissa Proctor turned her head to find a seat, I produced the silenced gun. I shot her in the back of the head twice. When her body fell, I shot her twice more.

***

At exactly 2:53 p.m., a silver Audi A6 pulled into the McDonald's parking lot.   A minute later, a woman wearing a different version of a McDonald's uniform exited the car.   Her uniform shirt was long-sleeved and white, with blue pinstripes.   I got out of the car quickly and walked across the parking lot to meet her, my North Face beanie pulled down over my head.   The police jacket was gone, replaced by a North Face bubble coat.   I called out the lady's name.   "Hey, Kayla?"

Kayla Jones stopped in her tracks.   "Who is that?"

I pulled the gun out of my jacket pocket.   "It's death."   Kayla Jones screamed, but it didn't matter.   I shot her several times and then ran.

***

Under the Newburgh Beacon Bridge, Gunz set fire to the Chevy Traverse hybrid SUV that he'd used to get to Chadwick Gardens and the McDonald's on Broadway.   Rah Rah did the same to the rental he had.   I had already dropped off the Durango back at the rental place and so did Tye.   I didn't want all four vehicles not returning to draw too much attention.   The LaQuinta Hotel was about thirty blocks from the underpass near the bridge.   We walked the thirty blocks easily.   Back at the motel, we packed everything up and headed home.   Mission accomplished.

Chapter 15

Aziz Navid

Montpelier, NJ

Eisenhower Gym

The gymnasium was almost full to capacity.   Supporters of the children participating in the gymnastics competition.   My daughter, Azizah, beamed with pride as she completed a difficult routine on the uneven bars that had made the crowd crazy.   The bars had been lowered to accommodate my daughter's small, seven-year-old frame.

"That little girl reminds me so much of myself at her age," Nadia leaned into me and said, "But she's a much better gymnast then I was, though."

"I doubt that, knowing you," I replied.

"No, it's true, Aziz.   At seven, I was running around the gym like a banshee.   And you must remember our gyms were nothing like these in America.   They were small, cramped places that doubled and tripled for uses of all kinds, a Masjid, a hospital and a school.   I was often distracted by a lot of different things.   I only went to the place seeking out gymnastics to escape the life I had at home.

"Several of my young friends took gymnastics so I figured I could do it, too.   But I found out quickly the misery of home was embedded in me too much to succeed at gymnastics.   I was very miserable as a child, and it came through in my preparation at the gym.   My parents bickered all the time.   My father would hit my mother often.   To this day, I still cannot figure out why they decided to marry and have a child."

"I thought you loved your parents."

"I did love them.   Very much.   And I love them still.   But that doesn't change the fact that my home was broken, Aziz.   My father was raised a Shiite and my mother was raised a Sunni.   Love or lust, whichever it was that attracted them, is not always enough to surmount religious differences and politics. My father was Bahrain, through and through. He believed in the monarchy that ruled my homeland in the sixties and seventies. My father was a staunch advocate for Emir Hamod Bin Issn Khalifa, who eventually became king in the eighties.

My mother was born in Qatar but migrated to Bahrain as a child with her parents, who supported sectarian groups and the force now known as Al-Qaeda. Bahrain was one of many Saudi-led nations that broke diplomatic relations with Qatar, citing its support of groups they labeled as terrorists.

Bahrain then entered into an agreement that led the nation to Israel and bothered my father to no end. While my mother supported the alliance. My parents loved each other, but also hated each other. And I had to grow up in the middle of that emotional tug of war. I found solace in the gym. But also, mischief ZiZi, is way more focused than I was at seven."

"You've never told me any of this before."

"And I wouldn't have today but seeing ZiZi there made me nostalgic."

I was about say more, but my cell phone vibrated loudly. I pulled the phone and looked at the screen. The caller was my nephew, Andre. I ignored the call. But before I could pocket the phone, a ping alerted me to a text message. The text was from Andre. I read the text.

Uncle Aziz, please call me. It's urgent.

"It's Muhammad again, isn't it?" Nadia asked.

I shook my head. "No, it's my nephew, Andre. His text says to call, it's urgent."

"Well, call him then, Aziz."

Andre calling me from Newburgh one day after Muhammad Shahid learned his business had been targeted wasn't a good sign. I called my nephew back. "Andre, what's the problem?"

I listened to everything he said and dropped my head. By the time I ended the call, my eyes were full of tears. Nadia noticed immediately.

"Aziz, what happened?"

I rose from my seat on the bleachers.   "I have to get to New-burgh."

"Go to Newburgh? Why, Aziz?"

"Because my entire family is dead."

***

Newburgh, NY

Three hours later

Eleven missed calls from Muhammad Shahid.   I tossed the cell phone into the passenger seat of the Benz as I raced on Interstate 87.   Exit 17 appeared and I took it, almost too fast.   Steadying the car and my nerves, I crossed the George Washington Bridge and let my mind wander.   There was no way possible my family could be gone.   How? I thought about the one call from my nephew telling me his mother and sister were dead.   In between his tears, I could've sworn I heard him say everybody was dead.   I'd hung up the phone too quickly.   I should have asked more questions.

By the time I came out of my reverie, I was at the intersection of William and Renwick Street.   The storr on the corner brought back memories of my youth.   I hadn't seen this area in years.   I hadn't been back to Newburgh in over ten years. To avoid it, I'd always flown my family to New Jersey.   If I had any doubts about what I was told on the phone, turning on Chambers Street killed them.   The police activity was crazy. Yellow crime scene tape sur-rounded my mother's house, the house I had been raised in.

I had to park all the way at the end of the street and walk down. People I'd known my entire life lined and crowded the block lead-ing to my mother's house.   As I walked by, most of them just dropped their heads, neighbors congregated with the police.   I spot-ted my nephew Andre leaning on a car with his hands repeatedly wiping away tears.   He looked up just as I rushed him.   I grabbed him around the collar.

"What the fuck did you do?" I screamed. "What did you do?"

Andre wrestled my hand from the collar of his coat. "Me? I ain't do shit!"

"What the fuck happened then?"

"I don't know. I wasn't even here. I was in Brooklyn. Me and some friends were in the studio for a week making music. Ma…Ma called me and told me to come home…"

"When?"

Tears flooded Andre's eyes. "I don't know…a couple days ago, I think. I-I-I didn't come immediately. Thought she was just…thought she was on some bullshit. Tryna…tryna control me still, even though I'm grown. I-I-I-should've came home! I should've been here. Should have been here." Andre broke down. "Wouldn't have happened had I been there."

I grabbed my nineteen-year-old nephew and held him tight. His tears stained my cheek. My own tears stained my cheeks. Our pain was the same.

"T.J.?" a voice called out.

I recognized my teenage nickname and turned to see my childhood friend, Michael Collier, standing there. His coat was open to reveal a multicolored sweater and a gold detective shield hanging around his neck. Mike had become a police officer after getting out of the Navy when he was twenty-three years old. It had been at least twenty years since I'd last seen him.

"Yeah, Mike?"

"I hate that we have to meet after so long under dreadful and tragic circumstances, but it really is good to see you, T.J."

I wiped tears from my eyes and released Andre from my grasp.

"Andre," Mike greeted my nephew, "sorry about Angie and Maya."

Andre nodded his head and leaned back on the car, still crying.

"T.J., Mrs. Mona and Doug, Kayla—I'm brokenhearted about this. I ate at your mother's table on several occasions. Doug owned the store on Grant Street when we were kids. And Kayla…" Mike choked up. "When the call come in about Angie and Maya, I prayed Andre was okay, Then the call come in about your mom and

Doug. Then Kayla. I'm not assigned to any of these cases, but you can rest assured I am going to catch these…This may not be the best time to ask both of you this, but we need as much leeway as possible, for we're going to find out who did this. It's easier to solve in the first forty-eight hours if we have the clues. Do either one you have any idea who might've done something like this?"

"No," Andre replied.

I shook my head.

"Was somebody in the family beefing with somebody that you know of, Andre?"

"No."

"You, T.J.? Know of any beef?"

"No beef," I replied.

"How about enemies? Anybody who'd want to kill every-body?"

"Can't think of anyone," I said.

"Me neither," Andre stated.

"Listen, this situation…these murders were coordinated. and by multiple people. The initial investigation reveals somebody went from place to place, to place, the McDonald's on Broadway where Kayla worked. This was calculated, thought out and well executed. Which leads us to believe somebody pissed off some-body and we need to know how pissed off somebody is."

Andre covered his face with his hands and cried.

"I don't have a clue," I told Mike.

Exasperated, Mike Collier said, "T.J., let me speak to you for a minute—alone." He walked up the sidewalk and I followed him. One we were halfway up the block and out of range of all prying ears, Mike said, "I could lose my job for telling you this, but I got to. I owe that to your family…I know all about you and Melvin."

"Melvin?"

"Yeah, Melvin. As in Mel Jr., Melvin Proctor's son. I'm not calling him no fucking Muhammad Farid Shahid. Just like I've never called you Aziz. No disrespect to y'all's beliefs, but I don't know Aziz and Muhammad. I know T.J. and Melvin. And so does the local law enforcement here in Newburgh. We've heard all about this big drug organization the two of you are running. Connected to cartels and shit. The alphabet boys here know all about y'all, too, they've been watching your families for years..."

"Then they should know who did this shit, then."

"They don't and according to them, as long as you stay out of Newburgh, they aren't going to come after y'all. You and Melvin have been the topic of conversation around here for years. Rumors, speculation and myths. You've even been linked to ISIS and Islamic domestic terrorism, but nothing was ever confirmed. Until now. Both of your families all being killed on the same day? Shit! You don't know, do you? I assumed you did. Y'all pissed off somebody, T.J., you and Melvin. His family was killed today, too. Ms. Viola, Evelyn, Paula, Mr. Melvin Sr. —his daughter Marissa..."

"No! Can't be! Can't be!"

"It's true, T.J. Today is probably the worst day ever in Newburgh history. Altogether ten members of both families and Mr. Melvin Sr.'s healthcare nurse, Rebecca Fleming, were killed. Then, four more people unconnected to you and Melvin. That's fifteen homicides in one day." Mike looked down towards my mother's house. "See all of those guys huddled up by the entrance to the alley? All fed guys. They're all over this. Which means they've already made the same connection as me. Shit is about to get dicey, T.J. fast. You know why? Because shit like this ain't supposed to happen.

"Ten people, two families...all killed in one day. Mrs. Viola and Evelyn were gunned down in a fucking church parking lot, for Christ's sake. The smell of this reeks of cartels, Mafia...shit like that. We see a lot of murders in Newburgh, T.J. , usual shit. Bloods beefing with other Blood sets, Crips and Bloods beefs, domestic violence, smoked out drug users killing other junkies. A robbery gone bad. A home invasion turned to homicide. Regular everyday life in the city. But this," Mike emphasized by waving his hand towards my family home,"Shit like this doesn't happen here. People are afraid.

"The mayor's been at City Hall secluded in a room within state and out of state law enforcement since about 3:00 p. m.   I know you, T.J.   I know the man you are.   I've heard all the stories about the people you've killed back in the day.   Don't make the mistake of trying to go after these guys on your own.   If you know who's responsible for these killings…tell me.   Let me do my job—"

"I already told you I don't know who did this.   But I'm going to find out and I promise you that I will let you know before I do anything," I lied to Mike.

"For some reason, T.J., I just don't believe that."

"Good, because you shouldn't." I said and walked away.

"T.J.! T.J.! C'mon, T.J., talk to me!"

I ignored Mike Collier, walked to my car and left the scene.

***

Sixteen missed calls from Muhammad Shahid.   And now I know why.   I picked up the phone and dialed Muhammad's number.

"Aziz? Where are you?" Muhammad asked.

"I'm in Newburgh," I replied.

"Still think I'm being paranoid?"

"So, you know, huh?"

"Stay by your phone.   I should be landing in Newburgh momentarily." The line went dead.

***

St.   Luke's Hospital

Staff Parking Lot

"Assalamu Alaikum," Wakil Muhmin greeted.

"Walaakeem Assallam," I replied.

The security detail that guarded Muhammad Shahid had spread themselves out in the parking lot.   Darcel Faroog, Asa Abdul and

Carlton Musa stood around the only car parked in the area, a candy apple red Mercedes Benz C330. Wakil stood near its hood. I opened the door to the Mercedes' passenger side and climbed inside. Muhammad Farid Shahid sat behind the wheel of the luxury vehicle.

"This is the car I bought Marissa, Aziz," Muhammad said after a brief moment of silence. "Right after she finished nursing school. I wanted my only child to have something much better, but this is what she chose. I thought by staying away from her life I could shield her from mine. I only wanted her to be a better person than me. She had her whole life in front of her, Aziz, and now she's gone, at twenty-five years old. Killed at work. The job she loved."

After another brief pause, Muhammad said, "I called you yesterday and told you about my business being destroyed. I suspected the culprit was Najee and his men. You told me it was impossible, Aziz. You told me I was being paranoid when I told you I didn't believe in coincidences. My last words to you were for you to think about how my business in Newburgh and Newark could be targeted, my associates killed and those incidents not be connected.

"I told you to call me back. You never did. And now, not even twenty-four hours later, my mother, father, two sisters and my daughter are dead. All shot and killed on the same day, hours apart. Someone is at war with me—with you—us. Our organization. It is your job, Aziz, to protect the organization. Our families were connected to us. And we are the organization. Who is that doing this, Aziz, if not Najee Bashir and his men?"

"I lost my family, too, Ocki."

"I know that, Aziz. I was told of your misfortunes as well. But you still haven't answered my question, Aziz. Who is it that did this? That killed our families?"

"But how could it be Najee, Muhammad? Najee and his friends are street guys. How could they have found out our personal histories? Who knew where our families were? It makes no sense!"

"The answer is more simple than you think, Aziz. Someone is helping him. Najee Bashir is guided by an unforeseen head. Someone powerful. Someone like us."

"But who? What connections could Najee have?"

"Think about something for a minute, Aziz. Najee had been at odds with not just us. He's been pursued by the Trinidad organization in DC as well. That makes not one but two strong organizations that want Najee Bashir dead. But yet he lives, Aziz! How do you explain that?"

As baffled as I was, a thought hit me. "Hold on a minute, Ocki," I said and pulled out my cell phone. I called Khitab.

He answered on the second ring. "Assalamu Alaikum."

"Walaikum Assalam. Ocki, do me a favor. Check with your sources in Najee's camp and find out if Najee and any of his friends were out of town the last day or so. I need you to do that for me right now, Ocki. Khitab clicked over. About four minutes later, he was back on the line. "Khitab?"

"Yeah, Ock, I'm here. I just talked to my source."

"What did he say?"

"Four of the crew was out of town. They left right after the shooting at the candlelight vigil, they been gone for two days. According to him, they went to a place called Newburgh. A city in New York. He says they are on their way back now, if they aren't back already."

I couldn't believe it. Muhammad was right. Najee and his friend had come to Newburgh and killed our families.

"Khitab, listen to me, Ocki. Listen to me good. Get with your source. I don't care what you have to tell him, how much you have to pay him, extort, threaten him, whatever. But in a week's time, I'll be back in Newark. And when I get there, on the same day I need to kill Najee and all of his friends. No more playing games. No more back and forth. I'm not asking, I'm demanding that your source makes his friends available for my gun. And Khitab, if I cannot kill Najee and his friends after I bury my entire family in Newburgh, New York, I'm going to kill your source. And then I'm going to kill you, Khitab. Do I make myself clear?"

"Ocki— I'm sorry about your family. I had no..."

"Khitab, I'ma ask you again. Do I make myself clear?"

"You're clear, Ock. You're clear."

I ended the call with Khitab and dropped the cell phone on my lap. "You were right. I was wrong. Najee and his friends are responsible. I'm going to kill them all."

"You have to, Aziz. But I need you to do me a favor. Save Najee for me. Kill everybody in his crew and every family member you can find, but Najee belongs to me. I want to torture him before I kill him myself. Can you do that for me?"

"I can, Ocki. I will do that," I told my mentor.

"And while you do that, I will be finding out who's helping Najee. The moment I get out of this car, I will be putting the word out that I need a name. The name of the powerful person behind Najee's strength. When I get that name or names, I want to kill whoever it is."

"No doubt, Ock. That goes without saying."

"My daughter never harmed a soul in her life."

"I already know, Ock. I already know."

With that said, I opened the door and got out of the Mercedes. Muhammad Shahid needed to be alone.

***

"Nadia?"

"I'm here, Aziz."

"I love you."

"I love you, too, husband."

"Where's ZiZi?"

"In her room. In bed, asleep."

"Kiss her for me, please."

"I will. Are you okay, Aziz?"

"I'm not, Nadia."

"Please get some rest, husband. You need your rest."

"It was Najee, Nadia. Najee and his friends killed my family."

"Are you sure, Aziz?" Nadia asked.

"Postive.   It was confirmed it was him…them."

"Oh, my gawd.   I'm sorry.   I'm so sorry."

"Muhammad's family was killed, too."

"Aziz—I don't know what to say."

"Well, I do, Nadia. Killing Najee's family and his friend's family was a mistake.   I listened to Muhammad and I listened to you and now look."

"Are you saying that you blame me, Aziz?"

"No, Nadia. I blame myself. Because I could have refused the order from Muhammad. But I didn't. Now my whole family is dead. Muhammad's family is dead. It's the qadir of Allah."

Anthony Fields

Chapter 16

Honesty

Suitland, MD

"Angel is not here. She's in jail. At the CTF. She was arrested a few days ago during a traffic stop. The police found a gun in her car. She was looking for you."

The sunshine permeated the small curtains on the windows high on the basement wall. Another day was upon me and still Angel lived. Trigger stirred beside me on the couch bed and snored lightly. I laid in bed and stared at the ceiling. Sleep had been hard to find since I was forced to give Angel's daughter to the man named Benito. He said something to me in the parking lot that wouldn't leave my mind. He had answered the questions I had thought to myself and verbalized to Trigger the entire time I had the little girl. Where was Angel? Why couldn't her own daughter get in touch with her?"

"Angel is not here. She's in jail. At the CTF. She was arrested—"

All I could do was shake my head in amazement, lay there and smile. The bitch Angel must have a three-leaf clover up her ass. Her good luck puzzled me. Her ability to escape death vexed me. Her still being alive after all I'd done to end her, angered me. My whole plan to kidnap Angel's daughter and use her as bait so I could kill Angel had backfired. Backfired and resulted in a death, but not the death of the right person.

I thought about David Preston, my aunt Wanda's boyfriend who'd been killed by Carlos Trinidad's men. I'd met him on several occasions, and he wasn't a bad guy. He was actually pretty decent, and he doted on my cousins, Wanda's children. His only sin was that he'd fallen in love with the wrong woman. A woman connected to me. I felt terrible about Dave's death and the fact that Wanda and her children had witnessed his murder, and that they'd all been threatened and sworn to secrecy by the man who'd killed

Dave. All of which I'd learned from one of my grandmothers. My mother's mother. My entire family wanted answers from me. Answers that I couldn't provide. Refused to provide.

So, after talking to my grandmother briefly after returning from dropping Aniyah off to Benito, I turned my phone off. What was I supposed to say to Aunt Wanda to ease the pain about Dave? What answers would I give both of my grandmothers who endured the most terrifying night of their lives? Especially without revealing too much info into what I'd done and what I had to do in the future? One day I'd give them the answers they needed. But that one day would have to wait. At least until after Angel was dead.

"Carlos knew your father and so did I. He was a good man. Loyal to us. That is why we won't take your life. Not because you gave the girl back because of your father, Tony.

Visions of my father came to mind. Images of him in different aspects of fatherhood. I loved him dearly but realize how very little I actually knew about Anthony "Tony Bills" Phillips. I remembered all the newspaper articles after his death and how he'd been rumored to be a part of the Trinidad Organization.

The news people had said similar things after Angel was arrested and linked to his murder. But my mother and I had dismissed those rumors as false. But Saturday night I had learned those rumors were true. Tears welled up in my eyes and fell. Drug dealer or not, he still didn't deserve to die the way he had. At the hands of a beautiful killer. His beautiful side piece. Currently imprisoned on a gun charge. Suddenly, something else Benito said, came to mind.

"I respect you, Honesty. Really, I do. What man can't respect a daughter's quest to avenge her slain father? Especially when he was killed unjustly? Angel may be Carlos Trinidad's daughter's mother, but she is no friend of mine. Never has been. I believe she should have been killed for what she did to your father. But the decision was not mine to make. Angel is being held in custody for a seven-day period. She'll be released on Wednesday. A little more

than three days from now. I suggest you get to the Superior Court-house and surprise her as she leaves the building or somewhere near there. It's what I would do...

When I was in school, a friend of mine had called me gushing about a book series she had read and loved. It was entitled *The Ultimate Sacrifice* series. One of the books came to mind. I'd read the entire series and while I didn't love it as much as Chance, I thought it was realistic and entertaining. In the series' third book subtitled, *No Regrets*, the main character Khadafi was being released from jail one night.

Lil Cee, the dude who wanted to kill Khadafi, surprised Khadafi as he left the jail. It was essentially what Benito was implying I do. The only difference being that in the book Lil Cee surprised Khadafi at night as he'd left jail. I would be ambushing Angel in broad daylight as she left court. It would take some planning to get the job done. Even more planning to get away with it.

"But I'm definitely game," I said aloud. "I'ma kill her ass once and for all."

"Huh?" Trigger awoke and said, "What did you say?"

"Nothing, baby. Go back to sleep. I was thinking out loud."

Trigger turned over and sat up. "You gotta go and see the detective, right? That's this morning, right?"

"Yeah, it is. In a few hours."

"I'ma get up and get ready to take you."

"Now don't trip, baby. Get some rest. I'll drive myself there."

"You sure? Because I am tired as shit. You wore my ass out yesterday."

I leaned up and pulled Trigger to me, kissed his lips. "I did what I was supposed to do. What you said I always do. Fuck my man."

"True, I'm surprised you ain't pregnant."

"Me, too, baby. Me, too."

117

Chapter 17

Detective Mitch Bell

District Attorney's Office

Hyattsville, MD

After knocking on her office door, I walked into Dom's office. A bag of food and my Louis Vuitton man bag in hand.

"Something smells good, Mitch, what is it?"

"Just two turkey bacon, egg and cheese croissants," I replied.

"And this is for me?"

I nodded my head.

"Are you trying to bribe me, Detective?"

I sat the bag on Dom's desk. "Only if it works in my favor."

Dom smiled, reached for the bag and extracted a cellophane wrapped breakfast sandwich. She unwrapped it and bit into it. "Mmm, good. Damn good!"

"I knew you'd like them. They came from Ms. Debbie's Soul and Seafood Cafe. All their food is good as hell." I took the seat across from the A.D.A. and sat down.

"Remind me to stop by there one day. Sit, Detective, tell me what you've got for me."

"I got the DVD I told you about on the phone Saturday. It's footage from a home security set up across the street from Tina Brown's house. The footage is from the evening that Tina Brown was killed. The video footage shows a van—a balloon delivery van—pulling up and parking across from Tina Brown's house. It shows Tina Brown pulling into her driveway and going inside her home. A delivery man or woman, can't really tell which, goes to Tina Brown's front door with balloons in hand. The delivery person goes into the house and doesn't exit, until thirty-nine minutes later. I'm assuming Tina Brown invited the person into her home. In between time, Honesty Philips pulls into the driveway of her mother's house. She goes into the house. Minutes later, the delivery person leaves the house through the front door, sort of in a hurry, the person gets into the van and leaves quickly.   Minutes later, the police arrive."

"Hold on…wait, back up, Detective.   I'm missing something. Why did the police arrive?"

"My bad, Dom.   I got a little ahead of myself. So, Honesty Phillips pulls into the driveway and parks behind her mother's car. The delivery person is still inside the house.   He or she never left. Somehow, a shoot-out happens inside the house.   Neighbors called the cops.   The delivery person leaves the house about ten minutes after Honesty Phillips arrives.   Gets in the van and takes off.   And get this…the delivery person leaves the house with the same balloons he or she took inside the house thirty minutes earlier.   The cops get there and discover Tina Brown has been killed.   I get the call to go to Benedict Court."

Dom finished the sandwich and wiped her hands on a napkin. She opened a drawer on her desk and pulled out a small bottle of water.   After drinking half of it, she commented,   "I'm still lost. If the delivery person was in the house when Honesty got there, then she should be able to identify the person who delivered the balloons, right?"

"That's the thing.   Honesty Phillips never mentioned any delivery person to us.   All she told us was that she came home, only to surprise an intruder and her mother was already dead when she got home."

"She never mentioned the balloon delivery person at all?"

"No."

"Maybe she implied that the intruder and the delivery person were one and the same."

"She didn't imply that, say that or allude to that.   She never said anything about a delivery person at all.   We never knew about the van or the balloon delivery person until we saw the DVD."

"Detect…Mitch, listen to me, I graduated at the top of my class at Columbia.   I've always prided myself on being one of the smartest people in any room.   But I'm still failing to see the picture that you are trying to paint for me.   Help me out here."

"Okay, let me simplify this. Elucidate a little more. I was the investigation detective who arrived at the house on Benedict Court the evening Tina Brown was murdered. Checked out the scene. Interviewed Honesty Phillips and listened to her story about what she knew about her mom's murder. Her story didn't jibe with me or my partner, Sgt. Voss. Called her to the station and interviewed her again weeks later. She told me the exact same intruder story. All about how she surprised the intruder and how they had a shoot-out in the home, then the intruder escaped out the front door.

"She never mentioned anything about a balloon delivery person being in the house. I can't disprove her story, can't confirm it. Case goes cold. I came to you last week with the letter found…"

"A letter you lifted illegally from Kareemah El-Amin's vehicle."

"Correct. But the letter was obtained nevertheless and allegedly written by who? Honesty Philips. And in that letter, she implicates the person that killed her mother…Angel."

"Kareemah El-Amin?"

"Yep. She says in the letter Angel…Kareemah El-Amin killed her mother and her father. Where did I find said letter? In Kareemah's car. After you declined to get me a judge who'd sign off on an affidavit for a warrant to search, I called Sgt. Voss, who told me about the DVD. Apparently, he had the DVD but forgot to tell me about it because we were all working the John Hackett…"

"The P. G. cop killed on Marlboro Pike. Him and Agent Tom Chaney."

I nodded. "Right. We were consumed with finding their killers. And I was also working the Donte Stevenson case. I go to the station and view the DVD. I see exactly what I've been explaining to you about the delivery person being at the house that night Tina Brown was killed. Afterwards, I do my research and learn the van from the video footage and the balloon company is owned by a woman named Jenelle Kearney. Ms. Kearney is a native of DC. I went to her home on Saturday and spoke to her. Showed her The DVD footage. She positively identified her van and guess who she says she gave the van to on May twenty-third of last year?"

"Kareemah El-Amin."

I nodded my head and smiled.

Dom Oliver leaned back in her chair and closed her eyes. "Let me see—we have an illegally obtained letter allegedly written by Honesty Phillips, where she implicated Kareemah El-Amin in the death of Naimah El-Amin, who was killed last week. You have no evidence, other than the letter that connects Phillips to the El-Amin murder, correct?"

"Correct."

"And you have no evidence other than that illegally obtained letter that may or may not have been written by Honesty Phillip and a DVD…Security camera footage, that shows a delivery van and a balloon delivery person taking balloons to the murder victim's house on May twenty-third. The video footage doesn't give clear and convincing images that the delivery person was Kareemah El-Amin but the van, and company owner swears that she gave the van to El-Amin. There's no video footage from inside the house that shows us who committed the murder of Tina Brown, and Tina Brown's daughter, Honesty Phillips, isn't cooperating with authorities and saying that Kareemah El-Amin killed her mother. Is everything I just said accurate?"

Listening to the assistant district attorney sum up my entire load of evidence made my spirits tank. "Yeah, that's accurate."

Dom Oliver opened her eyes and looked directly at me. "Mitch, if we were actors on an episode of Law *and Order*, what you have would be enough for an indictment, but in the real world, it's not. The letter was obtained illegally. The video footage can be dissected and dismissed easily. The van owner saying she gave Kareemah El-Amin her company van on the day of the murder isn't enough to prove that El-Amin was the person driving the van and entered the murder victim's home on May twenty-third. And I did mention, Kareemah El-Amin is represented by J. Alexander Williams…"

"One of the best criminal defense attorneys in the country, Yeah, you mentioned that."

"So, you still don't have enough to make me go after Kareemah El-Amin or Honesty Phillips for murder."

I reached in my bag and pulled out the plastic bag that held the bullet fragments taken out of Samir Nadir. I laid the bag with the bullets in them on Dom Oliver's desk. "Kareemah El-Amin was arrested in DC, with a loaded Glock .40 weapon. These bullets were taken out of the male victim at the Deborah Drive crime scene. Samir Nadir was killed with a forty-caliber weapon. Kareemah El-Amin was inside the house on Deborah Drive the night of the murders. We can prove that. I need to have the ballistics…"

"Wait… I thought the male victim…"

"Samir Nadir."

"The male victim, Samir Nadir was Kareemah's uncle? Her mother's brother?"

I nodded "But for some reason, I believe she killed him. I believe Honesty Phillips killed Naimah El-Amin, took a child… I need your help in getting someone to let me test that gun—"

"I think I can do that, Detective."

"If the bullets right there do not match ballistics with the gun in DC, then I'll stop bothering you. If they do match, then you help me take down both Kareemah El-Amin and Honesty Phillips for murder."

"Okay, Mitch. I'm in. Leave the bullets with me and I'll get authorization to have the ballistics test done. Let me make some calls. I'll get back with you soon."

"Music to my ears, Dom. Thank you."

***

Second District Police Station

Oxon Hill, MD

Honesty Phillips walked into my office. The young woman was pretty. Her hair was pulled back into a ponytail. She wore jeans, Ugg boots and a bubble coat.

"Ms. Phillips, glad you could make it,". I greeted the young woman. "Please have a seat in that chair right there." Honesty took the seat opposite my desk. "First, I need you to tell me again what you remember about the night your mother was killed."

"It's been ten months, Detective. I can't remember all of the details of what happened that evening."

"Just do the best you can, Ms. Phillips. Please."

"Okay. I pulled into the driveway of my house…"

I listened to the story Honesty Phillips told. It was pretty much the same story she'd told us the night of the murder and the day I talked to her at the station.

"Ms. Phillips…Honesty, do you remember seeing a van parked near your house that night?"

"A van? What kind of van? No, not really."

"What about whether or not the intruder was a woman?"

"A woman? I don't think it was a woman."

"Never saw any balloons or flowers in the house that night?"

"Not that I can recall, no."

I thought about all the holes in the Honesty story. "And the intruder was wearing a mask that night, right?"

"That's what I said, yeah," Honesty replied.

"You retrieved a gun from the kitchen area and surprised the intruder. He fired his gun at you and then you returned fire?"

"Correct."

"Then at some point the intruder fled, correct?"

"Correct."

"And you just let him go, right? Didn't chase after him at all?"

"I didn't chase after him, no."

"So, you remember if anybody else was in the house that night?"

"Somebody else like who?" Honesty asked defensively.

"I don't know. Anybody. Do you recall seeing another person in your house that night?"

"No."

"Are you sure?"

"Of course, I'm sure. Nobody else was inside my house that night."

"And what door did the intruder escape out of?"

"Not sure, but I believe he left through the front door."

"How many exits are there to your home, Honesty?"

"Three. The front door, the back door, and one on the side of the house that lets out onto the patio."

"And you think that the intruders left through the front door. Why is that?"

"Because I came in through the back door. My back was to that direction. The side door was—wait, why is this even important, Detective? Where are you going with this? On the phone, you said you discovered something new in the case. What is it? Or did you call me here just to answer the same questions over again?"

"I apologize, Honesty…"

"Ms. Phillips."

"Right, Sorry, Ms. Phillips, but I'm a stickler for details. Comes with the job description." I grabbed my laptop and opened it up. I sat it on the table near Honesty and turned it to face her. After powering it on, I pressed play on the DVD. "This is what I discovered that's new. It's footage from a home security system installed on the house directly across from your house. Watch it." I stood beside Honesty's chair and watched the video. At the conclusion of the footage, I walked back around the desk to face Honesty.

"The van was there when your mother arrived home. She walks into the house. Minutes later, the person in the van gets out, holding balloons. The person goes to your front door and knocks. The door opens and the person with the balloons goes inside the house. And doesn't come out. Did you see that?"

"I saw that," Honesty replied.

"Almost thirty minutes later, you came home. You pulled into the driveway behind the Lexus, but next to your mother's Benz truck. You get out of the Cadillac truck and stop. Then you go to the Benz truck and look inside it. What were you looking for?"

"I don't remember."

"Right. Well, on the video, you did see here…after you went inside the house, minutes later, the delivery person walks right out your front door. Still carrying the balloons. Did you see that?"

"I did see that, yes."

"And you're sitting here telling me you never saw that person…the delivery person…inside your house?"

"That's exactly what I'm saying. I never saw that person in the house."

"Honesty, be honest with me. Do you want us to find the person that killed your mother?"

"Of course, I do. Why would I not?"

"Maybe you want to find the person who killed your mother yourself."

"What makes you think that, Detective? I'm not that kind of a person. I'm just a child of two murdered parents. I'm a young woman who graduated college last year and still hasn't found a job in my field. A job that aligns with my degree. "I'm just a little…""

"Honesty…Ms. Phillips, do you know a woman by the name of Kareemah El-Amin?"

Honesty Phillips' face flushed, becoming drained of all color. But only for a minute. She recovered it quickly. "No. Should I know her?"

"You've never heard that name before?" I forged on.

"Don't think I have," Honesty replied.

"What about Kareemah El-Amin's nickname Angel? Ever heard that name before?"

"Went to school with a couple of chicks with that nickname. Years ago."

"But you don't know any woman named Kareemah El-Amin also known as Angel?"

"Nope. Never heard of her. Is that it, Detective? Or do you have something else for me to see?"

"Unfortunately, that's all I have. You can go. But before you leave, I need one more thing from you."

Honesty Phillips rose from her chair. "And what's that, Detective?"

I pulled out the papers that I had typed minutes before Honesty arrived. "If you don't mind, could you please print your name on these papers? Then sign each one." Honesty did what I asked her to do. "These are release forms authorizing the release of all the things we took from your house the night of your mother's murder. On the last form, I need for you to carefully write out that you, Honesty Phillips, authorized and will take possession for all seized items taken from 12114 Benedict Court, then sign and date that."

Once that was done, I walked Honesty out to the lobby and bid her farewell. "I'll call you if I need anything else."

"You do that, Detective," Honesty said and departed. I almost ran back to the office at a full sprint. I pulled out the letter I'd found in Angel's BMW and put it alongside the page where Honesty had just written what I asked her to write. All I could do was smile. The handwriting on the form I gave Honesty matched the writing on the letter perfectly. It was undeniable that the same person had written both. The loopy letters. The signature at the end of the letter. It all matched. That proved what I'd said all along. Honesty Phillips was a pretty little liar. She'd lied to me through her teeth moments ago, then she denied knowing who Angel was. Honesty knew the delivery person inside her house on the night her mother was murdered, was Angel.

She'd seen Angel's face clearly. Knew Angel was her mother's killer. I thought about all the questions I had just asked Honesty, but one question stuck out more than others. The one I'd asked her about wanting to kill the person who' killed her mother. . Then I thought about Honesty's answer.

"I'm not that kind of person—"

"Oh, you are definitely that kind of person, Ms. Phillips," I said to myself. There was one thing I was absolutely sure of, and that was Honesty Phillips wanted to avenge the death of her parents.

To do that, meant she had to kill Angel. And it was my job to make sure that didn't happen.

Chapter 18

Honesty

As I left the police station and climbed into the driver's seat of the Caddy truck, all I could think about was the detective's questions about Angel. What made him ask me about her? What was my connection to Kareemah El-Amin to him? What did he know that I didn't know? I sat back in my seat, fastened the seatbelt, and racked my brain for answers to the questions in my head. But no answers came. I couldn't figure out for the life of me why Detective Bell asked me about a van and delivery person. Then I thought about the video he showed me. The footage captured the night Angel came to my house and the moments she left.

I was caught in lies on some things I said...but fuck it. I never even paid attention to what Angel had been wearing that night. Nor had I run to a window to see what she'd been driving as she escaped me. Images from that night came to mind...*at the exact same moment that my gun locked on her, Angel's gun locked on me.* Not even ten feet from one another, we both stood ready to kill.

"So, we meet again, huh, Honesty?" Angel said.

"It sure looks that way, huh?" I replied.

"The sad part is that we were never really introduced. Hi, I'm Angel."

"What did my mother do to you? Why kill her?"

"Your mother and I go way back. She sold me a rack of death many years ago. After I survived your attempt on my life, I always wondered if she had groomed you and sent you on that mission. But either way, she had to go because after I kill you, she would have become a bitter enemy. Besides, now she can be with your father."

"We're all about to see him again. Me, you and her. Are you ready to die? Because I am."

"Now, I have a lot more living to do before I die. But you can tell me what it's like once I get there. Be a good girl and put your gun down."

"Not in a million years."

"Well, go ahead shoot me then. Oh, my bad, you already tried that once, huh?"

"Even a cat has nine lives. You killed my father. Fair exchange ain't no robbery."

"Fair exchange?" Angel shouted. I could see the spit fly from her mouth in rage. *"You almost killed my daughter. I was pregnant. She was innocent."*

"And so was my mother. But you killed her anyway."

"I like your style, Honesty. You remind me of myself when I was your age. I killed my own father when I was fifteen years old. You tried to kill me and my unborn child when you was fourteen. So, we sorta have something in common. My father was a piece of shit that raped me and then tried to rape my little sister. All while hiding behind a beautiful religion. I killed your father because I needed his connections and I couldn't get it while he was still alive. I killed your mother because of what you did to me and for that same reason, I'm 'bout to kill you."

Something in my head screamed, *move.* I moved at the exact same moment Angel fired her gun…

I remembered the shootout we had like it was yesterday. I remembered diving on the floor and hiding behind stuff, the chipped pieces of wood that rained down on me were from the wood sculpture on a table near where I was. I remembered running and shooting, shooting and running. I remembered hiding in the kitchen, waiting for Angel to pursue me. As I waited, I remembered the silence. It was so loud then. Then the door slammed shut and I knew Angel had left the house through the front door. I never even thought to run after her. My instinct took me to where my mother lay dead. I collapsed beside her and cried until the cops stormed the house.

Seeing the video footage of Angel casually walking away holding balloons and flowers made my blood boil, but I couldn't reveal that to the detective. Instead, I'd simply played dumb. As I started the truck and pulled out of the station parking lot, I still couldn't figure out where the detective was headed with his investigation and how he'd know that the person leaving the house that evening was Angel. I turned onto Livingston Road and headed for the highway. I had to be careful. The black detective named Mitch Bell was a lot smarter than I had originally thought. And being smart made him very dangerous.

***

The Carl H. Moultrie Superior Courthouse was at 500 Indiana Avenue in Northwest DC. I circled the block a few times, surveying the area. The entrance to the courthouse was also its main exit point. Large cement barriers were erected around the building to prevent a vehicle from being able to crash its way into the building. Parking was allowed across the street from the courthouse but not directly in front of it. There were large, "No Parking At Any Time" signs that you couldn't miss. A steady stream of foot traffic went to and from the courthouse non-stop. If there was a way to ambush Angel as she left the courthouse, I would find it. I had to. My life depended on it.

Anthony Fields

Chapter 19

Carlos

"This gumbo is delicious," Benito gushed.

"Mila makes it from scratch, comrade. It's the Mexican version filled with pearly shrimp, sweet crab and cod swimming in shrimp stock seasoned with dried herbs, sliced serrano and cayenne."

"Delicious."

I bit into one of my tacos stuffed with chicken breast, roasted squash, peppery arugula and doused with lemon ranch dressing, garnished with toasted pumpkin seeds.

"Benito, you never told me exactly how you got my daughter back."

Benito backed away from the table and wiped his mouth. then he pulled a cigar from his jacket pocket and lit it. He pulled generously on the cigar then exhaled the pungent smoke into the air. "It was simple, mi amigo. I did what you would have done. I sent our men to every address you gave me. I chose to go to Honesty's aunt's house in Southeast. There I was able to speak Honesty and persuade her to give us back your daughter. But not before I killed her aunt's boyfriend."

"Honesty's aunt Wanda had a boyfriend present?"

Benito nodded and puffed on the cigar again. "His name was David. I needed the woman...Honesty, to know how serious I was, so I killed Dave while she listened on the phone. But that wasn't the only reason I killed him."

"What was the other reason, Benito?"

"He reminded me of a young Bill Cosby, and I hate Bill Cosby."

I laughed out loud, and it resonated throughout the whole kitchen area. "I thought you loved *The Cosby Show*. As teenagers, I remember you watched it often when it was on TV"

"I didn't like the show. I was in love with Denise, Lisa Bonet's character. I loved her even more after I saw the movie she made with Mickey Rourke..."

"*Angel Heart.* I remember it well."

"That cocksucka Bill Cosby fired her from the show after the movie came out, Because of the explicit sex scenes she did. Ruined her career. And here it is, all these years later, we find out he was drugging and raping women back then. Fucking hypocrite."

"Other than Dave, who looked like Bill Cosby, no one else was hurt?"

"No one. Honesty quickly agreed to give me Aniyah after hearing her entire family would die that day if Aniyah was not returned to us. She wanted to save her family. Smart girl."

"What did Honesty say to you? Did she ask about Angel?"

"When I met with her to get Aniyah, I could see she was visibly afraid. I believe she thought Angel would appear any moment and kill her. I had to dispel that by letting her know that Angel was in jail."

"And what did Honesty say when you told her that?" I asked.

"She asked me would you become involved if she killed Angel."

"And?"

Benito put his cigar out. Then he ate more of his food. "I told her that her personal feud with Angel was just that. A feud between the two of them and that as long as the little girl...Aniyah, was left out of it, then we wouldn't get involved. "I hope I didn't misspeak, mi amigo."

"You didn't, Benito. Continue."

"I told her I didn't kill her because she didn't know Aniyah was your daughter. I told her that her father was a good man and Angel shouldn't have killed him. And Angel should have been killed for killing Tony, but the decision was not mine."

"Her father was a good man, Benito. Loyal, honest, and ambitious."

"But yet you forgave Angel for killing Tony unjustly."

I thought briefly about what Benito had just said. "Tony had been dead for a couple of years and there was no way to bring him back. I always suspected that Angel had killed Tony. But I couldn't be sure of her guilt. When she got arrested for the murders she committed to avenge her sister, I respected her on a different level. To me, it was rare to see a woman…a young, black woman…with her level of dedication to the game, to the streets. The whole scheme she put together to meet me and get put on was something I hadn't seen before. It was cruddy, but courageous and daring. The way Angel handled business reminded me of Griselda Blanco."

"Don't you mean, Rosalie Zapanero?"

"Maybe. Maybe I did see a little Rosalie in Angel. I don't know. But at the time, I kinda respected the fact that Angel admitted she killed Tony. I had Dorothy next to me inside the sauna. She had a gun under a towel. It was pointed at Angel the entire time we talked. Dorothy's instructions were clear. If I turned and looked at her, she was to shoot Angel and kill her. When Angel told me why she killed Tony, for some reason, I respected it. I told her that what she did was something the American Mafia—"

"Or the Colombian cartels?" Benito interjected.

"Correct, comrade. The Mafia or the cartels would have done. What she did was something I would have done, had I been in her position."

"And what position is that, Carlos?"

"A woman, Benito. Simply her being a woman."

"So, that's why you let it go?"

I nodded my head.

"Well, you didn't just let it go, mi amigo. That night, you also let something else go…inside of Angel. And now you have a little girl who's almost ten."

Smiling, I thought about the little girl who was somewhere in the house with one of the housekeepers that catered to whatever she needed. My heart swelled with pride, with love. "Thank you, Benito, for bringing Aniyah home to me. I still can't believe how surreal life can be. I never knew that little girl existed until a week ago. But seeing her for the first time a couple days ago, brought me to tears…"

"Mi amigo, I already…"

"Let me finish, Benito. You've seen her. Aniyah looks just like my mother did as a child. Like twins, comrade. And all that is not my mother is mine...her facial expressions, her eyes, her smile."

"And just like Najee's, Carlos. She looks exactly like him, too."

"Benito, I have known you for forty years. I understand you. I know what you think."

"Do you, mi amigo? Do you?"

"I do," I replied with conviction. "I'm not naive or stupid. I see the look in your eyes when I mention Najee. Or when you hear me talking to people trying to get info on Muhammad Farid Shahid and his people for Najee. I know how you feel inside about him. And I understand why you feel that way. But I'm asking you, as your oldest friend, to empathize with me for a minute. To put yourself in my position. Imagine knowing you had a son out here somewhere. Then a cruel twist of fate puts that son in the crosshairs of your sniper rifle. As you look through the scope and you notice that son looks just like you, would you still pull the trigger?"

Benito stood up suddenly. "What about the promise that you made to Emanuel Vasquez, to always take care of his son, before he died for you? What about the sons and daughters we lost, that our friends and associates lost? All because Najee assumed you wanted to kill his girlfriend, Angel?"

"Benito, I'll ask you again. Would you pull that trigger if it was your son, your own flesh and blood in your rifle's crosshairs?"

"If my son committed the crimes Najee has, mi amigo, I believe I would."

Benito turned and left the room.

***

"My mother told me one day that my father's name was Carlos. "Aniyah said as she spooned Rocky Road ice cream into her mouth.

"She did?" I asked, totally smitten.

'Um-hmm. She said you are a businessman from Puerto Rico."

136

"Is that right? Well, Mommy was wrong about that."

"Wrong about what? The businessman part or the Puerto Rico part?"

I smiled at the little girl's precocious nature. "About me being from Puerto Rico. My family is from Nicaragua."

"Nicaragua? Where's Nicaragua?"

"It's in Central America. Sits right in the middle of Honduras and Costa Rica."

"Central America?"

I nodded "And the capital of Nicaragua is Managua. I was born there many, many years ago."

"Can I go there one day to see it? To Managua?"

"If you'd like. I can take you anywhere in the world. All you have to do is ask."

"Anywhere I want?"

"Anywhere."

"Can I go to Mecca to pray?" Aniyah asked.

'If you want to, yes."

"How about Dubai?"

"You sure can."

"Okay, You're a businessman, right? What business do you do?"

"Real estate. I buy and sell property, land, buildings, homes."

"Homes like the one we are in now?"

"Exactly like the one we're in now."

"I like this house. It's big. Takes a lot of people to clean it."

"I agree. Glad that you like it."

"Esmerelda told me it's big. I like Esmerelda."

"Is that right?"

Aniyah nodded. "She's nice. She helped me with my hijab. Showed me a good place to offer my salah. I like her."

"I'm glad that you like Esmerelda. I like her, too. Whatever you need, ask her. And she'll do her best to get you whatever you need. Okay?"

"Okay. Mommy told me you never knew about me. That's why you never came to see me or play with me. Is that true?"

I nodded. "Had your mommy told me about you, I would have been beside you your entire life. I would have loved you more and more each day."

"So, am I supposed to call you Daddy?"

"You can call me whatever you like, but I'd like it if you called me Daddy."

"You look like me," Aniyah said and giggled.

I laughed with her. "That's true, but it's the other way around. You look like me."

"Okay. Daddy, have you talked to my mommy?"

"Not yet, but I will soon."

"I miss my mommy and my grandma."

The sadness that registered in my daughter's eyes broke my heart. Her grandmother was dead, and she didn't know it. "Well, you'll be seeing Mommy soon. Are you ready for Esmerelda to take you shopping?"

"I'm ready," Aniyah replied and laid the spoon down on the table.

"I told Esmerelda to buy whatever you want."

"Whatever I want?"

"Whatever you want."

"Can I have a PlayStation and plenty of video games?"

"If that's what you want."

"Grandma wouldn't let me have a PlayStation or video games."

"Well, I say you can have one and as many games as you like."

"I like *Grand Theft Auto*."

"Buy it then," I told Aniyah.

Aniyah hopped off her stool and came to me. I stood up. She hugged me tight. "Thank you, Carlos."

"I thought we agreed you'd call me Daddy."

"Oh," Aniyah said and giggled. "I forgot."

I hugged her a little tighter. "I didn't."

***

Central Treatment Facility (CTF)

"What inmate are you here to see, sir?"

"Kareemah El-Amin," I told the C.O. inside the booth.

"Fill out these forms for me."

I grabbed the forms and filled them out. Then I passed them back through the window.

"Go ahead in, Mr. Tate. She'll be right out."

The visiting room on this day was almost filled to capacity. I found a seat in the back near the vending machines. A few minutes later, Angel walked into the room. She found me and headed my way. I stood. We embraced. Her demeanor was sullen.

"I came to bring you some good news," I said as soon as we were seated.

"I need it. My mother is going to be buried tomorrow. I'm worried about Aniyah, and I just learned some more bad news," Angel said.

"What bad news did you just learn?"

"I'll tell you later. Give me the good news first."

"Aniyah is with me. At my house."

"Oh...my...gawd," Angel exclaimed, "Carlos, thank you, thank you, thank you."

"Don't mention it. I'm glad I could get her back. She's been at my house since Saturday night, and I think I'm in love."

"Aaww! I'm so happy. I'm so grateful to you. She's special, ain't she?"

"More than special. And she's doing great. Honesty took good care of her. Told her that her name was Michelle, and she was a friend of the family."

"Does she know...know that—"

"Know what? That her mother's in jail or that her grandmother is dead?"

"Either one...both."

"She doesn't know either one. Honesty never told her and neither did I. According to Aniyah, while she was with Honesty, all she did was play video games. Since she's been home, she's spent a lot of time with one of my housekeepers, Esmerelda.

They're become inseparable. They are together, out shopping as we speak."

"Carlos, I can't thank you enough."

"Not necessary, Angel. I just wish you would have told me about her. You should have told me."

"I wanted to, but I didn't. Didn't know how you'd react to the news. Never knew if you actually wanted children or not. We had a one-night stand, Carlos. A situation based on lust. That's not a healthy recipe to condone bringing a child into the world. But I took it as a sign from Allah. With all the life I'd taken, here was a life given. I felt the baby had a purpose. So, I kept it. To raise and to love. To be honest, I thought you'd probably reject us...me and the baby. And had I told you and you'd done that, I would have risked my life trying to kill you. I didn't want to have to go through that, so I just kept quiet."

"I get that. Really, I do. It's just...it's just that, I feel like I've wasted so much time. Time I could've had loving her. You know what she told me earlier?"

"What?"

"She told me I look like her."

Angel laughed. "That little girl is something. I'm telling you. Grown as hell, but smart as a whip and all she likes is Chick-Fil-A. Has she been asking for me?"

"All the time," I leveled with Angel, "and your mother."

"It's gonna be hard explaining my mother's death to her. She's gonna take it hard, Carlos. My mother practically raised Aniyah. Has she been talking your head off? She loves to ask questions."

"I love to hear her talk. And she does ask lots of questions. But I got a question for you. Why did you tell her I was in Puerto Rico?"

"I don't know. I never knew where you were or where you were from. I just chose Puerto Rico because it's far enough away for me to protect Aniyah's feelings. She has been asking about her father a lot. Why doesn't he love me? That sorta thing. I just told her that you were in Puerto Rico."

"Well, just so you know, I'm from Nicaragua. That makes Aniyah, half-Nicaraguan and now she knows it, too."

"Does Najee know he's half-Nicaraguan, too?"

"I was wondering when you'd get around to that. To Najee."

"How could I not? I love him. I really love him, Carlos. And to complicate things even more, remember when I told you I just learned some bad news?"

"I remember."

"The bad news is I'm pregnant, Carlos. And Najee is the baby's father."

"Whoa!" I said and meant it.

"Whoa, is right. This couldn't have happened at a worst time. How is Najee? Has anything changed with him since the last time you and I spoke?"

I shook my head. "Nothing's changed, other than he's really taking out the Shahid Organization. With my help, of course, but he's good. We talk daily. He was in New York recently, but now he's back in Newark."

"In New York? Why?"

"His war took him there. He's safe though, I told him where you are."

"What did he say?"

"There wasn't much that he could say. He's focused on other things."

"And now he's about to be a father and doesn't even know it. This shit is crazy. I'm fucking in love with my daughter's half-brother. She's about to be a sister and an aunt to the child. How confusing is that? I wish I had another choice, but I don't. I don't believe in abortion. I'm keeping this baby."

"Do you plan to tell Najee, or are you gonna keep him in the dark like you did me?"

"Carlos, that's not fair," Angel said.

"I was just curious. Either way, the choice is yours. Let's just hope everything works out in his favor, and yours. Speaking of which, since you're about to have my grandchild..."

"Damn, I forgot about that. That shit is crazy."

"I agree, but it is what it is. What I was saying was, you being pregnant changes things with me. I was going to stay out of your little feud with Honesty, but I must intervene..."

"No!" Angel said emphatically. "You don't have to do shit. Honesty Phillips is mine. She killed my mother. I'ma barbecue her ass. Leave her to me. I'ma take care of Honesty, as soon as I get out of here. All I need is the resources you used to get Aniyah back. I'ma use those resources to find her and kill her."

"And what about the gun charge?"

"What about it?"

"Do you want me to take care of it?" I asked.

"Would you, please?"

"Consider it done. Can't let you go to prison with my grandchild. Aniyah needs you. Najee gonna need you when all of this is over, and the baby will need you. I'ma take care of the gun. Is there anything else you need me to do?"

"For now, no. Just take care of my...our...daughter, and don't tell Najee what I told you about the baby. I wanna be the one who tells him."

"Cool...I promise, I won't say a word."

"Good, now get me some food out of the vending machine. I'm hungry as hell.

Chapter 20

Najee

Newark, NJ

"Najee, wake up! Your phone keeps ringing."

I opened my eyes quickly and sat up. The last time I'd been awakened to those words, I found out Salimah was dead. I looked around the unfamiliar bedroom and remembered where I was. Aminah got behind me and massaged my shoulders.

"You must've been really tired. Your ass slept all day," Aminah said.

"What time is it?" I asked.

"It's 5:38 p.m. And your phone has been vibrating non-stop."

"Damn, I was tired as hell, huh? Where is the phone at?"

Aminah handed me my phone. "You need to go and handle that breath before you make your calls, return calls or whatever. Shit kicking like an old karate movie."

"Oh yeah?" I said and put my palm to my mouth and blew. "Damn, you right. You gotta have an extra toothbrush in here."

"Of course, you never know who might spend the night at your house."

"Is that right?"

"Naw, Najee, I'm just kidding. Ain't nobody never spent the night in this apartment, but you. No cap. I know we kinda fucked on the first day, but you're different. It ain't like I don't know you. Your girl doesn't get down on any random dicks. Anyway, I keep extra everything. The Dollar Stores is my best friend." Aminah left the room and returned with a towel and washcloth, toothbrush and body wash. "Use the bathroom in the hall. The one connected to this room is full of feminine products you'd don't need to be seeing."

I got out the bed. "Feminine products? Fuck you got in there? Dildos, lube and shit like that?"

"Maybe," Aminah smiled, winked and left the bedroom.

When I reached the hallway bathroom, I heard Aminah call out, "I don't know whether to cook you breakfast, lunch or dinner. What are you tryna eat?"

I sat on the toilet fully dressed and looked at my phone. I had twenty-two missed calls and a couple text messages from my crew. I scrolled through the text messages and was happy to see none of them were murder/death/kill texts.

"Did you hear what I said?" Aminah asked.

"I heard you. Cook whatever you want it and I'ma smash it," I called out to her. Then I took off my clothes and got in the shower.

***

When I got to the lobby of Aminah's building, I spotted a triple black Mercedes Benz AMG S65 at the curb out front. My antennas went up and I gripped one of the guns in my waist. The FN was fully loaded and ready to spit. The window on the Benz came down as I walked out the building. Gunz' smiling face appeared through a cloud of smoke. He mouthed the words, "Scared ass nigga," and laughed. I walked up to the Benz and hopped in the passenger's seat.

"I got your scared nigga, yo. You was about to get your ass roasted," I said and looked around the luxury sports car. "Who whip is this?"

"Mine, baby boy," Gunz replied and passed me a joint of weed.

I hit the joint a couple times and was transported to a far-off place instantly. I was high as hell. "Damn, yo, fuck kinda weed is this?"

Gunz laughed. "That's them moon rocks right there, son. Better than weed."

"New smoke, new whip. What's got into you, yo?"

"I don't know, yo. Just felt like spending some money today. A gift to myself. A congratulations present for getting away from the curb." I couldn't reply to what he said, because I was too, too high.

Angel 4

***

In the projects, the Benz was surrounded by hood niggas. I opened my eyes to find Tye staring at me. The window was down, and the cold air had me a little chilled.

"Fuck you looking at, yo?" I asked Tye.

"We in the middle of a war and your ass in the car sleep," he replied.

"Them moon rocks fucked him up, yo," Gunz said. He was outside the Benz.

I pulled my FN out. "Don't worry about me, son. I got me. You worry about you." Tye unzipped his coat.

"Nigga, you flashin' that weak ass FN. Look at this bad mutha-fucka." In Tye's coat sat a hybrid rifle slash machine gun called a SK8. I'd seen it on *YouTube* before, but never in person. It held a hundred and twenty 7. 62 bullets and would fire on auto, semi-auto or single.

"Where mine at, yo?" I asked, referring to the gun Tye had.

"I got you when Rasul and nem bring another one through the hood. Gunz told me you fucking Aminah, fam. Fuck is up with that?"

"Fuck you mean, what's up with that? And Gunz need to stop running his fucking mouth so much."

"I heard that, yo," Gunz said.

"Out of all the bitches in Brick City, you gon fuck your girl's cousin?" Tye continued.

"Yo, son, you need to mind your fucking business. And let me do me. Fuck is you, my father?"

"I wish, nigga. That nigga Carlos probably caked up for real, yo. But on some real shit, yo, we in the middle of some serious shit…"

I was starting to get a little pissed off because Tye was blowing my high. "Like the fuck I don't know that, yo."

Tye recognized he was walking down a dangerous road with me. "Just saying, fam, you gotta keep your head in the game. Can't be distracted by no pussy. You was tryna hide shorty while we were in Newburgh. Like niggas didn't know shorty was there in another room."

Gunz and Rah Rah laughed.

"Ayo, Tye, don't worry about me, son. I'm wired a little different from y'all. When I'm stressed out, I drink, smoke and fuck. That's what I do, but I still put that fucking work in. So, ease up off me. I feel good, right now. Better than I have since I found out about Limah. We just sent a helluva message to our enemies, yo. We just showed Muhammad Farid Shahid that nobody is exempt from death, from pain and suffering. Him and tha nigga Aziz Navid probably still crying over their loved ones' dead bodies. Just like we did, yo. Ain't no muthafucka untouchable, nobody. And now them niggas know that, too.

"And I hope the info on them niggas hurry up and come through so I can body them niggas and get on with the rest of my life. I'm tryna grab Angel and do some different shit. Fuck all them drugs. That kingpin shit ain't me. All that Jay-Z shit we was on in DC, that shit ain't me, either. When all this over, I'ma sign all tha record company shit over to you niggas and let y'all bubble, hang around with rap niggas and all that shit. I'm a simple dude with simple dreams. I'ma walk away from the game like Kobe did, after dropping sixty points on the Knicks at the Garden."

"I feel you on that, fam. Real talk. But on another note, the nigga Drama that got spilt with you and Limah, his funeral is tomorrow. We gotta go and pay our respect, yo."

"Why is that?" Rah Rah said. "We didn't even know son."

"Son was *live*, I heard. I think it will be a good look to fall through," Gunz said.

"Man, fuck that nigga, yo," Killa said. "What if niggas shoot the funeral up."

Shotgun spoke up then. "See, Gunz, I told you this nigga on some shook shit."

"Shottie, I already told you…you can see me, yo," Killa replied. "Don't try to show off…"

"Show off? Show off?" Shotgun said and reached for his gun.

Gunz calmly said, "Ayo, Shotgun, if you pull that hammer, you have to kill me too, homie.   So, make up your mind.   Then act."

"Y'all always taking that nigga side, yo.   I'm out," Shotgun said and walked off.

"Ayo, Killa the lil homie got a point though, yo.   What you just said about the funeral for Drama was some scary shit.   Don't let me hear it again.   Feel me?"

"It wasn't even like that, Gunz…"

"I asked you, did you feel me?" Gunz said.

"I feel you, yo.   I feel you."

"I'm with Tye on the funeral.   Everybody ain't gotta go, but I'ma fall through.   Son got murked because of my beef with Muhammad Shahid.   I'ma pay my respects," Najee stated.   "When is the funeral?"

"Tomorrow at one p. m.   It's the church on Evergreen.   Holy Redeemer or some shit," Tye said.

"Cool, I'm there.   Speaking of funerals, yo, we gotta give some money to all the families that lost somebody out here Friday.   I need one of y'all to find out everybody who died and let me know.   Goo, did you get that money to Hasan's cousin and nem for their families that gotta be buried?"

"You already know, son.   I gave Saleem and nem the bread you left.   It was more than enough for six funerals.   I took money to Yasir's aunt for ya and his people, too.   Been done that, yo.   Been done it."

"I ain't doing no funerals for my peeps, yo.   I'm cremating nem," Gunz said.   "What about you, Naj?"

"Grandma had a sister I never met.   She gon fly in and take care of everything.   I'ma give her the dough.   Sis is already in the ground.   I did that one dolo on some incognito shit."

"And before I forget," Killa said.   "BeBe's father was coming though, while y'all was gone.   He's been asking questions about BeBe's death.   What are we gon tell him?"

"We ain't telling him shit, yo," Gunz spat. "He needs to chill…"

"Yo," Najee jumped in. "I need to holla at son anyway to see what he knows about Muhammad Shahid and Aziz Navid.   Get with him, Killa, and set up a time for him and me to talk. I wanna see what he knows and check his temperature about BeBe. Depending on the vibe or the info I get, he might get to keep breathing. If I don't like his vibe…y'all already know what it is."

"We did what you told me to do." Goo explained later when it was just me and Gunz in the hallway of the 715 building. "We went to that resource joint first. Killed like eight muthafuckas. We hit the Medina spot next. Wasn't nothing but one muthafucka in there. We bodied him. Next, I believe we hit the City Trendz spot, put the work in on a couple niggas and last, we hit the grocery store. That shit was all over the local news while y'all was gone."

"That's what's up," I commented.

"Yo, what the fuck is up with Killa and Shotgun?" Gunz asked.

Goo shook his head. "Yo, they wildin', son. Both of them niggas. I had to get in between them niggas in the truck that night. On some real shit, though, Killa be buggin. He blowing that shit yo, and Shottie called him on it. Told him he was gone tell both of y'all Killa gettin high. Killmonger lost it. Got to poppin' some slick shit about Naj and Gunz ain't my father and all this and that. Then son got on some real goofy shit about BeBe. I ain't gon repeat that shit, yo, but son felt some kinda way about BeBe getting murked."

"Is that right?"

Goo nodded. "Yo, listen, I fucks with Killmonger and the whole nine, and I don't wanna see son get hurt, but I think that shit he sniffing fucking with his head. Son shit is a little off. And Shottie knows it. Been peeped it. So, he is saying shit to Killa, and they are at each other's necks. They gon be aight, though."

I looked over at Gunz, and Gunz looked over to me.

"Yo, you two muthafuckas act like I don't know y'all. I know y'all too well. I saw that look y'all just gave each other. I didn't just tell y'all what I told y'all to have y'all body Killmonger. Let me holla at him, yo. Tighten him up. I think Ha's death fucked him up, then Yasir and BeBe really fried him. That's why I think he fuckin with that dope shit. Son was in love with Limah. Her being gone, Lil Haleem, Donnell Dyson getting killed the other night…"

"I get what you saying, yo. I'm a compassionate guy," I said, interrupting Goo.

"I'm not," Gunz said. "Ayo, Goo, somebody in the crew is working against us."

"Get the fuck outta here, yo."

"That's a big fact, yo," I told Goo.

"Somebody told them Muslim niggas Yasir knew where Limah lived. Shahid's men snatched Yasir and made him take them to Limah's house. And then ask yourself how did them niggas know where my family lived and Hasan's family."

"And my grandmother, Yasir's family. How would they know?"

Goo smacked his forehead and ran his hand down his face. Then he looked me in the eye. "Don't make sense, if y'all think it's Killmonger, yo. Yasir and Limah got spilt before y'all came back and you killed BeBe. From what I heard, Killmonger is fucked up about BeBe. BeBe was his partner in crime. Why would he…Killa…be a turncoat before BeBe getting split? If it was all done after BeBe, I could see where y'all coming from, but it was before. Why would Killa give up Yasir, Limah and y'all folks before you killed his man? Our man?"

"Good question, yo," Gunz said. "And I swear on my mother's grave, that's the only thing saving his ass right now. But from now on, he's your responsibility, son. Keep your eye on him."

"Say less," Goo replied. "Say less."

***

"Ayo, I'm really feeling the Benz, son. I think I'ma go and cop myself something, too. Them used joints we be in gotta go," I told Gunz as he dropped me off at Aminah's. "I'm thinking 'bout the new Porsche joint."

"The Panamera? The four-door?"

I nodded. I'ma get Aminah to put it in her name."

"That's what's up, baby boy.   Do you."

"Naw, yo, I can't wait to do Muhammad Shahid and Aziz Navid.   Do both of them niggas real dirty."

"It's gone happen, yo."

"I sure hope so."

Chapter 21

Angel

"Thank you for joining us this morning on *Good Morning DC*. The top story of the morning is crime in DC. It continues to rise, despite all efforts to stop it. Homicide levels have soared in ways not seen in decades. Authorities elaborated on why violence has soared amid a proliferation of guns used to settle disputes. Such as deadly road rage, neighborhood feuds and killings over French fries, in one case. A steady stream of firearms are pouring into the city, increasingly guns built from home kits that cannot be traced. And 3-D printers make it easy to modify weapons to fire in fully auto-mode, allowing a rapid spray of gunfire from one squeeze of the trigger. DC 's new police chief, Bob Conner, had this to say yesterday."

"The days of gunmen firing ten bullets are long over. The city is seeing a rise in shootings with multiple victims and a great share of people dying from their wounds. More victims are being struck multiple times. We now have criminals operating with a hundred and fifty rounds of ammunition that prey on the streets of our communities. And most of the disputes are trivial. This guy ticked off that guy and that guy decided he needs to die. It's ridiculous."

DC Police say trash talking at a flag football game in Southeast recently prompted an opposing player to fatally shoot an opponent. Two girls, age thirteen and fifteen carjacked and killed a sixty-six-year-old man working as an Uber driver. A seventy-six-year-old man was fatally beaten over a dispute about vacating an apartment in N.W. Of the nation's largest thirty cities, at least nine have record-breaking homicide tallies, including Austin, Texas, Portland, Oregon, Indianapolis, Denver, Baltimore, Philadelphia, Newark and Charlotte, North Carolina. In small cities, homicide rates are rising as well. Newburgh, New York, recorded over fifteen homicides in one day alone this past weekend. The District's two hundred killings in 2015 as of Friday evening represent a fifteen percent increase from 2014. But that is far from the levels of violence seen decades ago, when a record of more than five hundred people were killed in the city in a single year.

The city's still recovering from the death of a six-year-old girl, Nyiah Courtney, killed by stray bullets on Martin Luther King Jr. Avenue in Congress Heights. In the months leading up to Nyiah's death, police said there were six non-fatal and then fatal shootings in the immediate area where she was killed—"

"Angel?" Bay One called out from the top tier.

I walked out of the TV room and said, "What's up, Bay?"

"The C.O. is looking for you. She said you gotta legal visit."

"Aight. Thanks."

***

I expected to see Jay when I walked into the small visitation room. But it wasn't him. The person I was looking at was Latesha Garrison, my old cellmate at the DC Jail in 2002. Latesha was also Carlos' niece.

"Hey, Angel," Latesha said and smiled. "It's been a long time."

I walked over and embraced Tesha. "Girl, fuck you doing here?"

"I'm here to see you."

Breaking the embrace and stepping back, I said, "Yeah, I know that, but…" I furtively looked around the area where the legal rooms were.

"But, what? How did I get in here?"

"Duh, yeah. You ain't no lawyer. That's for damn sure."

"Let's just say I'm connected to some powerful people and speaking of me not being a lawyer, I'm not an ex-con, either, Angel. Carlos told you who I was?"

I nodded. "Yeah, told me you were his niece."

"So, he didn't tell you who I am. I'm not his niece. He told me he told you that, but he lied. Why, I don't know. I was put in that cell with you to make sure you never got weak and mentioned his name. I'm just an employee to him. Just like everybody else that works for him."

"Hold up…wait a minute…so, your job was what, had I gotten weak and said his name?" I asked, suddenly irritated.

"Angel, you better than anyone should know that everything or everyone you see are not always what they appear to be. I have a certain set of skills…but hey, listen, let's not get into that. It's neither here nor there. You didn't get weak. you never folded. And that's all that matters."

"Did Carlos send you here to see me?"

Latesha nodded. "He said he saw you yesterday but needed to get a message to you, so here I am. With good news and bad news. Which do you want first? And for the record, I hate that tired cliche. "Sit."

I pulled out a chair from the table and sat down. "Is Latesha your real name?"

"Yes. Latasha Garrison is my real name. Only my charges and reasons for being in the cell with you were fake."

"Understood. You got good news and bad. Gimme the bad news first."

"As you wish. A detective in Maryland…in P.G., a homicide guy named Mitchell Bell is on your line. Something about the gun you got caught with being linked to a murder at your mom's house in Clinton. A prosecutor in P.G., Dominique Oliver, made calls all day yesterday, trying to get authorization for the detective to do ballistics. They're going to test the gun you had to see if it matches bullets removed from one of the victims found at Mom's crib. The gun you had was a forty cal, and the bullet fragments they removed were forty cal…"

"Shit!" I muttered. "I was worried about that. But I thought I'd be out of here before that connection was made."

"And, according to Carlos, that detective also has a letter—"

"He searched my car! How could he search my car?"

"So, you're familiar with this letter, then?" Latesha asked.

I nodded. "It was a letter left at my mother's house by the bitch that killed my mother."

"Carlos also told me about that, Angel, I'm sorry to hear about your mother."

"Yeah, me, too. That's why I gotta get outta here, so I can kill the bitch. I left the letter in my car and the detective must've found it. How in the fuck did he get a search warrant to come to DC and search my car that fast?"

"To be honest with you, I don't think he had one. Because the scumbag would have had to get a search warrant for your house and business."

"He can search all he wants, because there's nothing in any of those places. I'm clean. Have been for years."

"What about the gun? Will the ballistics match the bullets?"

"Yup. Carlos already knows that. We already discussed what needs to be done. So, I'm curious as to why he felt I needed to know all of that right now?"

Latesha shrugged her shoulders. "I'm just the messenger."

"Okay, so what's the good news??"

"The good news is that your daughter is beautiful, and she misses you. And whatever you need to ask Carlos before you get out, you can."

"Ain't no more visiting days, and I go to court tomorrow."

Latesha responded by opening her briefcase. She fumbled around its edges and revealed a secret compartment. From that compartment, she produced a small cellphone. A small flat screen smartphone with an even smaller charger. "Here." She passed the phone and charger to me. "It's the latest design in future technology. Designed specifically for undercover agents in law enforcement. It's light, made of all plastic components, so it's undetectable. The batteries made into the charger are lithium and last forever. It never needs to be plugged into a wall socket. There are numbers already programmed into the phone. You'll see that once you power it on. My number is in there as well...Just in case you don't get out tomorrow and should need anything. And I do mean anything."

"Thank you, Latesha, for everything. And what you said about Aniyah."

"Angel, that little girl looks just like Carlos. I think I'm jealous. But listen, you're not going to be able to just walk out of here with that phone and charger, so you need to put it up. Where you put it is up to you, but it needs to disappear right now."

"Baby girl, you ain't said nothing slick to a can of oil." I examined the phone and charger for a minute. It was awkwardly shaped. But I could manage. My hand went under the table and into my panties. I pushed the phone into the wetness and then the charger. "I hope it's waterproof."

Latesha laughed. "As much as it costs to make, I don't think pussy juices will hurt it."

"Thank you, Tesha."

"Don't trip. Call me later."

***

Inside the cell, I pulled the phone and charger out of me and wiped them off. Then I called Bay One into the cell.

"What's up, Angel?"

"This," I said, showing her the cell phone.

"Damn! A phone? That's what's up."

"When I leave in two days, it's yours. But right now I need to make some calls. So, I need you to hold me down and watch out for the CO's for me."

"You got that. No problem. Handle your business. I'll be right outside the door. If the pigs come and make rounds, I'll come in and let you know. But you should be good for a while. That bitch Shipley lazy as fuck and she ain't on no hot shit. The other bitch working with her is hot as shit for no reason. Gotta watch her. I got you, though. Do you. "

"Thanks, Bay."

"Shit ain't shit. I'm outside," Bay said and left the cell.

I powered the phone on and familiarized myself with how to work it. I found the contact list. There were two numbers programmed into the phone. Carlos and Latesha's. I touched the number for Carlos.

Seconds later, Carlos' voice comes on the line. "Hello?"

"Carlos, it's me, Angel."

"Hey, Angel. Glad to see that we're connected."

"Me too. Thank you for everything."

"No worries. But before you and I talk, let me put someone on the phone that's been dying to talk to you. Hold on."

My heart rate quickened. A smile crossed my face in anticipation of talking to my daughter.

"Mommy?" Aniyah's voice came through. "Assalamu Alaikum!"

"Aniyah, baby! Hey, baby! Walaikum Assalam."

"Mommy, I miss you! I love you!" Aniyah said.

For the next twenty minutes or so, my daughter gave me life. I couldn't get a word in. She told me everything about her experiences last week. She told me about the time she'd spent with Honesty, who she called Michelle. She mentioned Michelle's boyfriend Rock. Then she started talking about my mother. How much she missed her, and she didn't understand why she couldn't talk to her. I assured her that her grandma was okay, even though I knew she wasn't. My heart broke for the both of us and tears fell down my eyes. I smiled through my tears when Aniyah told me how much she liked Carlos and the housekeeper named Esmerelda. She told me all about her new clothes and toys.

"I wanna see you, Mommy."

I wiped at the tears in my eyes. "You're going to see me soon, baby. I should be back in town in a day or so. I can't wait to see you. I'ma hug you to death."

Aniyah giggled. "Uh-uhn, Mommy. You can't because you love me too much."

"You got me, baby. I won't hug you to death, but I will hug you a lot."

"Okay, Mommy."

"I love you so much, baby. Never forget that. Now let me speak to your father."

"Daddy," Aniyah said in a sing-song voice. "Mommy wants you."

"Hello, Angel," Carlos said.

"Aniyah calls you Daddy, huh? How did that happen?" I asked.

"It was her idea. She is a precious little girl. I love her to death already."

"Has she been offering her prayers, every day?"

"All five of 'em. Sometimes, I wanna join her."

I laughed at Carlos. "Maybe you should. Might do your soul some good."

"My soul can never be saved, Angel. Done too much bad shit in my life. I got a for-sure date with the devil. But when I listen to Aniyah recite the Quran, it just seems so pure and majestic. Touches me in a place where I thought I couldn't be touched."

"It's been a while since I offered the salat. But I know the feeling. On another note, though, this detective that's on my line, do you know his story? Or how he got onto me so fast?"

"All I know is that he's assigned to your mother's case. He's the investigation detective. According to my source, you threw up in the bathroom the night of the murders and they were able to pull your DNA from that. That places you at the house that night. Somehow, he was alerted to your current situation, and he's been all over it ever since."

"The letter he has is the one I told you about. He got it out of the BMW. How could he get a warrant to search my car in three or four days?"

"That's a question you'll have to ask Jay tomorrow when you talk to him. But either way, don't stress it because I'll take care of everything. Even the woman who told the detective that she loaned you a work van..."

"Cheeks did that? How the fuck do they know about her van?"

"I don't know all the details. My source says they have video footage of someone driving a van the night of Honesty's mother's murder. They investigated and the owner of the van, a woman named..."

"Jenelle Kearney."

"Right. She told the detective you were driving the van she loaned to you that day."

"Damn! Look...don't worry about her. I'll talk to her. You just focus on that detective," I told Carlos.

"Consider it done. You have my word. I'm looking at nine different reasons to make sure you never see the inside of a jail cell again."

"I really appreciate it, Carlos. You didn't tell Najee about me being pregnant, did you?"

"I said I wouldn't and I didn't. That is a conversation for the two of you. Hopefully, tomorrow you can get one step closer to having it in person. You and him, face to face."

"Yeah, I guess so. Let me get off this phone. I got a lot of love for you, old man. I appreciate everything."

Carlos laughed. "Old man, huh? I guess I deserve that. Keep your head up."

"I will. Bye." I ended the call.

Chapter 22

Gunz

We were in five different cars, pulling into the church parking lot on 7th and Evergreen. There were people on every side of Holy Redeemer AME Church, most of them Blood gang members. Most of them dressed in different variations of red.

"It's a lot of muthafuckas out here, son," I said to my crew.

"And probably even more people in the inside," Tye remarked. Najee hopped out the Porsche Panamera and caught up to us as he put away his phone. "This joint looks like a sold-out Kanye West event."

There were dudes and females I recognized from all over Newark. "You ain't see that nigga that wrote all them books, son? Standing over there by the church entrance."

."."Yeah," Goo said."That my old head, Al-Saadiq Banks. Son was a helluva boxer back in the day before he started writing books."

Tye smiled. "I read all of his books in the feds. He kept some Blood niggas in them joints. And now he's here. He must be Blood."

"Naw, he ain't never gang bang."

"How do you know?" Rah Rah asked.

"I just told y'all that my old head. He used to roll with my uncles back in the day. Them nigga was gangstas, not gang members," Goo replied.

"I saw him get out of that new Aston Martin SUV over there. He better be glad I ain't on my bullshit," Killa chimed in.

Everybody burst out laughing.

"Fuck is y'all laughing at?" Killa asked.

"You nigga," Najee said, "talking 'bout he better be glad you ain't on your bullshit. I catch your ass sniffing that bullshit, I'ma get on my bullshit. Ayo, Gunz, ain't that the nigga Rich from Spruce Street that just got out of that Bentley truck over there?" He pointed.

"Yeah, that's him," I said with a bad taste in my mouth.   "I can't believe it."

"Well, it looks like a good day just got even better.   He's the one that got away after that shit with Bones and nem in Atlantic City last year."

"The night that Hasan got killed?" Goo asked Najee.

"Yeah, he is…Was Hashim and Big Rock's right-hand man. He was with—"

"I thought you said Mu was behind all that shit, yo?" Killa interjected.

"He was.   He put the pieces on the chessboard and set everything up, but them niggas put that work in.   Rich's name came up on several occasions after the night in A. C.   but I couldn't find his ass.   I guess he think he's in the clear."

I pulled my automatic Colt .357 out of my waist and put it in my coat pocket.   "Well, he thought wrong."

We ran into Drama's homeboys that Tye knew.   After chopping it up in the church's lobby, we got in line to view the body.

***

"Don't lose him, big boy," Najee said.

"Let me fuck this cow, baby boy.   You just hold his head," I replied.   As I maneuvered the Benz's 560 horsepower around the streets of Newark behind Rich.   "He ain't getting away from me."

"His blinker just came on.   He's turning into the Jiffy Shack up on the right." There were two cars in front of us.   When they went straight, I turned right, into the Jiffy Shack's parking lot behind the Bentley SUV.   Rich was engrossed in a call on his cell phone as he exited the SUV.   Wrong move.   Najee and I got out of the Benz. When Rich looked and saw Najee, he dropped the phone and tried to run.   He ran right into me.   I pushed him back a few steps while lifting the cannon from my pocket.   Rich's eyes grew as big as saucers.   Me and Najee wore his ass out.   Another broad day murder in the big city.   I took Najee back to Holy Redeemer to pick up his car.   Then we raced back to the hood.

***

Brick Towers Projects

One hour later

"Who the fuck's that right there?" I asked as I saw a tall, brown-skinned dude dressed in all-black clothes approaching us. My hand gripped my gun.

"That's BeBe's father," Killa said. "Naj said he wanted to talk to him."

"I recognize son, yo," Najee said. "I forgot that was BeBe's pops. He used to come through all the time with the old heads, Damu and Saboor."

"Young boy Najee, I've been looking all over for you," BeBe's father said.

BeBe's father had to be at least six foot four. His salt and pepper, low-cut Caesar matched the big beard he wore.

"I've been looking for you, too, yo," Najee told him.

"Is that right? I haven't been hard to find. Ain't that right, young Killa?"

Killa nodded his head. "Yeah, that's right, Mr. Bullock."

"Well, son, you found me. What can I do for you?" Najee asked.

"The last time I talked to my son, he told me he was on his way to meet you and your man Gunz. Said something about your sister getting killed and a couple of y'all's friends. My son looked up to you, Najee. You, your man Gunz, Tye...he always spoke highly of you. From that, I could tell he loved you. But I ain't feeling that love in return. Which leads me to believe somebody here knows something about his murder."

Najee smiled a dangerous smile. One I'd seen hundreds of times. "Mr. Bullock—."

"We're all friends here, right, Najee?" BeBe's father asked.

"Of course, we are."

"So, unlike young boy Killa over there, I'ma ask you to dispense with the formal names. Mr. Bullock was my father and grandfather. My name is Umar, but the streets call me Tall One. I'm hipped to you and your crew, Najee. I got ears and I keep one of them to the ground at all times, to hear what's going on the streets. Why? Because I have been killing shit in Newark and beyond the State of New Jersey since the eighties. Me and Akbar Prey was terrorizing these projects back when you were riding on a Big Wheel. And excuse me for cutting you off, that was a little rude, but I just wanted you to know who it is that you're talking to. Now, please, finish what you were about to say."

"Your son was my man. BeBe grew up under us in the Towers. I'm kinda lost as to why you ain't feeling no love for us. What exactly does that mean?"

"It means none of y'all, but Killa, has been to his mama's house to offer condolences or to pay respects. Ain't nobody reached out to me to say shit about my son's untimely demise. Ain't nobody riding for BeBe. Ain't nobody died behind his death. I need to know two things, youngin. And I pray I can find some answers I can live with. Because if I can't, then I'm gonna have to assume the worst. The worst being that somebody in this circle lined my son up for a back door play, or somebody here knows who killed him and y'all ain't goon enough to respond to it. And if that's the case…it's gon be a bad day for a lot of niggas out here. You feel me, youngin?"

"I feel you, son. I feel you. What are the two things you wanna know?"

"One, did BeBe meet up with y'all the day he was killed? And two, if he did, did he say where he was going when he left y'all?"

Knowing Najee like I did, we were all looking at a dead man talking. I could read the expression on Najee's face. I could see the calm before the storm.

"Mr. Bullock…my bad…Tall One, I was about to lie to you until you opened your mouth. I was looking for you to ask you about Aziz Navid and Muhammad Farid Shahid because BeBe said you knew them…"

"What do they have to do with this? Did one of them kill my boy?"

"They gotta lot to do with this.   but no, they didn't kill BeBe. I killed BeBe because he got on my nerves."

I could see the expression on BeBe's father's face change.   His hands moved to his pockets.   "Uh-uh," I said and pulled my gun out.   "Don't move your hands like that, yo.   Makes me think you are reaching for something.   You're making me nervous."

BeBe's father looked at me then down at the chrome .357 in my hand.

"BeBe's mouth got on my nerves, so I closed it for him," Najee continued.   "So, to answer your questions, I hope that you can live with my answers.   Yes, BeBe met up with us.   And when he left, he went to meet his maker."

BeBe's father hand moved again.   Everybody standing around pulled guns then.   Everyone except Killa.

Najee laughed.   "If your ears were really to the streets, you would've heard I don't appreciate subtle threats.   And if you were smart, you would've known it's stupid to come around here and throw around tough talk, talking about you been killing since the eighties.   You and Akbar Pray.   I killed BeBe for being stupid and talking too much.   Now I see where he learned that shit from."

"Y'all gon kill me in broad daylight, youngin?"

"You killed yourself.   Stupid."

I fired my gun first, then everybody else followed suit.   BeBe's father was dead before his body hit the ground.

Chapter 23

Najee

"Oooh...Gunz! Ooh...oooh...ohhh, Gunz! Fuck this pussy, Gunz! Fuck it, young nigga! Fuck it!"

I laid on Latoya "LaLa" Snowders' couch and laughed. LaLa was like fifty-two years old, but her body never got the memo. She was built like a woman half her age. She sold dinners out of her apartment on the sixth floor. When I went to sleep on the couch an hour or so ago, LaLa was in the kitchen cooking lamb chops, collard greens with smoked turkey, macaroni and cheese and Texas toast. I woke up an hour later and she and Gunz were fucking. I shook my head, then went back to sleep.

***

Gunz and I sat at the table eating. LaLa was in the back room asleep.

"You and Tye keep tryna get on me talking about I ain't focus. Look at you."

"Look at me, what?" Gunz asked.

"Look at me, what?" I mimicked. "We came up to LaLa's to get some food and you ended up fucking her. How the fuck did that happen?"

Shaking his head and laughing, Gunz said, "Don't ask me, that shit just happened."

"Yeah, right. I wonder if the cops are still outside?"

Gunz got up and walked to the window. "You better believe they are. And BeBe's pops is still out there, on the ground. Cops in Newark fucked up, yo. Got that man still laying out there. It's been like two hours, the ground out there cold as fuck. And I'm still tryna figure out what the fuck is the white sheet for?"

I ate my food while shaking my head. "You bugged out, son. Facts."

"I'm bugged out? Did you peep Killa outside earlier?" Gunz asked.

"How could I not? Killa Keith is living on borrowed time, yo. Believe that."

My cell phone vibrated. It was Carlos. "Yo?"

"Good to hear your voice, and know you're okay," Carlos said.

"Same here, Pops. How you?"

"I'm good on this end. I got something for you."

"Is that right? What?"

"Aziz Navid's home address."

I put the fork down. "No bullshit? Ayo, Carlos, I need that ASAP."

"I'm texting it to you right now. I'm still looking for info on Muhammad Farid Shahid."

"Yo, that one right there... It's coming through right now. I got that, yo. You already know that I appreciate that, son."

"Pops, son, you are confusing me with all the slang."

"You know what I mean. Stop playing, yo."

"I do know what you mean. Handle your business...but be safe. Navid is a natural born killer. Don't underestimate him. Get in, get out. Don't play around with him."

"I got you, yo. I feel that. What's the word on Angel?"

"Should be getting out of jail tomorrow morning. I'll have her call you as soon as I see her."

"That's what's up. I'ma holla back. Get that info on Shahid for me."

"I'm on it, son," Carlos replied. I'm on it."

I ended the call and put the phone down on the table, picked up the fork and ate my food.

"So, what's the deal, baby boy? What's Carlos talking about?"

"Same old shit. But he did get an address we needed."

"Whose?" Gunz asked.

"Aziz Navid's," I replied.

Gunz looked at me as I looked at him, then we both smiled.

***

Angel 4

13217 Oakwood Lane

New Brunswick, New Jersey

"Aziz Navid has a wife named Nadia and a seven-year-old daughter."

The address on the door of the large house on Oakwood Lane matched. I looked down at the text Carlos had sent. "Muthafuckas think just because they move out in the suburbs where the white people live, they can't be touched."

"You saying that made me just think about Salimah," Gunz said.

"Why's that, yo?"

"Because I wonder if she thought the same thing when she moved out into the suburbs, into that big house you paid for. She thought getting out of the Towers would probably keep her safe and untouched, but Aziz Navid proved her wrong."

I thought about what Gunz said and decided he was right. "Well, I'm about to prove to Aziz Navid that what goes around also comes back around," I said, eyes on the tan brick house. Three vehicles parked in a driveway adjacent to the house, a Mercedes Benz G-Wagon, a new model Genesis sedan, and a Ford F-150 Harley Davidson edition pickup truck.

"How much do you think that G-Wagon cost, baby boy?"

"That's the new joint. Probably about three hundred thousand."

"You think Aziz got a rack of money in his house?"

"Don't know and I don't care, son. Fuck his money. All I want is his life."

"Why don't we just come back in the a. m. with the police shit on. That way we gain entrance—"

"Fuck all that. You mentioning Limah just refueled my thirst for revenge. I'm going in there tonight. Here's how. The G-Wagon has an alarm, I'm sure. I'ma hit the wagon and make the alarm go off. If Aziz is in there, he'll come outside to investigate what made the alarm go off. If he's not in there, then the wife will come out. If no one comes out, then we know ain't nobody home. but I can tell by the lighting in the house that somebody's in there. If Aziz is in there and he comes out, then we are crushing his ass. Simple as that. The moment of surprise is still on our side. He won't think it's us, because he's probably arrogant and what else?"

"Thinks he can't be touched."

"Exactly."

"How do you know the G-Wagon even has an alarm?" Gunz asked.

"That muthafucka cost a lot of money, son. It comes equipped with all kinds of security features, the best being an alarm. You supposed to know shit like that, big boy, we live in the stolen car capital of the nation."

"They got you believing in the *New Jersey Drive* shit, too, huh?"

"You fucking right." I walked from the side of the house, down the driveway to the Benz truck. I kicked it. An alarm sounded immediately. I darted back to the side of the house. I gave Gunz the, *I told you so* look, and then peeked around the side of the house. The porch light came on. The screen door on the house opened and a woman's head appeared. The lights around the house come on. "Shit!" I exclaimed. "Too many lights. Somebody's gonna see us."

The woman's arm appeared next. Her hand pointed in the direction of the Benz truck and the alarms blaring ceased. Then she disappeared back inside the house.

"Now what?"

"If that was the wife, then at least we know Aziz ain't in there. But either way it's all good because somebody's dying in that house tonight. I'ma wait a while then hit the truck again. This time, she'll come outside to see why the alarm keeps going off. When she does that, we got her," I told him.

"And what if she doesn't come outside, Sherlock?"

"Then we go to plan B."

"Plan B? What's that?"

"You'll see. Just wait."

Five minutes later, I repeated myself and set off the G-Wagon's alarm. And just like I predicted, the woman came outside to investigate. In clear view, the woman looked young and exotic. She was definitely Middle Eastern or East African. She was beautiful. The woman looked around quizzically and beelined straight for the Benz SUV. I walked out from the side of the house, Gunz on my heels. In my hand was my gun.

The look on the woman's face went from surprise to resignation.

"Let's go inside the house and talk," I told the woman. Her eyes dropped to the gun in my hand. They lingered on the silencer attachment on the barrel's end. "Who are you and what do you want?"

"I'll tell you everything when we get in the house." When the woman made no move to head towards the house, I said, "Or you can make me mad and die right here. Your choice."

"There are no real valuables in my home. A little money, some credit cards, some appliances and gadgets. If you want the truck, you can have it. Here's the key fob. Take the truck and leave."

I shook my head. "Sorry, ma, but it ain't the truck I want. I didn't come here for debit cards, money or gadgets. I came here for Aziz Navid. Let's go inside and talk about Aziz or like I said, I can kill you right there, then go inside kill your daughter. She's seven, right?"

Panic crossed the woman's eyes and then recognition settled in. A slight smirk appeared on her face. "Najee Bashir."

I was genuinely surprised the woman knew my name, but I nodded my head anyway. "Since you know my name. I'm assuming you're Aziz's wife, Nadia. Is your husband in the house? My beef is with him, not you and not your daughter."

"Aziz is not here. He's in Newburgh burying the family you killed."

"Let's go inside and make sure he's not there."

The woman led the way into the house. Once inside, Gunz shut the door behind us and locked it.

***

I wanted to kill Aziz Navid so bad, I could taste it. But it wasn't meant to be. Not yet, anyway. His wife was telling the truth. Her husband isn't at home. Gunz had searched the entire house.

"How do you know my name?" I asked Aziz's wife.

"I have heard a lot about you within the last twelve months," Nadia said.

"Is that right? Some good, I hope."

"Some. Great men are stymied by your resilience. My husband actually admires you."

I laughed. "He admires the fact that I'm still alive and avenging my slaughtered family." I pointed at Gunz. "His slaughtered family. My friend Hasan's family. Yasir and his family. The people they killed at the candlelight vigil. Your husband should admire me. I'm the man who's going to kill him."

"Perhaps," Nadia Navid said.

"Gunz, did you come across the daughter while you were searching the house?" Gunz nodded. "Take her upstairs to get her daughter, then bring them both back here."

"You heard the man," Gunz told Nadia. "Let's go get the girl."

I stood in the spacious living room and marveled at its decor. It was like something out of a magazine spread. The furniture, the tapestry the paintings on the wall, the sculptures, the pottery, the books that line the vast bookshelves, the carpeting. I respected Navid's style. He had a beautiful wife, a beautiful home, luxury vehicles, obvious wealth. "And a beautiful daughter," I said to myself as Nadia, her daughter and Gunz walked back in the living room.

The little girl's pajamas had cartoon characters all over them. She was groggily holding onto her mother, her twin. Mother and daughter took a seat on the couch.

"Do you have your cell phone on you?" I asked Nadia.

Nadia nodded and pulled out her gold cased cellphone.

"Call your husband, Nadia. I need to speak to him."

Nadia did as I requested.   Second, I could hear a male voice answer on the other end of the cell phone.

"Aziz, Najee is here," Nadia said

"What? Here, where?" Aziz Navid responded.

"Here in our home."

"No!"

"Yes, husband.   And he wants to talk to you." Nadia handed me the phone.

"Hello? Aziz?" I said, glad to finally talk to my enemy.

"Najee...please, Ock. Please listen to my..."

"This was too easy, Ock. For real. Your organization is supposed to be a powerful one.   Where is the security on wifey and your daughter? You grew lax in your arrogance, huh? I can dig it."

"Najee... I'll do whatever you want.   Give you whatever you want.   Your beef is with me, not them.   Spare them, Ocki.   By the grace of Allah, let them go."

I laughed out loud.   "Never in your wildest dreams did you ever think I'd be standing in your living room, did you? Never thought that I'd find your family members in Newburgh, did you? You underestimated me, Aziz.   Bad move. Now you want me to spare your wife and daughter. Did you spare my sister? My grandmother? Did you spare Gunz' grandmother and mother? What about Hassan's family or Yasir's family?   Did you spare them?"

"It wasn't me, Najee! It wasn't me! Somebody has told you..."

"You're lying!" I exploded.   Aziz was pissing me off.   "It was you!"

"Najee, listen to me.   We can work something out."

I pulled my silenced gun out, tired of playing games.   I pointed the gun at Nadia Navid.   Her and her daughter both screamed. "Najee! Nooooooooo!"

"Mu was a piece of shit. The coke and money could have been replaced. The lives of our loved ones can't." I fired the gun, killing both mother and daughter instantly.   I emptied the clip into them. "Your daughter and wife's deaths are on you. Live with that."

"I'm never going to rest until I've killed you and all your friends."

"Not unless I kill you first," I said and ended the call.

"Let's get out of here, baby boy.   Our job is done."

I turned to Gunz and said.   "If I know Aziz Navid like I think I do, he's on his way here.   He has to confirm his family is dead. It takes two and a half hours to get to Newark from Newburgh. Add about forty minutes to get here to New Brunswick.   A little over three hours.   I'ma wait for him. yo. I need to finish him now and then that leaves only Muhammad Shahid."

"I'm with you, son.   But where do we wait? Here or outside?"

"Somewhere Aziz will never expect.   Outside in his G-Wagon," I told Gunz and flashed the key fob to him.

All Gunz could do was smile.

Chapter 24

Aziz

"Najee, listen to me. We can work something out." I heard my wife and daughter scream. "Najee! Noooooooo!"

"Mu was a piece of shit. The coke and money could have been replaced. The lives of our loved ones can't."

My heart broke as I heard the unmistakable spits of a silenced weapon. My trained ear was never wrong. Nadia and ZiZi's screams were cut off. An immediate pain settled in my stomach, and I knew they were gone. My eyes filled with tears.

"Your daughter and wife's deaths are on you. Live with that."

"I'm never going to rest until I've killed you and all your friends."

"Not unless I kill you first."

The line went dead. My hand shook as my chest tightened. *You gotta make sure they're dead*, a voice in my head said. I quickly dialed a number in my phone. After a couple of rings, a female voice came on the line. It was my neighbor, Rayna De-loach.

Hello?"

"Rayna, hey, it's Aziz."

"Hey, Aziz. Is everything okay?"

"That what I'm trying to find out. I've been calling Nadia and she's not answering her phone. I've been out of town."

"Speaking of that, my condolences on your parents, Aziz. Nadia told me they passed away recently and that you been in your hometown arranging their funerals."

"Thanks…but listen, do you still have the spare key Nadia gave you a few years ago?"

"I do, Aziz. Do you need it?"

"No, Rayna. I'm still in Newburgh. I need you to go next door and check on Nadia. Can you do that for me? Check in on her and ZiZi?"

"Sure, Aziz. When do you want me—"

"Now, Rayna!   Can you go to my house right now?"

"I'm…well, yeah.   Just let me put on my shoes on.   And grab my—"

"Keep me on the phone, Rayna.   Please."

"Okay,   Aziz, I'm putting my coat on now and leaving out." There was a brief pause, then Rayna said.   "I'm opening the door now, Aziz.   Nadia? Nadia? Nadia? ZiZi?"

The next thing I heard was a loud wail, then screams and I knew.   In a blackened rage, I destroyed everything in my mother's living room.   My screams pierced the night.   My fists were bleeding from punching the walls and ground.

"I'ma kill you…I'ma kill you…I'ma kill you…"

I imagined the bullet riddled bodies of my wife and daughter. The images I saw hurt me in a place I never knew existed.   I couldn't believe the lights that shined so bright in my daughter's eyes were gone.   Nadia's love and warmth, her humor, her eclectic style, her intelligence…gone.   In the blink of an eye.   All I could do was fall to my knees and rock back and forth as I cried and cried and cried.   In one stroke of a masterful pen, the entire script of my life had changed in five days.   Everybody I loved was gone.   Dead. Killed by Najee Bashir.

"Why are you crying, Aziz?" the voice in my head said.   "You killed his family first.   You drew first blood."

I put both hands over my ears and shook my head to clear it of the voices I heard.

"The Holy Quran sanctions the hudud, Aziz.   An eye for an eye.   You killed Najee's family and several other families you reaped what you sowed."

Squeezing my eyes shut, I tried to focus and drown out the voices, but they continued.   Then images of the people I'd killed played in my head.   Hafizah Kareem laying in the hospital bed. Anwar, Musa and Imran, the three Muslims in the organization that I'd killed at the behest of Muhammad Shahid.   I saw Najee's sister Salimah and the man called Drama.   I saw Yasir Rahmen and Najee's grandmother.   An old woman I killed as she slept.   I killed everyone Najee loved and he simply returned the favor. Just like the voices said.

Then suddenly, I could hear the other voices. Muhammad Shahid's and Nadia's. When they both told me the innocent lives lost were collateral damage and needed in times of war. I heard Muhammad instruct me to kill Najee's family in order to bring Najee back to Newark from DC. The killing of Najee's family had indeed brought him back to Newark. But what he did once he returned wasn't expected. Or was it?

My mind started to question everything I'd been told. About everything. Then the questions started. How had Najee gotten my home address? How did he know about my family in New-burgh? Get all of their addresses? How did he know Kayla worked at McDonald's? How did he know about Muhammad's family? Where they lived? Where Marissa worked? I remembered then the last conversation I'd had with Muhammad Shahid.

"Someone is at war with me, with you, us. Our organization…Who is it that did this…killed our families, if not Najee Bashir and his friends?"

"I lost my family, too, Ocki."

"I know that, Aziz. I was told of your misfortunes as well, but you still haven't answered my question, Aziz…who is it that did this?"

"But how could it be Najee, Muhammad? It makes no sense."

"The answer is more simple than you think, Aziz. . Someone's helping him. Najee Bashir is being guided by an unforeseen hand…"

An unforeseen hand…Someone was helping Najee…Someone powerful. Who could it be that was helping Najee against us? Muhammad Shahid promised to find that out. I silently prayed he did find out. I need to know who that person is so I could kill him. Him and everybody he loved. There was no way I was going to live in a world where Nadia and Azizah weren't with me. And as bad as I wanted to end my own life, I couldn't. There were too many lives I had to take before leaving the world. And Najee

Bashir's topped that list.   I got up off my knees.   I needed to see an old friend.

***

Brookhaven, NY

Several hours later

Muhammad Farid Shahid's home was located in upstate New York near the Catskill Mountains, the house sat on over a hundred acres of land.   Its all-brick facade greeted visitors and led you down a walk and driveway to a ten-car garage.   It boasted spiraling staircases, a cathedral style ceiling and wall to wall windows to give it a panoramic view.   The house was gated around the entire prodigy.

A security booth sat at the entrance, manned twenty-four-seven by guards, brothers in the organization.   There were also security stations strategically placed all around the property outside the gates. Muhammad Shahid's position afforded him around the clock security inside his home as well.   The brother manning the front booth embraced me warmly.

"Assalamu Alaikum, Aziz."

"Walaikum assalam.   Gabriel, I know it's late, but I need to talk to Muhammad and it can't wait.   The phone was no good.   He doesn't know I'm here.   Call him and tell him, then open the gate."

"Right away, Ocki," Gabriel Mahdi said, getting on the phone. Minutes later, the gate opened.

I got back in my car and entered the grounds.

***

Muhammad Shahid walked into his study, dressed in silk pajamas and a robe.   "Aziz, I would've prepared food had I known you were coming.   What could be so important to bring you here this late hour?"

"I apologize for the inconvenience, Ocki, but I had to come. I didn't want to talk over the phone, and you are the only person who can provide me with the answers I need."

"And what answers could that be, Aziz?"

"You told me someone was helping Najee. Someone powerful, you said, is providing him with information about us, about our families. You said you'd inquire and find out who that someone could be. That was on Sunday. It's Tuesday about to be Wednesday. Have you found out who that someone is?"

"I was going to call you tomorrow…today and tell you I have a name."

"Well, I saved you a call, Ocki. Who was it"

"Aziz, your eyes. They look different. Something about you is different, off. Has something new happened since we last spoke?"

I nodded my head, then my tears come. "Yeah, Ocki. Something did happen since we last spoke. Najee killed Nadia and ZiZi."

The expression on Muhammad Shahid's face changed. "It can't be! No! No!"

"Yes, Ocki. It's…they…they're gone. My wife…my baby!"

"I'm sorry, Aziz. I'm sorry. So sorry."

"It's kinda too late for sorry, Ocki."

"What can I do, Aziz?"

I laughed a short, deranged laugh. "What can you do? Can you bring back the dead, Muhammad? Can you give back life once it's been taken?"

"Brother, don't be insolent, impudent and blasphemous in your grief."

"Impudent? Insolent? *You* asked me what you could do. I asked you a question. But here's the thing…*brother*. You've already done enough and that's the problem. Muqtar Kareem getting killed set into motion a series of events that led to all of this happening. Can't you see that, Ocki? Or are you blinded by greed? By power? Allah is punishing us. Our families…my family, your family, are all dead because of *you*.

"In the beginning, you said things were bigger than Muqtar's death. That it was about the coke and money taken. Then you ordered me to kill Hafizah and three brothers...Muslims that were closest to Muqtar, all because you felt slighted. It was personal to you. To recoup the stolen money and cocaine. We...you...made three times the amount back that Najee took. It was supposed to end there, but no—"

"Aziz!" Muhammad exploded. "Have you lost yo mind? Where is this all going, because we've had this conversation before. It's redundant. I understand you're hurting because of Nadia and Azizah..."

I laughed again.

"Hurting? Oh, Ock...that's an understatement. I'm beyond that. Words cannot describe what I'm feeling." I wiped tears from my eyes repeatedly. "What I can describe is one emotion, though, Ocki, and I feel several. I'm pissed. I'm pissed because none of the people we lost had to be lost. None of their deaths had to happen. Your pride, your greed...that's the reason our families are dead. The reason that Nadia and ZiZi are gone."

"You're wrong, Aziz!" Muhammad Shahid moved closer to me. "Najee Bashir and his friends are the reason they're dead. Not me. But again, I ask you, where is this conversation going? Is this why you've come to my home in the middle of the night? To blame me for Najee having killed Nadia and Azizah?"

"I don't blame you for Nadia, Ock. Nadia knew that it was wrong. I was never supposed to kill all those innocent people. Casualties of war as you called them, or was it collateral damage? I do blame you for ZiZi, though. She was a little girl. Truly innocent of everything. All she wanted to do was be a gymnast like Simone Biles. But now that will never happen. All because you couldn't just leave things alone—"

"Leave things alone?" Muhammad repeated, then laughed. "I couldn't leave it alone. I couldn't let the shit go unpunished, unanswered. You, of all people, should understand that." Muhammad's laugh chilled me to the bone. The bile in my throat threatened to come up and out my mouth.

"This ain't about me, Ocki. It never has been. This is about you and your enormous ego. Organizations take losses all the time. Robberies happen. Kidnapping. Murders. It's all a part of the life we live. That's what I understand. Killing almost thirty innocent people for the actions of one man, I can't understand. But I did what you told me to do, like always. For nine months we couldn't find Najee, then we learned he was in DC.

"In those nine months we got richer. Richer than ever and we never lost face for what happened to Muqtar. So, it could have been left alone. But you're right about one thing. Playing the blame game ain't going to bring my ZiZi back, or my family and Nadia. Earlier, you told me you were going to call me and tell me what you learned about who could be helping Najee. Who was it?"

"For reasons I can't understand, I learned the person who's been asking for all the information on us is Carlos Trinidad. Apparently, Carlos and Najee have joined forces. I…"

My face registered shock. "Carlos Trinidad? Najee's enemy? Why would someone like Carlos Trinidad join forces with someone like Najee? And why would Trinidad go against us? When he insisted that we not come to DC, we didn't go. We respected his organization in every way."

"Something happened in DC that we knew nothing about. But the channels I used, the people I talked to, they aren't wrong. Carlos Trinidad willingly gave or sold Najee information about us."

"It doesn't make sense, Muhammad. None of this makes any sense."

"I can continue to dig and hope to come up with different answers, Aziz. Maybe something different that would mollify you, but I think what I was told is accurate. Najee took sixteen thousand keys of cocaine from us and an indeterminate amount of money. Maybe Najee paid Trinidad for his life or to let their beef go. Then paid for the info on us, after his sister was killed. So, instead of standing here blaming me for all that's happened, you should be finding Najee and his friends, confirm what we've learned about Carlos Trinidad and then go to DC and kill him."

"I will do exactly that, Muhammad. But answer me this, do you still deny your hand in all of this?"

Muhammad laughed again. "How could I ever deny my hand in this? I gave the orders. But you carried them out, Aziz. Your hands, your goons. You shoulder some blame, too, Ock."

I thought about everything Muhammad Shahid said. He was right. A lot of the blame could be laid at my feet. I could have refused to commit all the murders Muhammad told me to commit. I could have left it on others to do. It was my choice and I'd chosen to do everything. Guilt overwhelmed me then as I envisioned Nadia and ZiZi at a morgue on a cold slab of metal, their bodies mutilated. Then Muhammad's laugh echoed inside my head. My anger took over. My eyes filled with fresh tears. I remembered again why I drove hours to Brookhaven. I pulled my gun and quickly screwed on the silencer attachment.

"Killing me won't change anything, Aziz," Muhammad Shahid said, eyes on the gun in my hand. "Sticking together, getting answers and seeing this through, will."

My father was never a real father to me. Muhammad Shahid was the only father figure I had ever known. I loved him more than I did myself. "Killing you won't change this, Ocki, but it's sure gonna make me feel better," I said and shot my brother. His arms flailed as his body fell back. I covered the space between us and stood over him. His eyes searched mine for mercy, but there was none there to find. I wiped at the tears falling from my eyes. Then I fired again. The bullet entered Muhammad Shahid's right eye. His body became still, and I knew he was dead.

I'd been to the house several times, but never had I been upstairs to the bedrooms. I climbed the stairs until I reached the top floor. I searched all the rooms until I found Hawa, Muhammad's wife, asleep in bed. I killed her without qualm and descended the stairs.

On the first floor, in the security room, three men gathered. They were good men. Men I had trained in martial arts when we were all a part of the Fruit of Islam as teenagers. Taking all the men by surprise, I killed them all.   I grabbed one of the men's radio off his belt.

"The big house to Gatehouse One.   Over."

"Gate to House One."

"Gabriel, this is Aziz.   Who's manning Gatehouse Two, Three and Four?"

"That would be Omar, Mikael, and Rafael."

"Have the three of them meet at the main gatehouse where you are.   I need to speak to the four of you and it might as well be at once, together."

"Okay, Aziz.   I'll do that now.   Assalamu Alaikum."

"Walaikum Assalam.   I'll be there in about ten minutes."

***

The security booth at the front entrance was known as Gatehouse One.   When I got there, all four of my men were huddled together inside that small booth.   I tapped on the glass and Gabriel opened the door.   I stood outside with the door open.

"Assalamu Alaikum," I agreed with the men.

"Walaikum assalam," they returned the greeting.

"What's up, Ock?" Mikael Shakur asked.

In response, I lifted the silenced gun and shot all four of the men repeatedly.   I made sure all four of them were dead, then I shut the door and walked back to my car.

***

In the car on the way to Newark, I called Khitab.   He didn't answer the first time, so I called again.

Khitab answered on the third ring.   "Assalam Alaikum."

"Walaikum Assalam.   Sorry to wake you, Ock, but this is important.   I'm just leaving Muhammad's house in Brookhaven.   Something came up.   I need to see you when I get back to Newark."

"How long, Ock?" Khitab asked.

"I'm just leaving Brookhaven. I'd say in about two hours. Meet me at the detail shop. Do me a favor and wake up Amir. Tell him we got something to do and not a lot of time to do it. Have him meet you there at the shop. Both of you be ready to ride when I get there."

"Insha'Allah, Ocki. I'll be there. I'm calling Amir now."

I ended the call.

***

Star and Crescent Detail Shop was owned by Khitab and used as a place to move drugs distributed by the organization. When I pulled up, the metal grill that was the door front of the shop was pulled up. A black Range Rover Sport sat parked near the entrance grill. The headlights on the Range Rover flashed. I parked and got out of the car. I approached the Range Rover on the passenger side. I opened the door and fist bumped Amir, who was in the passenger seat, then reached over him and fist bumped Khitab after giving them both the Islamic greeting.

"So, what's the mission, Ock?" Amir asked.

"I know where Najee and Gunz are right now. Muhammad threw his hat in the arena and put somebody on it. We gotta go now if we're gonna get 'em."

"Let's get it," Khitab offered.

"Which one of you has the source in his camp...in Najee's camp?"

"It's my source," Khitab said. "But he talks with Amir the most."

"Who's the source in the camp?" I asked.

"His name is Killa," Amir said.

"Okay, cool." I pulled the gun from behind my back and shot Amir first. His brains splattered all over Khitab. "Don't look surprised, Ock. I told you I was gonna kill you." I shot Khitab as he tried to get out of the truck. He never made it. His body's weight made him fall out of the Range Rover's driver's seat. I walked around the truck and shot him in the head, killing him. I checked his pockets and found his cell phone.   Then I did the same with Amir.   I put both phones in my pocket and left.   I needed to rest before my next missions, and I knew exactly where to go.

Chapter 25

Angel

El-Amin! El-Amin, wake up! You got court!" the C. O. hollered through my cell door.

"Aight, bitch, she hears you!" Bay One responded angrily. "Making all that muthafuckin 'noise early in the morning!"

"Fuck you, Lake!" C. O. Jennings replied.

"Naw, bitch, fuck with me!"

"Whatever, Lake. Whatever."

I climbed out of the top bunk. My bare feet hit the cold cement floor and chilled me to the bone. I grabbed everything I needed for the shower. I smiled as I thought about Bay One's grumpy demeanor. She'd been on the phone all night talking to her girl-friend, Lisa. As soon as Bay thought I was asleep, she'd initiated phone sex with Lisa. I laughed to myself as I thought about women bumping pussies. There was no way in Allah's green earth that I could ever be about that life. I was strictly-dickly and would re-main that way until I died.

"Angel, do whatever you need to do. I ain't sleep," Bay One told me. I sat on the toilet and answered the call of nature. "I'm good, Bay. I'm about to go get in the shower and get ready to bounce. We already talked about everything, so you already know what it is. I'ma hold you down from the street and play my part. Keep the phone. My number's already in it. Everything I have in here is yours. Other than that, ain't shit left to discuss. So, get you some rest. I'ma holla back before I leave for court."

"That's what's up. I'ma do that."

Seconds later, the cell door popped and opened. I walked out of the cell and headed straight to the shower. In The shower, I adjusted the nozzle then put the water on hot. I did the dance under the water until my body got acclimated to the temperature. I al-lowed the hot water to relax me, warm me up inside and out. As always, my thoughts ran rampant. I thought of Najee making love to me.   Then the images in my head changed to Carlos fucking me in the sauna.

Before I could protest, my hand moved down my body and settled between my legs.   I began to massage my clit vigorously.   I imagined Najee's tongue on me.   I imagined Carlos's lips on me where my fingers were.   I imagined myself fucking both Najee and Carlos together.   One deep inside me, the other one in my mouth.   Soft moans escaped my mouth.   I put the fingers of my left hand inside my mouth to stifle the moans.   My hormones were raging.   I imagined my fingers were Carlos' dick.   With the other hand, I slipped two fingers inside my wetness.

The tightness of my pussy gripped my fingers and pulled at them.   I used them like a dick—Najee's dick—to satisfy myself.   I felt a sudden fullness, then a crescendo.   My legs closed tightly on my hands.   I climaxed so powerfully that my entire body shook.

"Damn," I said to myself.

I leaned back on the shower wall and waited for my shaking to subside.   I was naked, wet, and horny.   I was vulnerable.   I felt nasty and unsatisfied.   I need to cum again.   So, that's what I did.   Started my self-seduction all over from the top.

***

There were six of us waiting to be seen by the judge.   There were four men in a cage beside us, and just me and another woman in my cage.   The door to courtroom C-10 opened and in walked Jay.   He was wearing a dark gray pinstripe suit, a dark pink shirt and matching tie.   He walked over to my cage and put his hand through the bars.

I took his hand and shook it.   "Good morning, Jay."

"Good morning, kiddo.   How you feeling?"

"About as good as possible.   You?"

"I'm great.   I filed a motion this morning the judge can't get around.   The case law is in your favor.   The hold the judge granted that kept you in jail for the past week was wrong.   The prosecutor and judge are both in error.   Today, we correct that error.   You ready to go home?"

"Of course, I am," I replied.

"Good.   Your case will be called shortly, and you'll be getting out of here."

"Sounds good, but I got a question.   Do I get released from here or CTF?"

Jay Alexander Williams smiled.   "Kiddo, you're going to walk right out those double doors out there.   Any other questions?"

"Naw, that's it.   Thank you, Jay.   I appreciate you."

"Thank me, later over breakfast or an early lunch."

***

"J.   Alexander Williams, Your Honor, representing Kareemah El-Amin, who's present."

"Doug Barone, on the behalf of the government, Your Honor."

Judge Wilma Rolerk's glasses, were perched at the end of her nose.   She pushed them back further only her nose as if it was a habit to do so.   "Counselor Williams, I'll start with you."

Jay got up from next to me and approached the podium.

"Your Honor, my client, Ms.   El-Amin was improperly held on a B1-A last week, when the statute under the   DC   code clearly states that a defendant cannot be held on a B1-A hold under the presumption of other crimes or for past convictions.   And I remind this court that my client has never been convicted of a crime in the District of Columbia or in any other state in the United States.   Ms. El-Amin was charged in 2002 with multiple counts of first-degree murder.   But those charges were ultimately dismissed.   In light of that, it was a blatant error on the part of the government to ask for a B1-A hold and an abuse of discretion on the part of your honor to grant that hold.   In Malik versus the United States, the holding case…"

"Mr.   Williams," the judge interjected, "I am familiar with the existing case law that governs when and when not to grant a B1-A hold.   I am also familiar with recent opinions of the   DC Circuit Court of Appeals in the United States versus Basil Malik.   So, I don't need to be reprimanded by you.   Nor do I need a dissertation on pertinent case law. In a case that was decided after Malik, the U.S. versus Jamal Pinckney holds that as long as exponential circumstance exists, the court can use this broad discretion when deciding whether or not to hold a defendant for five or seven days under the B1-A statute.

"AUSA Barone presented factual evidence to the court about Ms. El-Amin being considered by this court, a clear and present danger to the community at large. Ms. El-Amin constructively possessed a loaded firearm in which the U.S. Attorney's office ballistics expert conducted a test and concluded that the firearm had recently been fired. 'We read your motion, Counselor and it was and still is the position of this court that the B1-A hold placed on Ms. El-Amin last week was justified and legal, according to Pinckney. If you disagree with the ruling, you can file all necessary appeal motions to the Court of Appeals, today. We're here for the status of Ms. El-Amin custody…"

"Your Honor," Doug Barone stood and said," It is the government's position that Ms. El-Amin is still a threat to other communities, and we ask that the B1-A held be extended."

"Counselor Barone," the judge said calmly, "you may not nor or ever again interrupt me."

"My apologies, Your Honor."

"And your verbal motion to continue the B1-A hold is denied. Seven days ago, it made sense to hold the defendant, but today, that is no longer the case. Ms. El-Amin is hereby released into her own recognizance with the understanding that she is required to appear before this court in sixty days. How does the twentieth of May sound to both counsel?"

Jay checked his phone calendar. "The twentieth of May is good for the defense, Your Honor."

"The twentieth of May is good for the government as well," Doug Barone added.

"So ordered," the judge concluded. "Ms. El-Amin, you are free to go. Good luck."

"Now that you're free, I gotta tell you, there's reporters and news cameras everywhere outside the courthouse. I'm not a hundred percent sure, but I'd wager and say they are here for you. Unless Paul Manafort is in the building somewhere. So, I'll lead, while you follow out of the courtroom, through the hall, up the escalator and out the front door. My car is parked outside on Indiana Avenue, down near 7th Street. When we get away from this side show, you can tell me where you like to eat at. Okay?"

"Okay, Jay. Let's do it."

"You ready, kiddo? Let's go."

***

"Ms. El-Amin? Can we get an interview?" the reporter nearest to me shouted.

"Can we ask you a few questions, Ms. El-Amin?" another on the side asked. A stylishly dressed woman that resembled Gabrielle Union stepped right in our path. "Is it true, Ms. El-Amin, that you are still trafficking cocaine into the city for Carlos Trinidad?"

I politely ignored the woman, stepped around her and followed Jay down the hall and up the escalator. As soon as we reached the top lobby floor, reporters swarmed us.

"Ms. El-Amin, did you kill your mother?"

"Ms. El-Amin, what were you planning to do with the loaded firearm you were arrested with?"

"Is it true that you've changed your life, Ms. El-Amin?

"My client does not wish to speak to the press," Jay shouted as he pushed past reporters. "Please respect her wishes to remain silent."

"Mr. Alexander Williams, how long have you been defending Ms. El-Amin?"

"No comment," Jay replied.

"Ms. El-Amin, who killed Fatima Muhammad?"

"Ms. El-Amin, did you kill your uncle and mother in Maryland?

"Ms. El-Amin, do you still have the name Angel?"

"Do you think you're going to do time for the gun case, Ms. El-Amin?"

I dropped my head and continued to ignore all questions the reporters asked. Outside the Superior Courthouse, the cold hit me immediately. I looked up into the sky to see that the sun was high in the sky shining bright. I was happy to be free. The press eventually left us alone.

"Angel, I'm going to get the car. Sit here," Jay said and crossed the street.

I watched Jay walk to a midnight blue Jeep Trackhawk and get inside. As he made a U-turn on Indian Avenue, I thought about a turkey half-smoke from the hot dog stand on the corner. My stomach started to growl at the thought, The Jeep pulled in front of me. I walked down the path leading away from the courthouse and hopped in, I was fastening my seat belt when Jay screamed, "Angel, get down!" Instinctively I ducked low. I felt Jay throw himself over me as gunshots rang out. I expected to die at any moment. I could hear the windshield's shattered glass rain down all over the place. I squeezed my eyes shut with every gunshot. Then as abruptly as they started, the gunshots ceased.

"Jay, it's okay. You can get up now," I told Jay.

Jay didn't move.

"Jay, get up. You're heavy."

The door to the Jeep opened and hands reached in. Jay was pulled off of me and it was then I saw that Jay was hit. Blood stained his shirt and suit jacket from the back. He was placed down on the sidewalk. Jay's blood pooled beneath him.

"He's dead," someone said.

I can't feel a pulse," another said.

Ma'am, are you hurt? Are you shot?" a man asked me.

I shook my head.

Sirens blared nearby. I tried to get out of the car.

"Don't move, baby," a woman said,"An ambulance is on the way."

I nodded my head and then I blacked out.

***

When I opened my eyes, I was in an observation room at a hospital.

"Glad to see you back with us," a beautiful, black nurse said.

"Jay...where's Jay? Is Jay okay?"

"I'll get the doctor for you, baby," the nurse said and disappeared.

Minutes later, an Asian doctor entered the room. "Hello, young lady. How do you feel?"

"I'm good," I replied. "Jay...how's Jay?"

"The police are outside. They would like to speak to you. We checked you out thoroughly and you have a clean bill of health. I believe you blacked out from shock and stress. You were not hit with any bullets. Thank God. So, whenever you're up to it, you're free to leave."

"Thanks, Doc."

"You're welcome," the doctor said and left the room.

The door to the room opened and three detectives walked in. One, tall and black, looked like Karl Malone. Another was short and white, and the third was fat and Hispanic.

After a brief introduction, the questions began.

"Did you see the shooter?" fat Hispanic cop asked.

"No."

"What happened before the shots began?" this from the short, white cop.

"I had just got in the Jeep."

"Who do you think was the target? Witnesses say the lawyer dived to provide cover for you?"

"Ask the witness, then. I don't know," I replied.

"Do you know of anyone who might want you dead?"

I shook my head.

"What about your lawyer? Know anyone who wants him dead?

"Ain't that y'all job to find out?"

"Chico, we got ourselves a smart ass right here," white cop said.

"Naw, Bobby, we got ourselves a cold-blooded killer right here," Hispanic cop said. "Ain't that right, Angel?"

Ignoring the words coming out of their mouths, I sat up and swung my legs off the bed. I found the boat shoes that CTF gave out and put them on. I stood up, ready to leave.

"Whoa...pretty lady," the tall black cop said. "Where do you think you're going?"

"Am I under arrest for something?" I asked.

"You're not under arrest, but this is a murder investigation. Your lawyer didn't make it. We still need to..."

"You can talk to my new lawyer as soon as I get one. I'm leaving."

"Go ahead and leave, Angel," white cop said. "We'll be in touch."

"Or we'll be back to scrape you off the permanent when someone kills you the next time," Hispanic cop added.

"Scrape that dick out your ass, fat boy," I said and left the room.

***

The house behind the black cast iron gate was huge. Guards opened the gate and the Jaguar I was in rode on the grounds. At the entrance to the house, Carlos and his longtime companion Benito were there to meet us. I climbed out of the back of the Jaguar.

"Angel, you look like shit. What happened?" Carlos asked.

"Someone tried to kill me," I told him. "Jay leaped on top of me. He saved my life...but lost his."

Carlos looked at me directly. "Honesty?"

"Had to be her. Nobody else is that bold."

"I'ma going to kill her," Carlos hissed.

"No, you're not. I am. Where is Aniyah? I need to hug and kiss her."

Chapter 26

Carlos

"Muhammad Shahid is dead. It's all over the news up here," Najee informed me. "His wife and several of his men were all found dead, in and around his home in upstate New York."

"That's good news then, right? You did what you needed to do. It's over," I replied.

"It wasn't me, son, it wasn't us. We didn't kill him."

"If it wasn't you, then who was it?"

"Your guess is as good as mine, but I got an idea about what might have happened."

"Your phone secure?" I asked.

"About as secure as yours," Najee answered.

"What do you think happened?"

"After leaving bodies all over Newburgh, New York, we went to Aziz Navid's spot in New Brunswick. His wife and daughter didn't survive the night. I think Navid snapped, went to Shahid's spot and killed everybody. Have you heard anything about somebody else wanting to take out Shahid or his organization?"

"No. As a matter of fact, I hadn't even heard Shahid was dead."

"Well, he is and whoever did it, I think it was Aziz Navid, did me a favor. But that still leaves Navid alive, and I need to find him and end him. Because if it was him that offed Shahid, he's headed my way with a lot of bad intent."

"I agree. Shahid was the brain and Navid was the brawn. Once Navid is dead, you're safe. You're cut from the same cloth as me, I got faith you'll get it done. Then you can come and get your woman."

"Who, Angel?" Najee asked.

"Yes, she got out earlier today and the girl tried to kill her again."

"What? The girl? Who, Honesty? She tried to kill Angel again? Already?"

"Yep. Caught her leaving the courthouse earlier. Shot the car up. Missed Angel, but killed her lawyer, J. Alexander Williams. I'm fucked up about it in a lot of ways. Jay was a friend of mine. I sent him to represent Angel. The girl…Honesty, is about to cease to exist. But Angel still needs you, she loves you a lot."

"Damn! Woman can't catch a break. If y'all can't find her, when I get back then I'ma kill that bitch myself."

"She'll be long dead by the time you get here. Maybe you should call Angel."

"On what phone?"

"Damn, I forgot. She doesn't have one. I'll have her call you."

"Cool. But where is she? Is she…"

"She's okay…shaken up, and stirred, but okay. She's here in the house."

"In your house?"

"Yeah. After the shooting, I had her brought here. She's been with Aniyah all day, thought that would cheer her up. Besides, they needed to see each other."

"No doubt. Get her to call me whenever she is free. I got some shit I need to figure out. I'll call you back tomorrow. See if there's anything else you can get me on Aziz Navid."

"I'm on it. In the meantime, you be safe, kid."

"I will. Give Angel my love. Tell her to call me. I'm out."

"Again, be safe. And call me. Love you, Najee."

"Same here, son. Same here."

***

"Qul-al-uthubil-rabil nas, malik nas uliheen nas…"

When I looked in on Angel and Aniyah, I was surprised to find them both praying. I was even more surprised to find Aniyah reciting surahs from the Holy Quran as she led Angel in prayer. I watched as my daughter bent at the waist and placed both hands on her knees, before kneeling completely and placing her forehead into the carpet.

"Subhana rabbiyal ala, subhana rabbiyal ala…"

I stood and watched the entire Salah until Aniyah looked to her right shoulder and said,"Assalamu Alaikum wa rahmatullah." Then turned to her left shoulder and repeated the same thing. Then she rose, as did Angel and they both embraced.

***

Later

"I spoke to Najee. He wants you to call him."

Angel walked over to the refrigerator and opened it. She pulled out a bottle of water, twisted off the cap and drank from the bottle. "I'll call him after I'm done."

"After you've done what?" I asked curiously.

"Killing," Angel replied, looking me straight in the face.

"Angel, you don't have to do that anymore. That's why you have me. I can send someone to do it..."

"No! I don't want you to send anybody, I have to kill Honesty Phillips myself. I understand the risks that come with that. After she killed my mother, I promised myself that I would kill her and her whole family. I gotta keep that promise. For me and for all the tears I've cried over my mother. Aniyah is safe. All of this shit with Najee happened for a reason...Can't you see that? In Islam, we call it the qadir of Allah. It's his will.

"Had I never met Najee in Newark and brought him here to DC, I wouldn't be here...standing in your kitchen right now. And you wouldn't know shit about your daughter. I had no way to reach you and I probably would have never told you about her. Why? Because there was never a reason to after so much time had passed. But I'm here. Aniyah is here for a reason. Think about this. Had I never gone after Honesty last year and killed her mother, I would never have gone to Newark. Never met Najee. Never brought him here. And you would never have met him.

"I'm saying all of this to say that Honesty killing my mother and taking Aniyah was written, preordained to happen. The Qadir. You found Aniyah, now she knows you and loves you. If something happens to me, this is where she belongs. With you is the best possible place she could be right now. Not with me. Not while Honesty lives…"

"Let me kill her for you, personally," I pleaded.

"No. Haven't you heard a word I just said? I have to be the one who kills Honesty. Me. I know you. I know what you're capable of. With the snap of a finger, you can have her killed, while you, me and Aniyah play Connect Four for hours. But that ain't what I want. This bitch is unbelievable. If I wasn't committed to killing her, I'd want her as a best friend. She tried to kill me not once, not twice, not three times…but four times, four muthafucking attempts on my life and I'm still here. For a reason. To stop her, to kill her. This bitch just killed Jay, Carlos. Has that sunk in for you, yet?"

By this time, Angel was openly crying, and I felt her pain.

"I need all the information you used to go at her family members. I want this bitch to die knowing her entire family died because of her. That's why I'm killing them first, then her."

I didn't know what to say to Angel in response, so I said nothing at all. I pulled out my cell phone that had all the info on Honesty's family and passed it to her.

"Thank you, Carlos."

"Don't thank me until all of this is over, and you get back here safe. And one more thing…"

"What?"

"I found out all I need on the detective that's chasing you. If you won't let me take care of Honesty, at least let me take care of him and the letter situation."

"Permission granted, Carlos. Please take care of that for me."

"My pleasure."

Chapter 27

The News

"Good evening, Maria and everybody watching at home. Behind me is the Carl H. Moultrie Superior Courthouse, where nationally known, African American, criminal defense attorney Jarvis Alexander Williams was tragically gunned down earlier today. At a little before eleven and according to authorities, Attorney Williams had just pulled his Jeep Trackhawk vehicle up to the curb here on Indian Avenue and waited for a client to get into the vehicle. Once the client got into the vehicle, a lone person walked up and opened fire on the vehicle.

"Metropolitan police are investigating this broad daylight shooting that caused the death of the prominent attorney. Miraculously though, Maria, the client inside the vehicle was not injured. According to witnesses close to the scene, Attorney J. Alexander Williams allegedly threw himself over the client to shield her."

"Okay, Aniyah, let me stop you there. Does the Metropolitan Police Department know whether or not Attorney . Williams was the intended target? It's been well documented over the years that the famous attorney often represented clients of ill repute. Does anyone know if this daylight murder of J. Alexander Williams can possibly be motivated by someone seeking revenge due to him getting someone off on a case?"

"Well, Maria, due to the newness of the investigation, local authorities are not revealing much to the press. But sources close to this scene tell us the client J. Alexander Williams had just represented and gotten a judge to free on personal recognizance, was none other than notorious drug queen pin, Kareemah 'Angel' El-Amin. As you know, Maria, Ms. El-Amin was arrested last week during a traffic stop, where a loaded firearm was found in her vehicle. Several outlets of news people had gathered here today in hopes of getting an interview with Ms. El-Amin.

"Once released from custody earlier today, Ms. El-Amin and her attorney, refused all questions thrown at Ms. El-Amin. After walking past the media, Ms. El-Amin stood about there," Aniyah pointed, "behind me I'm told, and waited for her attorney to pull the car around. Once the vehicle, the Jeep Attorney Williams was driving pulled over and Ms. El-Amin got inside the vehicle, the gunman appeared and fired at the vehicle.

"Moments later, passerbys attempted to aid both people inside the Jeep. According to witnesses, Attorney Williams was pulled from of the vehicle and determined to be unresponsive, suffering from several gunshot wounds to his back and head. Kareemah El-Amin was pulled from the vehicle unharmed but was taken to a local hospital for observation."

"Aniyah, has there been any implication that Kareemah El-Amin was in fact the intended target of the brazen shooting?"

"As I said earlier, the investigation is ongoing and relatively early. So, authorities haven't said much, but according to the witnesses we at *CUS Fox News Five* spoke to today, that implication may well be the case, Maria. But as of yet, nothing has been confirmed..."

Chapter 28

Honesty

"What the fuck?" I got mad and screamed.

"True, you gotta chill out with all the screaming and shit. You already know how my grandmother is about a lot of noise," Trigger reminded.

I paced the basement floor in a near-rage state of mind. "Why can't I kill this bitch? Huh? Why? Every time I try…she's right there…and it just doesn't happen! Muthafuckas get stabbed one time and die. Get shot once in the leg and die. They fall down, hit their head and die. Kids and shit get beatings and die. Niggas gets hit with one stray bullet and die. Car accidents. People crash into a pole or a fence and die. Muthafucka pop one E pill and dies. Blow some fentanyl and die instantly. But no…not this bitch! I had the bitch cornered like a rabid dog, a sitting duck…and still couldn't kill her!"

"I already know that. Loud as you are, my whole fucking house gon know you just committed murder."

"The wrong fucking murder!" I exploded.

"True, if you would have done it my way, she'd be dead. I told you to hop out the truck and run up on her while she stood on the sidewalk. But your ass wouldn't listen. Talking about, 'Let her get in the car first. She can't get away. I don't want her to run…' Well, guess what? She got away. The lawyer threw himself in the line of fire and paid for it. Her surviving yet again is the price you pay for not listening to me. You should have caught her out in the open and got her."

I turned and glanced at Trigger. As mad as I was, the thought of killing his ass crossed my mind for a second. "So, it's my fault again, huh?"

"Who else's fault is it, True? Mine? Angel's? Whose?"

"I didn't mean it like that…"

"Well, how did you mean it? All I did was drive the getaway vehicle…like you asked me to. Just like you did that night you tried to hit her in front of her store. Everything else was all you, True! When you were fourteen, you tried to kill Angel. Shot her a few times, but you never stayed to finish her. She survives and for some reason she disappears, eight years later, Angel returns out of the blue and kills your mother. You're strapped that night, but so is she. Y'all shoot it out and she escapes. Okay, shit happens. You do your homework and find out about her store. We go there that night and basically do a drive-by. You hit her, but don't kill her. Months pass by. We go back to the drawing board…"

"Trigger, I'm really not in the mood for a history lesson. I lived everything you're say…"

"See that's your problem, True! You don't fucking listen. You think you know everything! I can't talk to you. I can't get through to you on certain shit. Everything I say, you second guess and then tell me your parents were killed and not mine. So, guess what? I'm done. It's over for me. I can read the writing on the wall—"

"And what writing is that, Trigger?"

"The writing that says I got other shit I can be doing. That I'm taking penitentiary chances, all in the name of love. But from a penitentiary prison cell, love don't mean shit. Love ain't going to buy a nigga an Oodles of Noodles when he broke and hungry. Love ain't gon stop time and keep me healthy while I'm doing fifty years. I said this to you before, but I swear to God, I mean it this time, True. I'm sick of this shit. This 'cloak and dagger,' 'vengeance is mine,' says the Honesty Phillips shit. This shit been going on for almost a year now. Ever since you graduated college. With little to no success. The writing on the wall says at some point you gotta realize it is what it is."

"It is what it is? Are you serious?" I asked, dumbfounded.

"Yup. It is what it is. You can't kill her. You tried four times. It's obviously not in the stars for her to be dead. If it was, Angel would have been dead a long time ago. Nine years ago. Think about this…you walked over to that Jeep and put over twenty bullets in the car. Twenty. I watched you shoot into the passenger seat then move around the side door. All you didn't do was open the door. And what happened? You killed her lawyer and not her. Did you see all the news cameras and shit?"

"You know I saw them. We both saw them."

"But as far as we know, none of them saw you. How long do you think your luck is gonna last? All these broad daylight shootings and getting away. We went to Angel's mother's house, and you killed her mother and got away. Took her daughter. Got away with it. Shot Angel on two other occasions. Got away with it. Tried to kill her in your house. Got away with it. Tried to kill her today, killed her lawyer instead. Got away with it. How many more chances do you think you get? So, my thought is, when does all of this end?"

"You know when all of this ends for me. It ends when Angel is dead," I said petulantly.

"That's what I thought you'd say. Well, good luck on that. Because you know what happens next, right?"

"Naw…you tell me, Trigger, since you seem to have all the answers."

"Despite whatever Benny…Benito told you, Carlos Trinidad's loyalty to your dead father is not gonna supersede his loyalty to his baby's mother. He's going to give Angel his notes on where your family lives and she's gonna kill them all to get back at you. Believe me, by now, Angel's figured that the person who fired those shots today was you. She might even have seen you. So, she's gonna kill your family, or use them the same way Carlos' men did to bring you out in the open, so she can kill you once and for all. That's what's about to happen, but your book smart, street stupid ass is so blinded by revenge you can't see it.

"So, when you're all in here pacing, screaming and being bent outta shape because you missed Angel yet again, you need to be thinking about what you gon do when that call come through, telling you either your family members are dead, or will be killed if you don't do such and such. Either way, True, shit is about to be all bad and I'm out before it comes back to affect my family as well. And now that I'm thinking with my head and not with my dick, it ain't that much love in the world to make me sacrifice them. I'm out."

I thought about everything Trigger said as he left the basement. I had to admit it all had a ring of truth to it, and it made sense. Perfect sense. My entire family was in grave danger and there was really nothing I could do about it. Or was it? With Trigger adamantly taking the position he now took, I realized I was now on my own. Actually, I preferred it that way. Angel was my problem and I had to deal with her my own way. Before leaving from the basement door of the house, I looked around one last time.

"I love you, Trigger. But I can't live while Angel still breathes." I grabbed all my bags and walked off into the night.

Chapter 29

Detective Mitch Bell

Meshawn Tate had a thing for morning sex she just couldn't shake and that was fine with me. I laid in the bed with my eyes on Meshawn. She was on her knees, in between my legs, with my dick in her mouth. I was halfway down her throat as she sucked me noisily. Her neck gyrated while her hands twisted. Her eyes were on me the entire time. That was the ultimate turn-on to me and Meshawn knew it. When a woman as beautiful and sexy as Meshawn gave up head early in the morning, gagging and attempting to deepthroat you, it made you feel immortal, empowered.

As her eyes bore into my soul, I knew what Meshawn wanted, which. turned me on even more. Meshawn wanted my seed, in her mouth, on her tongue. According to her, she lived for the explosion that followed her favorite sex act. She wanted to swallow the life creating semen that came from me. And I wanted her to have it, to walk around throughout the day, knowing part of me was inside her still. I had already cum once, but Meshawn didn't care. It wasn't enough for her. She wanted to eat me until she was full. And who was I to deny her that?

***

"Did you hear about that famous, black lawyer that got killed in front of the Superior Court yesterday?" Meshawn asked me afterwards, as she lotioned her legs and feet.

I was moving around the bedroom getting dressed for work. Yeah, I heard about it. Everybody at the station was talking about it. But I was too busy to catch the details on the news."

"It's a damn shame. You work all your life to reach the pinnacle of your profession. You get rich, get famous and then get killed, before you can really enjoy the fruits of your hard labor. That man wasn't even from DC and got killed there. Muthafuckas don't care who they kill. They just kill."

"I'ma homicide detective.   I investigate why people kill for a living.   You preaching to the choir."

"I'm just saying…It's crazy that a person can't just live their life without hating muthafuckas coming along and killing you."

"It's sad," I told Meshawn. "But it's the way of the world.   Pass them socks off the dresser."

Meshawn got the socks off the dresser and passed them to me. "The news people said that the boss bitch Angel was probably the intended target…"

I stopped in my tracks by the bed.   "Angel was there?"

"Yup.   In the car with him when somebody walked up and shot up the joint."

"You sure about that?" I asked, wondering how nobody at the station had mentioned that part of the story.

"I'm positive.   Shit been all over the news since it happened. And you know I love that bitch, Angel.   That's my bitch right there."

"Why is that?"

"Because ain't nobody ever done shit the way that bitch did back in the day.   I grew up in the Southeast.   Angel was the shit where I'm from.   But anyway…fuck all that.   Are you still taking me and Ebony to Cadillac Ranch out the Harbor tonight?"

"As soon as I get off work.   I promised Ebony I would."

"Don't pull no dumb shit then, Mitch.   Talking about …uh, something came up.   I don't like it when you break a promise to me.   I'ma fuck your ass up if you do that to my daughter."

"Is that right? You gon fuck my ass up, huh?" I asked as a devilish thought hit me.   I got up off the bed and grabbed the lube out of my drawer. I squeezed some into my hand while Meshawn wasn't looking.   Then I reached into my boxer briefs and put the lube on my dick.   I pulled my boxer briefs down.

"Fuck is you about to do?" Meshawn asked.

Ignoring her, I walked around the bed and wrestled Meshawn down, until she was laying on the bed on her stomach.

"Stop, Mitch!"

Ripping Meshawn's underwear off, I said, "Shut up, you talk too much." I laid on top of her as she continued to protest and forced my dick in her tight ass.

"Oooww! Mitch…stop!"

Meshawn wiggled around in an attempt to dislodge me from her ass. I wasn't having none of it. I went deeper into her. "You…raping me, Mitch! Stop it! Sto-o-o-p-p!"

"You can file a police report when I'm done," I said and kissed Meshawn on her neck.

"I hate you!"

"Good. I hate you, too."

***

As soon as I got to the station, I beelined up to Sgt. Voss's office.

"Sarge, what if the person that fired those shots into J. Alexander Williams' Jeep was Honesty Phillips, trying to kill Angel?"

Sgt. Able Voss' attention was elsewhere. Without looking up from his desk, he replied, "Mitch, how many times I gotta tell you, we got enough homicides to solve in Prince George's County, without worrying about homicides in other jurisdictions like DC?"

"I get that, Sarge, but we're still law enforcement, right? No matter what jurisdiction. But what if I'm right? What if the shooter was Honesty, trying to kill Angel? The news said that the lawyer leaned over to protect her…"

"What news said that?"

"*City Under Siege Fox News.* I watched it on my phone on the way to work."

"If you really think Honesty Phillips killed that lawyer guy, but was really trying to kill Kareemah El-Amin, call DC and find out who's on that case. Once you find out who's on the case, fill them in on everything you have. It's called interdepartmental, interagency cooperation, it's done all the time. Let the dicks in DC solve their own crimes. You still have to find out who killed two people in a house on Deborah Drive. You have the murders on

Walker Mills Road to solve.   Polensky, Davis, and Fotham still need answers on that Hasket and Chaney case from Marlboro Pike. And this just in…the little eight-year-old girl killed last night on Homer Avenue was just assigned to us.   Have you spoke to Dom Oliver again, yet?"

"Yeah, yesterday.   She's supposed to meet me later and give me the results of that ballistics test for the gun Angel got caught with in   DC. I already gave her the paper Honesty wrote that matches the letter I found in Angel's BMW…"

"You've taken to calling Kareemah El-Amin, Angel.   You don't think you're taking the aspect of this case a little too personal?" Sgt. Voss asked and looked at me.

"Maybe…but that's just the hard-working detective in me," I replied.

"Okay then, Mr. Hard-working Detective.   Take your hard-working ass over to Homer Avenue and see what you can find out about last night's shooting."

***

"It was Taco Thursday in the household, Mitch," Detective Art Machado said.   "The little girl had just gotten second place in the school spelling bee.   The family is celebrating that.   Mom let her pick out her favorite tacos.   Cately Dunbar was only eight years old.   Shot in the fucking head by a stray bullet.   So sad."

"Bullet came through the window?" I asked Art.

"Yeah. White sedan captured on camera, pulled up to the front of the building. Man steps out and opens fire on the crowd gathered on the front porch, four men and a woman.   None of them were injured.   Only the little girl.   I was here last night on the scene. Saw the little girl laying on the floor with a hole in her head. I'm starting to hate this shit, Mitch."

"Where's the girl's mother?"

"Hospital. Had to be sedated last night. Overcome with grief. The girl was her only child."

"Mom's name again?"

"Priscilla Dunbar. Thirty-seven years old. Works at the Census Bureau across the street."

My cell phone vibrated. I pulled the phone out and answered. "Mitch Bell."

"Mitch, it's me…Douglas," the female caller said.

Majorie Douglas was a homicide detective in my unit. "Hey, Marj, what's up?"

"Gotta call a few minutes ago on the landline phone. An anonymous caller asked who's working the Clinton murders from Deborah Drive. When I asked why the caller wanted to know, the caller…a female by the way, claims she can solve the case for you. I was kinda tempted to tell her I was working on it just to secure the info, but I didn't want to blow the source. I gave her your name and number. She wants to meet and talk. So, that's the heads up. I can usually spot a quack from miles away. Don't think this chic is a quack. This might be the real deal. Keep me posted, Mitch."

"Will do. Thanks for the alley-oop, Marj. Did the caller say when she'd call?"

"Nope, didn't say. She just said that she'd call. I believe she will."

"I'll be looking for the call. Thanks again, Marj."

"Thank me if you close the case, Mitch. Bye."

***

Applebee's Restaurant

Donne Drive 5:50 p. m.

Dom Oliver was seated at the bar when I walked into the restaurant. I joined her at the bar. I could see she had an almost empty beer in front of her. Her attention was on a basketball game as I sat on the stool next to her.

Dom glanced at me briefly and said, "Hey, Mitch."

"Hey, Dom. Good game?"

"Hell no. I'm a big Wizards fan, but they break my heart every year. The Lakers are beating them by twenty in the first quarter."

"Dayyum."

"You're telling me. Here." Dom slid a manila envelope down the bar towards me. "You were right about El-Amin and that gun. The bullets pulled from Samir Nadir and ones in her .40 caliber weapon she got caught with, are a perfect match. Still doesn't prove she committed at least one of the murders, though. But I guess it's a start in the right direction."

"Thanks a lot, Dom. I owe you one."

"No, actually, you owe me two. Tomorrow, you can take an affidavit applying for the search warrant you wanted…on both Honesty Phillips and Kareemah El-Amin's homes. Kareemah lives in Potomac, Maryland, by the way. My judge in Upper Marlboro is going to sign off on them. I faxed him everything you gave me, and he says even without the letter, it's enough probable cause for the searches."

"Damn, Dom, I'm speechless. If this works out, how can I ever repay you?"

"You can start by buying me another beer."

***

The call I'd been waiting for came in as soon as I reached my car in the parking lot of Forestville Mall,

"Hello, this is Detective Mitch Bell."

"I called the station earlier and was given your name and number," the female caller said. "I have information about the double murder on Deborah Drive."

"That's what I was told, but listen, we get crank calls all the time. You're gonna have to tell me something…anything…that makes me take you seriously—"

"Does the name Angel ring a bell to you?"

"It does. Is she—"

"She's involved in this, yeah."

"Can we meet somewhere and talk tomorrow? I'm definitely interested in whatever you have to say."

"Tomorrow? Tomorrow might be too late. I'm free tonight."

"Thoughts of Meshawn and Ebony came to mind. The promise I made to them. "Uh…tonight's not good. I got a dinner date I can't get out of."

"Not asking you to break your dinner date. Just to meet up with me afterwards."

"Didn't think about that. It might be kinda late. Does that matter?"

"Not if it is tonight. I need to get what I know out of my head tonight. If I wait until tomorrow, I'll chicken out."

"Tonight it is, then. I'll end my dinner date early and come to you. How do I reach you, with this number on my phone?"

"Yes. This number is good. Call me when you are ready to meet."

"Okay, but I don't know your…" the call ended.

I made another call. "Hello, Alex? It's me, Mitch. I need you to run a phone number for me and see what you come back with. You're ready? Okay, 202-555-7650. Got it? Good, hit me back when you have something. Thanks, bye."

***

Four hours later…

The phone the woman called me from earlier turned out to be a burner phone. Those were pretty normal these days, because people wanted to avoid cell phone contracts and monthly fees. After leaving the National Harbor and dropping Meshawn and her daughter off at her condo, I called the number back.

The phone rang twice and was answered. "Hello?"

"Hi, it's me, Detective Bell. Still want to meet up and talk tonight?"

"Sure, I do. I told you it's either tonight or never."

"Well, I'm available now. I can meet you wherever you want," I told the woman.

"I live on Cricket Lane in District Heights, but I can't have you come here. My dude is here, and I can't let him see me with no cop. If he even thinks I'm ratting his friend out, I'm dead. Do you know where the Hostess Bakery used to be on Addison Road in Fairmont Heights? Not too far from Eastern Avenue in DC?"

"I know exactly where it is," I replied.

"Meet me there in that parking lot across from Addison Chapel Apartments in like twenty-five minutes," the woman said. "I'll be in a Chevy Traverse SUV."

"I'm driving a blue Chevy Impala unmarked. I ain't too far from there, I'll be there when you get there."

"Okay. Twenty-five minutes."

***

Headlights blinded me momentarily as a vehicle pulled into the parking lot and headed straight towards my car. It was the Chevy Traverse. The small SUV parked a few feet away from me. Then a woman stepped out. To my surprise, the woman was white, with long blonde hair. Even in the dim light of the lampposts outside, I could see she was beautiful. She reminded me of Carmen Electra. I watched as the woman approached my car on the passenger side. The passenger door opened, and the woman stuck her head in the car.

"Detective Bell?" the woman asked.

"That's me. Are you getting in, or should I get out?" I asked her.

"No, you stay right there, Detective," the woman said and pulled a gun.

Chapter 30

Angel

Eastover Shopping Center

Forest Heights, MD

The weather forecast for the next few days was a wintery mix, even though it was fast approaching spring.   I turned the heat on in the car to warm me as I sat outside the Family Dollar.   It was scheduled to close at 11:00 p. m.   Having called ahead of time, I learned Wanda Brown was working today.   Then I walked into the store and made a purchase just to put a face with the name.   Wanda Brown was an older version of her sister, Tina.

I smiled as I thought about how different Wanda was gonna look after I finished with her.   I fingered the Ruger .45 in my lap and then the sound suppressor attachment that screwed on the barrel.   The sound suppressor was another thing Carlos gave me before I left his house.   My phone vibrated and the caller was Carlos.

"Hey, Carlos."

"Hey.   I'm sending you a video text to your phone.   Thought you might wanna see it."

"A video text I need to see?"

"Yeah.   It's the news broadcast from thirty minutes ago.   It confirms I took care of what I promised you I'd do.   It is also safe to say the evidence the P.G.   County police was building against you is in my possession.   And then the gun you got caught with is also missing from the evidence room at Fifth District Police Department."

I breathed a long sigh of relief.   "I really don't know how to thank you…"

"Don't sweat it, Angel.   I already told you we have nine, almost ten reasons to keep you out of prison.   Aniyah's gonna need her mother.   Keep that in mind as you move about the rest of the night and tomorrow."

"I will. Don't worry about me. I visited one family member already and I'm about to drop in on another. By tonight's end, I hope to have completed my mission."

"That's good news, but it's not you I'm really worried about. I know that you know how to handle your business. It's the unforeseen events that pop up from time to time that's got me worried. I'ma tell you like I told Najee, be smart, be safe and be careful, and always remember that you have people nearby that need you."

"I hear you. I'll remember that. Anything else?"

"No, that's it. Call me later."

"I will. Bye." I ended the call and saw the video text come through. Before watching the video text, I closed my eyes and thought about the murder I committed about an hour ago…

The information I'd gotten from Carlos told me Honesty had two grandmothers. Her father Tony's mother, Portia Phillips and her mother's mother, Desiree Brown. Her mother had one sister, Wanda Brown. I needed all the info on my phone and for some reason, I decided to visit Desiree Brown first. Maybe it was because she was the most liable to be at home since she did not work. Having grown up in the area, I knew exactly where the 3000 block of Fort Davis was. Once I got there, it was easy to find 3317, the two-story house near the end of the block, closest to 34th Street.

There was a short black gate that connected to the three-foot brick walls at each end of the front of the house. I parked down the street and got out the car. In my hand was a bag of food. Once I entered the yard, I could see most of the home's lights were out, but in a couple rooms the light was on. I opened the screen door and knocked on the door with my free hand. Then I pulled the elongated handgun and hid it by mid side.

"Who's there?" a female voice called out from inside the house.

"It's Uber Eats, Ms. Brown. I have a food delivery from Wanda Brown, sent to you from Pimento Grill."

The locks on the door clicked. "Pimento Grill? Wanda sent me food this late?"

I watched as the door opened a little and Desiree Brown stood behind it.   She was a few inches shorter than me and thick.   I lifted the bag to show her the food.

"Are you sure Wanda sent that for me—"

Instead of answering the question, I rushed to the door.   I put my whole hundred and forty-five pounds into a bull rush and surprised the woman.   The door slammed into her and knocked her back a few feet.   That's all I needed.   I stepped into the house, the bag of food in one hand, the gun in the other.

Confirmation and alarm gripped the woman in front of me as her eyes fell to the gun in my hand.   "Is this about my granddaughter again? I haven't seen her or spoken to her."

"This is about your granddaughter, Ms.   Brown.   She tried to kill me yesterday and I'm still pissed off about it.   Honesty killed my lawyer…"

"The man on the news?"

I nodded my head.   "Yup.   Your granddaughter is a killer, Ms. Brown.   Did you know that?"

"No."

"Well, she is and unfortunately, you have to pay the price for her sins."   I upped the gun and shot Honesty's grandmother in the chest and face.   Then I stood over her body and shot her again.

Killing Honesty's grandmother felt right, even though I knew it was wrong.   It was wrong for the same reasons that Honesty had killed my mother.   And the reason why I had killed her mother.   I glanced at the time on my phone and then looked at the entrance to the Family Dollar.   The store would be closing soon. I opened the video text that Carlos sent.   It was a clip from *Channel Nine's Eyewitness News* at ten.   I pressed play.

"In tonight's breaking news, Prince George's County is mourning the deaths of two of its brightest stars.   At approximately 6:45 p.m., P. G.   Police were called to the 1200 block of Cecily Court in Lanham, Maryland, where they found a woman suffering from gunshot wounds, near a car in front of a home.   The woman was unresponsive.   She was pronounced dead at the scene.   That woman has been identified as thirty-seven-year-old, Assistant District Attorney Dominique Oliver. Oliver prosecuted some of the biggest cases in the county's history. Authorities say ADA Oliver's car was ransacked, and her purse was taken.

"Sources close to the scene tell us the ADA's murder appeared to be targeted and not a random case. Then hours later, at approximately 9:23 p.m., a passerby discovered the bullet riddled body of a man in a car on Addison Road. P.G. Police responded to the scene and determined the man's identification revealed him to be Prince George's Police homicide detective Mitchell Bell. Spokesman Lt. Jonathan Perry on behalf of the P.G. Police Department had this to say moments ago…"

"Tonight, we mourn the death of one of our own. Mitch Bell was an eighteen-year member of the Prince George's Police Department. He was a dedicated public servant in this county. We will work tirelessly to bring the people responsible for his death to justice. There will be no stone left unturned until whoever is responsible for this tragedy is in custody. At this time, we are asking for the public's help…"

I stopped the news clip. I'd seen enough. Carlos Trinidad and his organization was serious. Relentless, remorseless and dangerous. Having both the detective who was on my line and the prosecutor who was aiding him killed was bloody, but a stroke of genius. The man known as Carlos Trinidad never ceased to amaze me. He issued no threats, no warnings, just death.

***

At 11:14 p.m. all the employees of the Family Dollar, three women and two men, left the store. Wanda Brown hugged everybody before walking across the parking lot to a late model Buick Sedan. Minutes later, the Buick pulled out of the parking lot, headed to Southeast. Before going home, Wanda Brown stopped at a Popeye's Chicken drive thru and ordered food. Afterwards, the Buick went straight to Chesapeake Street. Quickly, I parked on Barnaby Street and ran up the block to catch Wanda before she got inside her house.

I approached her just as she was putting keys in the door and holding the bag of food. "Wanda."

Visibly startled, Wanda Brown faced me. "Who the fuck is you?"

"Somebody you don't want to fuck with. Go in the house."

"Here we go again with this shit."

Inside the house, one of the children ran down the stairs calling for Mama. It was the last words a child ever said. I killed Wanda and the other three children with no mercy. The fifth child wasn't there. It was the oldest girl. Her absence saved her life. I picked up the bag of Popeye's Chicken and walked out the door.

In the car, I ate a thigh. The chicken was greasy but good as hell. After a while I pulled away from the curb. Next stop, Gale Street, NE.

***

I looked at my watch. It was close to midnight. How do I get into Portia Phillips' house? I couldn't use the food route or any type of delivery. I could knock and if the lady answered, I could shoot her through the door. But what if Honesty had already warned her? As far as I know, she hadn't warned Wanda and Desiree Brown. I pulled out my phone and called Carlos.

He answered quickly. "Angel, hey."

"Damn, Carlos, do you ever sleep?"

"Very little. You okay?"

"I'm good. I got a question for you, though."

"Shoot."

"When your men came to Honesty's grandmother's house in Northwest, how did they gain entry?"

"They broke in. Well, not broke in, but one of my men picked the back door's locks."

"Interesting. Do you think whoever that was, can do it again? For me?"

"I don't see why not. When do you need—" Carlos asked.

I cut him off. "Now, Carlos. Right now."

"Let me send somebody out there.   Stay by the phone."

Chapter 31

Honesty

The living room was enveloped in darkness.   My grandmother, Portia, was upstairs asleep.   I sat on her couch and wondered if I was wrong for being there.   I wondered if Trigger was wrong about what he'd said about Angel.   About Carlos Trinidad giving Angel the addresses for my family members and that she'd want to kill them all.   Even though, it was late, I decided to call my grand-mother Desiree's phone again to make sure she was okay.   There was no answer on that end.   I couldn't jump to conclusions about that because of the late hour. The woman could very well be knocked out, asleep.

I dialed Aunt Wanda's phone then. Hers went straight to voicemail.   I couldn't read too much into that either, because Aunt Wanda was still grieving over her boyfriend Dave's death, and the traumatic events from the night he was killed by Carlos Trinidad's men.   She hasn't spoken to me since the incident and probably had my number blocked in her phone.   I pocketed the phone and said a silent prayer that everyone was okay.   After deciding earlier that what Trigger said could be true, I decided to act.   I couldn't be at three places at one time, so I'd simply chosen Grandma Portia's to camp out at, just for a few days.

I'd never told her what was going on hours ago when I got here. Just told her I was sorry again for what had happened, and I was gonna be around for a few days.   My eyes got heavy as time went on.   I pulled out both of my guns…mine and the one that I'd taken from Trigger before I left his house.   Both guns were fully loaded. I made a mental note to get rid of the Sig Sauer nine-millimeter soon, because it was the gun I'd used to try to kill Angel on Wednes-day, but instead killed her lawyer.   And knowing Angel like I thought I did, girlfriend was probably beyond pissed at me.   I knew she wanted nothing more than to watch me die.

When I was in college, I minored in History, World History, the stories about generals who commanded great armies intrigued me.

People like Napoleon Bonaparte, Hannibal of Carthage, Toussaint Louverture and Genghis Khan. What I learned from them was that you never leave an opponent at your back, once you've broken them. Genghis Khan and his army once spent an entire day killing the wounded and men who'd surrendered to an enemy army. They believed in order to beat an opponent, you had to think like them to preempt a potential strike against you.

I couldn't say I knew for sure what Angel's next move would be. But I believed I did. I didn't know where she'd go first, but there was one thing I knew for sure. And that was, Angel was coming at some point.

Something went bump in the night, causing me to react to sound. I hadn't even realized I'd fallen asleep. My eyes popped open, and I gripped the two guns in my lap. Getting up slowly, I had to let my eyes adjust to the little bit of light that streamed in through the window. I moved through the house with silence, then just when I thought that I was tripping, I heard the nose again. Couldn't place it, but I was sure that I heard it. As I moved closer to the kitchen, I heard it again. I raised both guns like O-Dog in *Menace II Society*. As soon as I turned the corner, I saw her. Angel stood in front of me with two guns raised as well.

Angel smiled. "This déjà vu is getting kinda old, huh?"

"I knew you were coming. Just didn't know when or where."

"I told you before, great minds think alike."

"Ain't no getting away this time. One of us is going to have to die tonight."

"Or both of us, who knows."

"You're one lucky bitch. The shit irks me to no end."

Angel laughed but didn't flinch. Her guns were aimed at me, mine at her.

"Came here to save Grandma, huh? Angel asked.

"Something like that," I replied. "Like I said, I knew you'd come."

"Well, guess you also knew I'd go to Chesapeake Street and Fort Davis Drive?"

"Did you?"

218

"I did. Killed everybody but Wanda's oldest daughter. She wasn't home."

Tears welled up in my eyes instantly. I hoped Angel was lying to me, but deep inside, I knew that she wasn't. "I could've killed your daughter when I had her, but I didn't. Now, I wish I had."

"Our minds think alike, Honesty. But our hearts beat differently. I'm glad you didn't kill my baby. I would have died inside had you done that. But I gotta tell you, had our roles been reversed, I would've killed your daughter in a heartbeat. The same way I did your little cousins."

My anger swelled. "None of them had shit to do with this."

"Amen, sister. Neither did my mother," Angel said.

"I really enjoyed killing your mother. Had one of the best orgasms ever that night."

Angel laughed again. "You too? I had one of the best orgasms of my life the night I killed your father. He ate my pussy, toes and elbows, then fucked the shit outta me...twice. Poor Tony. I talked him into letting me tie him up. He was a freak like that. I pulled a gun from under the bed while he was tied up. Never knew what hit him, blew his muthafucking brains—"

Bok. Bok. Bok. Bok.

I had heard enough. My trigger fingers had minds of their own. They, like me, just wanted to kill.

Pffft! Pfffft! Pffft!

I could see the flames erupt from her gun barrels, but no sound. The bitch had silencers attached to her guns. I could feel a burning sensation in my side and knew I was hit.

Getting shot pushed a button inside me. I went berserk. Angel back pedaled as she fired her guns. I moved around, impervious to her actions. My bullets found their mark and Angel stumbled. But she didn't fall. I advanced until I couldn't anymore. I was getting weak. Then bullets slammed into me. I kept standing. My bullets hit Angel. She fell back this time. Her guns went silent.

"What the hell is going on down there!" My grandmother shouted.

"Go back upstairs, Grandma!" I shouted back.

I could hear my grandmother's footsteps on the wooden stairs as she ascended them. I'd won. Angel was dead. I crept up to her body. Then I was hit again. I dropped to the floor. I could feel my life slipping away from me. And just like the Phoenix that rose from the ashes, Angel did the same. She stood over me now.

"Earlier, I told you great minds think alike," Angel said as she lifted her shirt to reveal a bulletproof vest. "I figured you might know what I had in mind. I assumed you'd be at one of these addresses. Anticipated you waiting at one. So, I decided to do something worthwhile. Wear one of these." Angel tapped the bulletproof vest. "This thing saved my life. I'm smart, had I not worn it, I'd be sorta where you are now. Up shit creek without a paddle. Say a quick prayer, Honesty. It's over for you."

I was doomed and I knew it. Despite my fear of dying, I embraced it like a real bitch. A bad bitch. "Fuck you, bitch. Do what you gotta do."

"This is for my mother and Jay. And you can die knowing I'm about to kill your grandmother next."

I heard the cough of the gun. Saw the flash and then there was darkness.

Chapter 32

Najee

"Najee, baby, I did it! It's over!"

"Angel?"

"Yeah, this is me, baby. I love you and I need you to come home. I gotta lot of shit I need to tell you."

"I gotta tell you a lot, too. But what's over? What did you do?"

"I killed Honesty. Nailed her ass to the floor."

"Damn, Angel. I'm happy for you, I heard about what went down on Wednesday after you got out of jail. I'm glad you finally bodied that bitch."

"Najee, I need you to come home. Come home, baby."

"Angel, I can't. Not yet. There's still one person left that I need to find. He's my Honesty. I can't relax until after he's dead."

"Najee, I need you," Angel pleaded.

"I need you too…but I can't leave right now. I gotta see this through up here. I can't leave Aziz Navid behind. I can't." I looked up and saw Aminah putting on her clothes. I quickly covered the cell phone. "Fuck you going at, yo?" I asked Aminah.

"I'm going home," Aminah sulked.

"Don't leave this room, yo. I'm not playing."

"Nigga, fuck you."

"Hello, Angel…my bad. What were you saying?"

"How long do you think it might take to find the guy you need to find?"

"It shouldn't be much longer. He knows I'm looking for him and he's looking for me, so our paths should cross soon."

Aminah sat on the bed and pulled her boots on one by one. Tears were in her eyes. I was still listening to Angel when Aminah got up, grabbed her coat, and put it on. Then without a backwards glance, she left the hotel room.

"Shit!" I mouthed.

"What did you say, baby?" Angel asked.

"Nothing.   I stubbed my toe on the table.   You know I miss you, right?"

"I miss you too."

"Well, in a minute, I'ma be able to really show you just how much."

"I can't wait, baby.   I can't wait."

"I'm in this trap spot in the hood.   Let me get off this phone and go see what's shaking around me.   I'ma call you back in the a.m."

"You make sure you do that.   I love you, Najee."

"I love you, too.   Always."

"Always…bye."

I ended the call with Angel, jumped up and ran to the door of the room.   I looked both ways in the hallway.   Aminah was nowhere to be found.   My boots were by the bed.   I quickly put them on and ran down the hallway.   I didn't wait on the elevator. I took the stairs.   Once in the hotel lobby, I walked calmly to the parking lot.   My eyes scanned the entire area for any sign of Aminah, but she was nowhere to be found.

I walked down the sidewalk to the Porsche.   The spot where I had parked it was empty.   I patted my pants pockets, for the key fob.   It wasn't there.   The key fob was gone and so was the Porsche.   All I could do was laugh.   After a while, I went back to the hotel room.   I called Aminah repeatedly, but she didn't answer.   I sat on the bed, then laid down and kicked off my boots.   My thoughts were all over the place.   But mostly, I thought about Angel.

Chapter 33

Aziz & Killa

"Have you seen the news lately?" Gerricka Dunn asked.

"Naw, Ma, I haven't. Should I have caught it?" I replied.

"I mean, I know you and your uncle weren't that close, but he's still your uncle."

I put the blunt out in the ashtray and handed the ashtray to India. "Ma, what are you talking about? Me and my uncle ain't close. What uncle?"

"Your uncle Eric, dumb ass. What other uncles you got on your father's side?"

"I didn't hear you say all that. Did something happen to him?" I asked.

"Yeah, something happened to him. That's why I asked you if you'd caught the news. He's dead. They found him shot to death in front of a detail shop. I don't know what the fuck he was into, but it caught up to him. I thought he had tuned over a new leaf once he got into that Muslim shit real hard. Changed his name and shit. I can't even pronounce that shit…"

"Amir Khan, Ma. His name was Amir Khan," I said, totally shocked.

"Well, you know what I mean. All that shit sound the same to me. Amir, Jamir, Rhamir, Shamir, Abdul, Abfool…all that shit sound the same. Assalamu Alaikum, assalamu Jamaica, assalaam you fakin. Peace, hair grease and a wild beast. Niggas always wait until they go to jail and start talking that Islam shit. I remember when your daddy came home and tried."

"Ma, I'm kinda busy right now. You called to tell me about my uncle. I'm sorry to hear that. Is there something else you wanted? It's one o'clock in the morning, Ma."

"Nigga, you rude as shit. Take right after your no-good ass daddy. But since you put it that way, no, that ain't all I wanted, I need some money."

"How much you need, Ma?"

"Just something to hold me over until I get my check. About a thousand dollars or something like that. Kita been acting up in school and Jerome's little fast ass got that lil heifer all up in..."

"Ma, I'm coming through in the morning. I got you. I'll give you two thousand."

"Okay, baby, thank you. Make sure you come through, too. Don't make me have to blow that damn phone up. And you know I will, too."

"I know that, Ma. You won't have to do that."

"Aight, baby. You be safe out there. See you in the morning."

"Okay, Ma. Bye." I ended the call and tossed the cell phone on the bed. "Damn, somebody killed my uncle."

"For real, bae?" India said. "I'm sorry to hear that."

"Man, fuck that nigga. He was on some bullshit anyway. Extorting a nigga. Just like a bitch. He deserved that shit. Fuck him."

I pulled out the gram bag of heroin and sat it on the table next to the bed. Using a twenty-dollar bill rolled up as a quill, I snorted the beige powder into one nostril and then took a generous sniff into my other nostril. Heroin was nasty as hell when it drained down your nasal passage, so I had to sip my fruit juice to dilute the taste as it went down my throat. I looked at India's body and my dick got hard.

"Suck my dick for me, baby," I told India.

The phone vibrated again.

India passed the phone. I looked at the screen. "Hello? Who is this? Aight, yo, I'm coming. I'm on my way, right now," I said and ended the call. To India, I said, "Hold that thought. I'll be right back."

***

Toyota Camrys and Honda Accords were the most stolen cars in America for eleven years in a row. So, my most obvious choice of stolen vehicle would be either of those. The first Honda Accord I came across in a neighborhood detail shop, I took it. Using the auto theft skills I learned as a kid, I sat in the Honda and watched the source pull into the gas station.   He parked away from the pumps, then went inside the station.   A few minutes later, he exited drinking a beverage.   He scanned the area.   I flashed my lights to get his attention.   The man nicknamed Killa turned and headed in my direction.   Once he reached the car, he opened the door and climbed into the passenger seat of the Honda.   His clothes and coat reeked of weed, cigarettes and some type of perfume.

"I don't know what type of games y'all playing, yo, but…"

"Games? Ain't nobody playing no games, Ock.   Somebody killed Khitab and Amir.   I think it was Najee and Gunz."

"It couldn't…then again, it could've been them.   But how would they know who Khitab and Amir were? And where to find them?"

"Listen, I need to find Najee and Gunz now.   Right now.   No more going back and forth, they shoot and kill ours, we kill theirs. Where is Najee and Gunz right now?"

"You listen to me, yo, because I don't even know who the fuck you are.   Najee moves to the beat of his own drum.   It's hard to pinpoint where he's gonna be.   Or where he is now.   He ain't never where he's supposed to be.   The last place he was where he was supposed to be was the candlelight vigil.   I did my part by giving Amir the info he needed.   And y'all fucked that up.   Not me.   When that happened that made Najee mad as shit.   He left and came back a few days later.   He's out for blood and he don't care where it comes from as long as it stained his hands."

"What kind of car does Najee drive? Gunz and the others?"

"The others like who, Najee's inner circle?"

"Yeah."

"That would be Rah Rah and Tye.   Najee, Gunz, Rah Rah and Tye are all the real hitters.   Me, Goo and Shottie are just window dressing.   Let me see.   Tye gotta Range Rover sport.   It's silver and black.   Rah Rah gotta Lexus and a Hellcat.   Gunz just copped a Benz.   The AMG S65 in all black.   Najee got a new whip, too. A Porsche Panamera, the new four-door joint.   It's champagne gold."

"Where is Najee laying his head at? Him and Gunz?"

"Since Gunz' family got killed, he hardly goes home anymore. He crib-hopping in the Towers. And Najee fucking with this chick named Aminah. She lives out by Weequahic Park somewhere. He might stay with her, he might not. I haven't seen him since Tuesday. Him or Gunz. Not since the day the old head Umar got killed."

"Old head Umar? Umar Bullock? Tall One?"

"Yeah, him. Najee killed his son BeBe, my man. And the old head came through asking questions about it. He said some slick shit to Najee and Gunz and nem killed him."

"I know Tall One. We were friends once. I remember his son, too. Damn. But let me ask you something. If Najee and nem are your friends, why have you been betraying them?"

"If I gotta tell you that, then you ain't in the loop. And if you ain't in the loop. . . ayo, who the fuck are you, yo? I ain't never seen you with Amir or Khitab. You called me from Khitab's phone, talking 'bout you need to see me, it's important. I get here and we been chopping it up for about twenty minutes and I don't even know who the fuck you is. Who are you?"

"I apologize for being rude. Let me introduce myself. My name is Aziz Navid." Killa's eyes found mine then. I gazed into his. In my eyes, he saw grief, pain, anger and death. In his, I saw reverence and fear.

"Khitab never goes anywhere without his phone. Neither did my uncle. If you called me from Khitab's phone…then you must've killed them both."

"You got me, Ock. I'm guilty as charged."

"Everybody I know is looking for you…Najee, Gunz, Tye—everybody."

I smiled as I produced the gun in my hand. I pointed it at Killa.

"That's where you're wrong, Ocki. They are not looking for me. I'm looking for them." Bullets exploded from the gun's barrel and entered Killa's face one right after the other. Blood and brains exited the back of Killa's head and coated the glass behind him. I calmly pulled out of the space I was parked in and drove a few blocks to a place more remote, more deserted.

Getting out of the car, I walked around to the passenger side of the Honda and opened the door. I rifled through all of Killa's pockets and pocketed everything I found, but the drugs. The weed and heroin I left for the police to find. His murder would be overlooked and pronounced as just another robbery gone bad. I took Killa's phone and saw that it was locked. It needed a thumbprint to open it. I used Killa's finger to open the phone. Then I went to the phone's settings and changed the security feature to an access code instead of a thumbprint to unlock the phone.

I closed the Honda's car door and walked blocks back to the gas station and Killa's car. The sleek Audi R8 was a beautiful automobile. The doors unlocked as I approached it. Once inside the Audi, the vehicle sensed the key fob in my pocket and came to life. I pushed the *push start* button and the engine roared. As I pulled out of the gas station, a thought crossed my mind. I smiled. A killer named Killa had just been killed.

I drove through the city, distracted by the phone in my hand. I scrolled through the phone's contact list and call logs. I found contacts for Najee, Gunz, Tye and Rah Rah. The four people that I was most interested in. A devilish idea came to mind. I pulled the car over and typed out a text, then sent that text to all four men. The first reply I received was from Tye.

"Wya, yo?"

My response. "Near the Towers. You?"

His response. "Around the corner. Be there in like fifteen minutes."

Rah Rah replied next. "Catch you in the a.m., yo. Peace."

Najee and Gunz never replied to my text. I waited a while and then sent a similar text to Goo and Shottie. Shottie never replied, but Goo did.

"I'm at Lyanna's in the Towers. Come through."

I had no idea who Lyanna was, but I did know my way around Brick Towers. I was twenty minutes away. The Audi would get me there in ten.

***

The parking lot near 715 was full of cars, but short on people being outside. I parked the Audi not far from the building's entrance. Minutes later, a car's headlights caught my attention. I could see it was a dark-colored Range Rover sport. Tye had arrived. I watched as the Range Rover drove down the parking lot headed in my direction. The Range double-parked and Tye jumped out. He jogged over to the Audi. I lowered the driver's side window.

When Tye got to the window and saw the driver of the Audi wasn't Killa, it was too late. The look on his face was priceless as the gun in my hand erupted. I shot Tye in the face, then calmly leaned over and out the window to shoot Tye again, to make sure that he was dead. I pulled out of the parking lot quickly. *One down, several more to go.* As I left, another idea hit me.

Block's away, I dialed another number on Killa's phone.

Jabari Akbar answered on the third ring. "Hello." His voice told me he'd been asleep.

"Jabari, it's me, Aziz. Assalamu Alaikum."

"Walaikum Assalam, ock. What's up, Aziz?"

"Najee and his friends killed Khitab and Amir. Get dressed and meet me on Prince Street near the projects. I have a job for you."

"I'm getting up now, ock. I'll be there in twenty minutes."

"What are you driving, ock?"

"A red Toyota Camry."

Chapter 34

Najee

V-v-v-v-r-r-b-b-b…

"Hello?"

"Naj, get up, baby boy!"

"What's up, yo?"

"It's Tye. Tye's gone."

"Gone? Tye's gone where?"

"He's dead, baby boy. Somebody rocked Tye an hour ago."

I sat up in bed, Gunz' words repeating over and over in my head. "What the fuck happened to Tye, yo?"

"Come to the Towers, baby boy. Come now."

"Aight yo, no…wait. You gotta come get me, son."

"I know you fucked up, but you can still drive."

"I can drive. I just don't have shit to drive. Aminah heard me talking to Angel. She bounced and took the car. I'm stranded. Come get me from the Ramada on Melbourne."

"I'mma hit you when I'm outside. One."

***

The tension and grief inside the small apartment in the Towers was thick enough to cut with a knife. I could hear Tye's girlfriend, Shadonna, in the next room crying loudly. I looked into the eyes of all the men present. Nobody held my accusing gaze.

"Somebody, tell me what the fuck happened? Who bodied my muthafuckin nigga, yo?"

"Like I told you in the car, LaLa called me and told me somebody got killed in the parking lot of 715. I called a few people and found out it was Tye. That's when I called you."

"I was sleep when I got the call. Ademu called me and I called Gunz, but he already knew. I made some other calls and texted Killa back again."

"Killa texted you?" Gunz asked.

Rah Rah nodded. "About thirty minutes before I got the call about Tye."

"He texted me, too," I announced.

"Ayo," Shottie offered, "I don't know if this means anything, but Killa texted me too, but I never responded. And when I got here, Choppa told me whoever killed Tye was in an Audi like Killa's. Same color and everything."

"Are you saying Killa killed Tye, son?" Gunz asked.

"Fuck no, yo. Everybody in this room knows I ain't been fucking with Killa, but I wouldn't put that on him. All I said was what Choppa told me."

"Where the fuck is Choppa at?" I asked.

"Around here in the Towers somewhere. He hangs in 645."

"Go get his ass and bring him here," I told Shottie.

The next person I spoke to was Moneybag Twan, one of my young boys from the hood. "I heard the same shit, big homie. But I dismissed it as a rumor. Niggas is saying Killa's Audi was outside parked, but he never got out. Minutes later, Tye pulled up in the Range. He got out and went to Killa's car. They saying the shots that killed Tye came from Killa's car."

I pulled out my cell phone and called Killa's phone. There was no answer. "I got a text from Killa at 1:02 a.m. He said he needed to see me about something important. I was on some different shit then and ignored the text."

"He sent me the same text, yo, "Gunz said. "I ignored it, too."

"My text said the same shit," Rah Rah added.

"Mine too," Goo chimed in.

"Has anybody talked to Killa since finding out Tye got rocked?" I asked.

Everybody shook their heads.

"I've been calling him like every ten minutes, but he ain't answering," Goo said.

"Ay, Rah, call Killa's house and see if he's at home," Gunz said.

Rah Rah made the call. The whole room got quiet and somber. Tye was loved by everybody in that room and in the Towers. The only voice that could be heard was Rah Rah's voice on the phone.

The door to the apartment opened, and in walked Shotgun and Choppa.

"Tell me what you saw, you. Everything," I told Choppa.

"I told Shottie everything…"

"Muthafucka, tell me. Do I look like Shotgun?"

Choppa went on to relay everything he saw. It was pretty much the same story we'd already heard. The same thing Money-bag Twan said.

"Aight, yo, you can leave now," I told Choppa.

"I'm already here now, I'ma chill…"

"Get the fuck out!" Gunz ordered.

As Choppa left the apartment, Rah Rah ended his call.

"That was Killa's cousin Melody, yo. She said the cops called her aunt right before I called. Killa's dead. They found him in a stolen car, shot to death on Springdale Avenue near Parkhurst."

"Damn, yo," Goo reacted with a head smack. "What the fuck?" I passed the living room as I unzipped my coat and pulled it off. Sweat soaked my clothes under the coat.

"Somebody got to Killa and made him text us…me, Gunz, Tye. I'm assuming he texted Tye, Rah, Goo and Shottie. Nobody responded but Rah Rah."

"I responded," Goo said. "Told him I was at Lyonna's spot and to come through. But he never did."

"I think Tye must've responded to his text and told him to meet him outside the building. Whoever killed Killa took his phone and car. That person came here to the Towers in Killa's car and killed Tye."

Gunz and I locked eyes and said in unison, "Aziz Navid."

"A dead man, yo," Rah Rah replied. "A fucking dead man."

***

Thirty minutes later…

There were three of us in the building's hallway, Gunz, Rah Rah and me.

"This hallway stinks like shit, yo," Rah Rah said and turned up his nose.

"These hallways always stink, yo. You act like you just realized that," Gunz retorted.

"Naw, son, I mean like really stink. Like somebody just pissed a few minutes ago, then shitted."

I leaned on the wall outside crackhead Milly's apartment and closed my eyes. Things were getting worse right before my very eyes. Aziz Navid had gotten to Killa and used him to get to Tye. And losing Tye was a helluva blow. Tears welled up in my eyes and fell down my cheeks. I couldn't believe my left-hand was gone. Cut completely off by my enemy. I thought of all the things Tye and I had done together. All the people we'd killed.

I saw Tye with me in DC as him and Gunz took my side and ripped up shit all over the nation's capital. I thought about the recent moves we had made in Newburgh. I could still hear his voice in my ear. I could hear his laughter. I could hear his cries as he commiserated openly about Salimah. I could see his tear-stained eyes, then I thought about the time Gunz and I had spent huddled in Aziz Navid's Mercedes SUV after I'd killed Nadia Navid and her daughter. We thought Aziz would come straight home that night, but he hadn't. After waiting hours, me and Gunz climbed out of the G-Wagon and went home.

The next move was Aziz Navid's to make. And man, had he made a big one. By killing Tye, he'd killed a part of me. "This nigga always seems to be one step ahead of us or one step behind us. How in the hell did he get to Killa so fast? Why pick Killa? And how in the hell did he even know Killa? When niggas mention our names, nobody mentions Killa."

"You already know the answers to those questions, baby boy. Killa was connected to them niggas some kinda way. This confirms to me that Killa was the leak in the crew. He was working with them niggas and they betrayed him. Aziz Navid is distraught about his wife, daughter and family in Newburgh. If we believe

Aziz Navid went to Brookhaven and killed Muhammad Sha-hid…and I definitely believe he did that…that means Aziz is a one-man machine now.

"No rules, no help, he's doing whatever he needs to get to us. I think he probably killed Killa and sent those texts himself. Tye responded, thinking it was Killa and he got rocked. The reality of it all is that anyone of us could've been Tye. All of us gotta text. Me, you and Shotgun never replied. That saved us from a potential ambush. Rah Rah replied he'd see him in the a. m. Goo said he replied to the text by telling Killa to come through Lyonna's crib. Aziz Navid didn't know who the fuck Lyonna was, so there was nothing for him to do to get Goo. Anything else, he risked exposing his hand. Tye fell for the bait. Aziz bodied him."

"And the crazy part is…we don't even know what the fuck this nigga looks like, yo. He could be anywhere, and we wouldn't even know it," Rah Rah surmised.

"Wait," Gunz said. He looked at me. "Najee, you still got the cellphone you took from Nadia Navid?"

I thought about the phone I took from Aziz Navid's wife before killing her. "Yeah, I still got it. It's at Aminah's house."

"You gotta get it. All this shit we been slaying and it never dawned on none of us to get a picture of Aziz Navid. There has to be a picture of son on his wife's phone somewhere."

"You're right, but the phone is locked. How the hell we gon get into the phone?" I queried.

"Don't worry about all that, baby boy. My man Papi at the Geek Squad spot on Evergreen can do anything with any device you give him. Just get me the phone tomorrow and I'll get it to Papi."

"I got you, son, I got you. We gotta get this nigga, yo. Before he gets another one of us."

We walked outside to Gunz's car then climbed in.

"I know how you feel, baby boy," Gunz said. "I feel the same way. I just haven't cried yet. I mean really cried. Losing Tye is a serious blow…I can't believe it."

"I can't believe it, either. My nigga was just here with us. Talking, laughing, joking, crying…all that shit and now he's gone.

I'm fucked up about it, son." Real live tears formed in my eyes and fell. "I read this book about Genghis Khan one time. When he was born and had a clot of blood in his right hand. The midwife who helped birth him told his parents what that meant. She said Genghis was destined to walk with death his whole life. I think I was born with a blood clot in my hand too, yo."

"You trippin now, baby boy. You buggin the fuck out."

"I ain't buggin, yo. That shit makes sense to me, everybody around me dies."

"This shit ain't just about you. Death surrounds us all. It's the life we live."

"I ain't gotta make it about me because it is about me. My actions have gotten everybody around me killed. When Reek and nem brought us that move in Atlantic City and Ha got killed, that was about me. They wanted to kill me. Supreme was in the Bentley with me. I got out to piss and niggas put mad bullets in the car killing Supreme. But they were trying to kill me. After I bodied Mu, I went to DC and death followed me there. Angel introduced me to some good niggas…Faceman, Doodie, George Foreman. Them nigga are all dead now because of who? Me!

Then the Mu shit explodes. He ends up being connected to an organization of Muslim niggas, they can't find me, so what do they do? They kill my family, your family, Yasir and his family, Hasan's family, and all the people who died the night of the candle-light vigil. We retaliate and body a lot of shit from here to New-burgh. From Newburgh to New Brunswick. I killed BeBe and y'all killed his father. Now this nigga Aziz done killed Killa and Tye. I definitely walk with death, son. It follows me around."

"You overthinking that shit, Naj. This shit comes with the streets."

"Did you hear anything I just said, yo? This ain't normal street shit. The one common denominator in everything I just said is 'me.' I'm the cause of everybody's deaths. I didn't want to say this around Rah Rah, yo, but you need to get away from me, son."

"What?" Gunz asked.

"You heard me, big boy.   Get the fuck away from me before I get you killed, too."

Gunz laughed in my face.   "Fuck that bitch Aminah putting in your food, nigga? Because you acting crazy right now, yo.   Talking bout get away from you before I get killed.   Before you get me killed.   Nigga, I'm already dead.   I died the night them niggas killed my mother and grandmother.   I died when the niggas killed Salimah, Hasan, Yasir and Tye.   We started killing when we were young.   I been by your side through all that shit.   You can't get rid of me, yo.   I'm in this, hard body.   Ten toes down.   When we kill that nigga Aziz Navid, then we'll talk about the future, but until then miss me with that sucka shit, son.   I ain't tryna hear that shit."

For a brief time, no words were spoken between Gunz and I.

Then my cell phone vibrated.   I pulled it out and saw the caller was Aminah.

"You talked up Aminah, yo," I said to Gunz, then answered the phone.   "What's up, Aminah?"

"Najee, I'm sorry for walking out on you and leaving you at the hotel.   I let myself get beyond myself.   I was upset and insecure and jealous and I apologize for that.   When we started this shit between us, I knew who you were with, who you loved.   I knew your feelings were with Angel.   I guess I thought I could do some-thing to change all that.   To capture your heart and mind, I thought I could kiss you away from her.   Sex you away from her.   And for a minute, I almost believed that it had worked.

"I tricked myself into thinking you were mine, then hearing you talk to Angel…what you were saying to her fucked me up.   So, I left.   I went home and tried to forget you, to hate you, to stop wanting you.   But I couldn't, then I heard about what happened to Tye and all I could think about was you.   How fucked up you had to be.   Whatever you need from me…I went back to the hotel to get you, but you'd left the room.   You're in the Towers, aren't you?"

"Yeah."

"Well, I'm coming to get you.   I'm about seven minutes away."

"Cool. But you don't owe me no apologies, Minah. I understand why you left. Why you got vexed. That shit ain't about shit, yo. We are good."

"That's good. I was worried I might've overstepped my boundaries or overplayed my hand. I know my position, Najee, it won't happen again."

"It's all good. You good, we good."

"Okay. Where are you, though? Inside or outside? I'm about to pull up."

"I'm in the parking lot in front of 715. Sitting in the Benz with Gunz. When you turn in, you should be able to see me. As a matter of fact, I'm getting out of the car now."

"I'm about to come down Essex Street right now. You see me?"

I saw the Porsche slowly come into view. But it wasn't the Porsche that had my attention, it was the red Toyota Camry that slowed as it saw the Porsche. When Aminah stopped to turn into the parking lot, the Toyota stopped parallel to it. A sense of foreboding hit me. "Minah...pull off! Pull off!"

"Najee, I..."

Gunshots rang out and pierced the silent night.

"No-o-o!" I screamed, pulled my gun and ran at the Toyota. I stopped and let off round after round at the Toyota as if pulled off. As I walked to the Porsche, Gunz' Benz shot past me in pursuit of the Toyota. I could see the driver's side window of the Porsche had been shot out as I got closer to it.

I ran a short distance to the Porsche and slung open the driver's side door. It was bad. Aminah's blood and brains were splattered on the passenger seat. Her head hung at a grotesque angle off her neck.

"I'm sorry, baby girl," I whispered as I grabbed Aminah's body and pulled from the car. "I was born with a blood clot in my hand." I laid Aminah on the ground in the street and climbed behind the wheel of the Porsche. My phone was in my hands in seconds as I pulled into the parking lot and then all the way around. Quickly, I dialed Gunz' phone.

"Yo?" Gunz answered.
"Where are you, son? I'm headed your way."

Chapter 35

Gunz

For a moment I sat in the car stuck. Couldn't believe what I was seeing. I was watching someone in a red Toyota fire bullets into Najee's Porsche. I watched it in real time, but it felt like I was watching the movie on TV. I could hear Najee as he shouted for Aminah to pull off, but it was too late, the gunfire had already started. Then Najee whipped out and popped at the Toyota. The Toyota took off. Something inside my head said, "Go! Go after the Toyota!" And that's what I did. The Toyota had me by a few minutes, but I quickly found it as it bent the corner on Cutler Street. In seconds, I was on its ass literally. The four-cylinder engine inside the Camry was no match for the AMG's 550 horsepower V12 engine.

The cell phone in my pocket synced with the car's Bluetooth and rang though the car's speakers. I answered the car. It was Najee. "Yo?"

"Where are you, son? I'm heading your way."

"We on 6th Avenue, approaching the Miller Street intersection. I'm right in back of the Toyota. On his ass. What's up with Aminah? She aight, yo?"

Najee's non-answer told me everything I needed to know.

"We are on Miller Street now, baby boy. Headed towards Dewey Street. He gotta turn either left or right…"

"Keep calling out streets, son. I'ma find y'all. Can you see inside the car?"

"Yeah. From what I can see, it's just one dude in the car. I think it might be Navid, yo."

"Stay with him, Gunz. Don't lose him. Whoever he is has to die."

"Facts. I got him, baby boy. He ain't going nowhere. He tryna hit the highway, though. I think he tryna hit the 1 and 9. we just turned down Sussex, near the Walmart."

"I'm tryna find y'all, yo. Just don't lose that muthafucka."

The driver of the Toyota had figured out that he couldn't outrun me. So he just drove fast and I followed. Then some shit I'd seen in the *John Wick* flick came to mind. Holding the wheel with my right hand. I pulled the four fifth from my waist. I lowered the window and put the gun out the window. Aiming as best I could with my left hand, I let off some shots at the Toyota. The back window shattered, and the Toyota's driver did some type of evasive maneuver, but it didn't work. I continued to let off shots.

"What were those shots I heard, yo?"

"That was me, son. I'm on my movie shit," I said and pulled my hand back inside the Benz.

"Be careful, yo, don't catch a wreck tryna to be the transporter."

"I'm good, baby boy. I'm good. This nigga is fuckin with the best."

The Toyota tried to lose me by making quick turns and unexpected turns, speeding up then slowing down. But he couldn't shake me. Wasn't going to shake me. I was in a real live high-speed chase through the city and couldn't believe that no cops had got on our line yet. Even if they did, it was going down. Whoever it was that was in the Camry had tried to kill Najee. He probably thought he had. The tinted windows on the Porsche had hidden the fact that the driver wasn't Najee, it was Aminah.

"Baby Boy, we on 3rd Street headed towards Martin Luther King."

"Okay, yo…I'm in the area. If I take 11th to North 6th Street, that'll take me to Belmont Avenue. I can hit MLK from there."

"We hitting it fast, yo"

"Just keep me posted on the streets. I'm coming."

"MLK is about…"

There was a small alleyway on the left side of the street. The Toyota tried to hit it too quickly and oversteered, then overcorrected and ended up crashing into the front yard of a house.

"Got his ass, baby boy," I shouted in glee.

"What's up, yo? Talk to me!"

"He just crashed. I'm about to…"

"Where are you at, Gunz? Huh?"

I looked around as I got out of the car after stopping. "I'm on 3rd Street, by…Giraldi Avenue. About three blocks from South Street."

"I'm on my way," I could hear Najee say.

Slowly I approached the Toyota with my gun out. Hopping the halfway fallen metal fence, I walked up on the driver's side of the Toyota. The airbags had deployed. The Toyota driver's face was smashed against the airbag. I stood at the window about to shoot, when a gunshot rang out and I felt a burning sensation in my gut. I looked down and saw feathers flying from my bubble coat. I could see the hole the bullet had put there. I went nuts and opened fire on the dude behind the wheel of the Toyota. The bullets he'd fired at me burst the air bag, and I could see his face as it turned towards me. Or tried to. The fourth-fifth bullets had hit him. Blood and brain pulp replaced what used to be the man's face. I moved the hand that I'd put near the hole in my coat. I pulled it back coated with blood. At the sight of the blood, I got light-headed. I turned and headed back to the Benz. I couldn't hop the small gate, so I took the long way around. Through the gate's entrance. Then a few different things happened at once. A dog barked. Lights came on in the houses in front of me. Cars raced down the street in every direction. The cars stopped, police officers hopped out and shielded themselves behind car doors. Guns were aimed at me from everywhere. Cops on foot walked towards me. And I was losing more blood by the minute. then they started to shout.

"Drop the gun!"

"Drop the weapon!"

"Put the gun down!"

"Put the weapon on the ground!"

A hundred different thoughts went through my head. My grandmother's face. My mother cooking in her kitchen. Salimah's smiling face. Hasan offering the salah. Yasir eating a sub from the Halal spot. Carlos Trinidad killing George Foreman. The Toyota's driver shooting into the Porsche. People at the candle-light vigil falling to the ground and the faces of the Muslims that were killed at the Masjids.   Then Najee's words to me from an hour ago came to mind.

"Get the fuck away from me before I get you killed, too.

"Put the gun on the ground! Now!"

"Drop the gun, sir!"

"Put the gun down!"

The fact that I had just committed a murder dawned on me. Then I thought about jail. Being jailed and injured.   My enemies trying to pounce.   Courtrooms. My gun being connected to other murders. Being sentenced to life in prison.   Dying behind bars. Tears rolled down my eyes. I made up my mind. I decided to die just like I had lived. I lifted the gun and screamed. Then fired at the nearest cop I saw.

Chapter 36

Najee

"Put the gun on the ground! Now!"

"Drop the gun, sir!"

"Put the gun down!"

I stood in the crowd and watched the scene unfold. Gunz stood not far from the Benz. His expression on his face was distinct. One of his hands clutched at his side. It appeared to be covered in blood. What happened before I walked up? Had Gunz been shot? If so, by who? I looked at Gunz as he stood there motionless. Cops were on every side of him with guns trained on him. I wanted to tell him to get down and to drop the gun, but I didn't, couldn't. I hoped Gunz looked around and saw me standing in the crowd. I wanted to understand what he was going through as he stood there.

But suddenly, his face told me what I needed to know. I watched as tears fell down Gunz' eyes. Then I knew what he was going to do. A scream pierced the night and then Gunz raised the gun and fired at the cops. Gunshots rang out from all directions, and I watched my childhood best friend go out in a hail of bullets. Tears filled my eyes. I turned and walked up the street. My heart was broken. Gunz and Tye were gone.

Two of the most important people in my life had died hours apart. And the crazy part was that I had no clue as to who was inside the Toyota. Whether or not the driver was Aziz Navid was yet to be revealed. I didn't wipe my eyes as I walked slowly back to the Porsche. I couldn't wipe my eyes. Didn't want to. All of sudden, a song played in my head. I could hear it well…

"Day after day, seems like I push against the clouds/they just keep blocking out the sun/it seems since I was born/I wake up every blessed morning/ down on my luck and up against the wind/don't you stop, don't you run, don't you cry/you'll do fine, you'll be good, you'll get by/right after night seems like I rage against the moon/but it don't never light the dark. I curse the falling rain/but it won't stop for my complaining/down on my luck and up against the wind/don't you stop, don't you run, don't you cry…"

The song, "Up Against the Wind" that played in *Set It Off* after Cleo and Frankie died, wouldn't leave my head as I thought about the scene when the police had killed Cleo. It was the same scene that had just played out in front of my eyes with Gunz. I got back to the Porsche and tried to ignore the broken glass, the blood on my clothes. Aminah's blood. I tried to not think about her being gone, but I couldn't. I sat in the Porsche with no driver's side window to keep out the early morning rush of cold air and cried like a newborn baby.

I drove through Newark, the city that birthed the animal in me and really looked at how much everything had changed. Nothing was as it had been years ago. The past could never return to confront the present. And the future was a naked bitch walking to and fro, being unsure of where she was headed. I had to wipe tears from my eyes constantly in order to see things clearly. The end of my journey found me right back where I had started, Brick Towers. Yellow crime scene tape cordoned off the area where Aminah's body had been. There were plain-clothed detectives still at the scene. I parked the Porsche and then proceeded on foot to the projects. Minutes later, police cars swarmed the area out of nowhere. They leapt out of the cars and surrounded me. A black cop I knew personally emerged from the crowd.

"Take your hand out of your pockets, Najee," he said. "And get on your knees. If you resist, we'll shoot you."

I didn't resist. I dropped to my knees and put both hands in the air. I was frisked and the gun I carried was pulled from my waist. Then I was handcuffed.

As I was being put in the back of the squad car, the officers said "Najee Bashir, you're under arrest for the murder of Richard Giles. You have the right to remain silent. Anything you say can and will be used against you in a court of law…"

***

Later that day…

After the processing, I was placed in a large holding cage. One that I hadn't seen since being arrested for shoplifting as a teen-ager. I pulled off my coat, balled it up and used it as a pillow on the metal bench. Laying there I thought about what the cop had said. I was charged with killing Richard Giles. Without having to be told, I knew Richard Giles was "Rich," the dude me and Gunz bodied at the gas station. The murder must've been caught on video, I thought.

"Najee Bashir?" a voice called out.

I opened my eyes and looked up to see an Asian detective at the bars. "Yeah, what's good, yo?"

"Wanna step up here for a moment?"

"Naw. Talk."

"Do you wanna talk about this case?"

"Naw."

The detective left quickly and minutes later, a uniformed lady cop appeared.

"Bashir, come on, you get a phone call."

I was released from the holding cage and led to a phone.

I dialed a number I remembered by heart. "Carlos? What's good, Pops. I'm in a jam. I'm in jail for murder."

To Be Continued…
Angel 5
Coming Soon

Lock Down Publications Exclusive Interview with Author Anthony Fields

Lock Down Publications (LDP): What's good, Anthony Fields?

Anthony Fields (AF): I'm good, bruh. And you?

LDP: We good, lil bruh. Killing the game right now, as you already know. Ain't no other publishing houses measuring up to us in the urban lit game. Like the logo says, *the game is ours*.

AF: Respect. You doing it like *Triple Crown* in the early 2000's. I appreciate the love, homie. The platform is well respected. Thank you for the opportunity to get on board the ship.

LDP: Come on, lil bruh, you're damn near a legend in the urban lit game. The pleasure is all ours. Thank you for choosing Lock Down Publications to put out your work. Speaking of which, for those that don't know you, introduce yourself.

AF: My name is Anthony Fields, but everybody knows me as Bucky Fields.

LDP: Bucky Fields, huh? A'ight. DC, stand up!

AF: (smiling) You already know. But I'm not to be confused with the other people that carry the name. One of whom is my father. Rest in peace to a real DC, street legend, Thomas 'Bucky' Fields, the man who raised me and taught me morals and principles. He passed away in August of 2005. I still mourn for him. Then there's my brother, Thomas Ali Fields, Sr. , who is also nicknamed Bucky Fields. The name was his by birthright, but he was using it wrong, so I took it and made it global.

LDP: Tell the readers where you're from, Bucky.

AF: I'm from your nation's capital, Washington DC, born and raised. Southeast DC, stand up. Ward 8 in the building! Barry Farms, Sheridan Terrace, Sayles Place, MLK. That's the hood to me, but I do it for the culture and my people, so I represent the whole DC, every quadrant. I gotta shout out the whole 69 Square Miles.

LDP: Do you rep the DMV as well?

AF: Of course, I do. Maryland and Virginia also stand up!

LDP: Okay, bruh, let's get down to it. You came to LDP in 2020. Tell the people how you got here.

AF: I gotta tell the whole story in order to answer that question.

LDP: By all means, fam, tell it.

AF: I went to federal prison in 2002 on a fresh fifteen-year bid. I was going through a lot mentally and needed an outlet to ease my mind. I was 29 years old at the time and already the official old head to the youngins. I used to sit around and tell them all the street and prison war stories. Someone suggested that I write a book. I had never thought about writing a book until then. They say the thought is the start of it all. I put my mind to it and ended up writing my first book. It was about my life. But then, I realized that outside of DC, nobody knew who I was.

I shelved the first book and started another one. A fictitious novel that I titled *A Fallen Angel*. It was about a woman who was beautiful, smart and feminine, but she was in the streets, and as dangerous and as hard as any man in the game. I finished that book in 2003. I was transferred from one prison to another (USP Coleman) in '04. It was there that I edited and prepped the book as much as I could. Then, I mailed it to *Urban Books* and Carl Weber, *Black Print, Triple Crown, Teri Woods* and several others. Then came the rejection letters.

I had completely given up hope, when in 2005, Teri Woods contacted me. She purchased the book from me, shortened the title to *Angel,* and released it in 2006 to great success and critical acclaim. *Angel* debuted on the *Essence Best Sellers* list shortly thereafter and remained on the best sellers list for eight months. That motivated me to keep writing.

I wrote *Ghostface Killaz* and released it through *Crystal Publications*, owned and operated by Crystal Perkins-Stell. Bad move. But I kept writing. I wrote *The Ultimate Sacrifice* in ninety days and then *In The Blink Of An Eye*. My homeboy from DC, Jason Poole, put me down with T. Styles. I signed to Cartel Publications in 2007. But T. Styles, who is also from DC, and I couldn't get along, so that deal fell through.

I was then introduced to Kiki Swinson, who promised to take me to Kensington (a major publisher) when she got on. That didn't manifest (it did for her but not for me). I reached out to *New York Times Best Seller* Wahida Clark, and the rest is history.

In 2016, I was released from prison. I started *N DA Streets Publishing*, put out a clothing line of the same name and promoted them both, nonstop. I re-released all of *The Ultimate Sacrifice* books (1 thru 4), *Angel and Ghostface*. Then, I released new books (*The Ultimate Sacrifice 5, Angel 2, In The Blink Of An Eye, Khadafi, and Bodymore Murderland* by Delmont Player). In February 2018, I was arrested and sent back to the feds. For years, I had always communicated with LDP boss, Ca$h. In 2020, during a global pandemic, I reached out to Ca$h and told him I needed a platform for *The Ultimate Sacrifice 6, Angel 3 and If You Cross Me Once.* He welcomed me into the LDP family with open arms.

Gotta shout out Ca$h. Thank you, big bruh, for giving me the opportunity to continue where I left off. I opened up the files and now LDP has my entire catalog. Shout out Lock Down Publications.

LDP: It's all love, lil bruh. You know that. You've been in the genre for nearly twenty years, what's your take on how the book game has evolved? Plus, you've been on both sides of the spectrum as publicisher and an author.

AF: I'm a part of the game, homie. Real live. Ten toes down. I live it, rep it and still respect it to a degree. But time is constant, always moving, not stagnated. In time, everything has to change. Even urban lit. The ways to get paid are few. It's just like the music game, artists had to find more creative ways to make money. So, now they're streaming music and doing all types of stuff to make a buck.

It's the same way with authors now. We have to find creative ways to keep readers in tune and spending money on books. The genre is saturated with authors who don't respect the craft. They're putting out bullshit books. They make it hard for good authors to eat. Amazon has platforms where they print books on demand. Anybody can publish a book and sell it on Amazon. You don't even have to be talented. Just write something, get a cover done and put it out. It's as simple as that. The game now is messed up.   Readers have purchased so many garbage books that nobody really wants to support urban lit the way it is now.   And to a degree, I can't blame them.

LDP: How do you feel about what Amazon is doing?

AF: Amazon founder Jeff Bezos is projected to be a trillionaire in five years.   It's hard to beat a person with that type of clout. His resources are unlimited.   Amazon is a behemoth company that has now become a publisher.   Mom and pop, independent bookstores can't compete with Amazon, so they are becoming extinct.   Walden's…Borders…all gone.   Barnes and Noble are closing stores monthly.   No one can compete with Amazon.

Let me ask you this: if Amazon puts out books on Amazon Direct Publishing through Kindle as an ebook, then allows readers to download those ebooks for free if they have Kindle Unlimited, how can the author make money off of the books?

LDP: Well, there's a formula where they pay the authors based on total pages read monthly, but I get the gist of what you're saying. The game has changed and the ebook and Kindle Unlimited has definitely affected our pockets.   So, you know who benefits most, don't you?

AF: Hell yeah! Amazon and Jeff Bezos! They're getting paid regardless.   Like I said earlier, authors have to find new creative ways to move books and get paid.   It's different than back in the day.   Teri Woods, Vickie Stringer, Nikki Turner, Wahida Clark, Kiki Swinson and others, they got their money when the game was good.   But how many of them are around today?

LDP: Facts!

AF: Everything I just said is nothing but *facts*.   And speaking of authors who got paid when the game was good, shout-out to Al-Saadiq Banks.   Good brother there.   I had the opportunity to meet him in Newark, New Jersey in 2016.   We were at a bookstore on Broad Street.   I respect that brother to the fullest.   And he's one of my favorite authors.   It's crazy, but I just recently read *Caught 'Em Slipping* again a few days ago.   He put that out almost 17 years ago.   Much respect to Al-Sadiq Banks.

LDP: What other authors do you read, like and support?

AF: Well, right now I'm set tripping hard.   I'm on some DC stuff. I'm supporting the homies.   Jason Poole, Eyone Williams, Nathan Welch, Rex (*Pressure Bust Pipes*), Rico (*King Of The Yo*), Huff The Great (*The Life Of A Savage*), Ducksauce Lassiter (*Cruddy Buddy*), Sean Branch (*Money, Murder and Mayhem*). And my Baltimore homies, Delmont Player (*Bodymore Murderland*), and Gutta Almighty (*Dante Bailey*) (*Emms Are Forever* and *Mr.   Don't Play*).   I like Ca$h's books and not because we're friends.   Big bruh can really get down with his pen.   He needs to stop playing and get that *Bonded By Blood 2* out to the people.

I like Askari's books, too (*Blood Of A Boss 1-5*).   Although, I still write in the genre and I love it, I've evolved mostly.   I don't read a lot of urban fiction for the reasons I mentioned earlier.   I like Conn Iggulden (*Genghis Klan series* and the *Julius Caesar series*), *The Game of Thrones* author and everything from the late Eric Jerome Dickey.   Shout out to EJD, and my condolences to his family.   May he rest in peace.   We just lost EJD to cancer, his death was a great loss to literature as a whole. Shout out to Sistah Souljah, but she throwing me off. I paid for *Life After Death* and that joint was weird as hell.

LDP: Let everyone know what's next for you, Anthony.

AF: I'm coming with *If You Cross Me Once 2, In The Blink Of An Eye 2*, the much anticipated *69 Square Miles* (*Ghostface Killaz Reimagined*) and Angel 5: The Finale next.

LDP: Is there anything else you want to say before we wrap up this interview?

AF: Yeah, and I know that people are gonna get tired of hearing me say this, but I'ma say it anyway.   On this new beef I caught that has me sitting in prison until 2031, I was charged as the leader of a conspiracy. I could've and should've copped out, but I didn't. I went to trial and lost.   Certain co-defendants are upset with me for not copping and getting them dropped from the case.   That opened the door for lies and slander to enter the picture.   This coward on my case named Lonnell Tucker, also known as "L", found out that I believed he was an informant for the feds.   So, after I got on the witness stand to testify in my own behalf about me, denying the conspiracy and any wrongdoing, the coward told dudes in the streets that I had Nino Brown-ed (his exact words) and told on the case.   He lied, just to get me back for calling him an informant. He's now denying that he ever said anything against me. But I endeavor to set the record straight because I'm gonna die to defend my name and legacy. And I want the dudes who are repeating the lies and slander to understand just how serious I am about that.

LDP: That's real, bruh. Coincidentally or not, I notice that in all of your books you kill off the rats of the human kind.

AF: I am dedicated to the Code Of Silence, the omerta. I've been back in prison almost five years; had I snitched and lied on dudes, I would be home by now, not in prison with a 2031 release date. I fervently believe the a rat anywhere is a serious threat to good men everywhere. Since I can't kill rats in real life, because I'm in prison, I do it in my books.

LDP: On that note, we're out of here. We wish you continued success.

AF: Thanks, bruh. I'm currently housed at USP Hazelton. P.O. BOX 2000. Bruceton Mills, WV 26525 if anyone needs to reach me. My fed number is 16945016. Thanks for the interview and for letting me get my story out there.

LDP: It's always a pleasure Anthony Fields. Until next time, stay up and keep writing.

AF: You too, big bruh. And as always ... D.C. stand up.

Disclaimer

The views in this interview expressed by the author appear as they were told to Lock Down Publications by Anthony Fields. As such, Lock Down Publications accepts no liability resulting from Anthony Fields responses to the questions in this interview.

Lock Down Publications and Ca$h Presents assisted pub-
lishing packages.

BASIC PACKAGE $499
Editing
Cover Design
Formatting

UPGRADED PACKAGE $800
Typing
Editing
Cover Design
Formatting

ADVANCE PACKAGE $1,200
Typing
Editing
Cover Design
Formatting
Copyright registration
Proofreading
Upload book to Amazon

LDP SUPREME PACKAGE $1,500
Typing
Editing
Cover Design
Formatting
Copyright registration
Proofreading
Set up Amazon account
Upload book to Amazon
Advertise on LDP Amazon and Facebook page

***Other services available upon request. Additional charges
may apply
Lock Down Publications
P.O. Box 944
Stockbridge, GA 30281-9998
Phone # 470 303-9761

Submission Guideline

Submit the first three chapters of your completed manuscript to ldpsubmissions@gmail.com, subject line: Your book's title. The manuscript must be in a .doc file and sent as an attachment. Document should be in Times New Roman, double spaced and in size 12 font. Also, provide your synopsis and full contact information. If sending multiple submissions, they must each be in a separate email.

Have a story but no way to send it electronically? You can still submit to LDP/Ca$h Presents. Send in the first three chapters, written or typed, of your completed manuscript to:

LDP: Submissions Dept
Po Box 944
Stockbridge, Ga 30281

DO NOT send original manuscript. Must be a duplicate.

Provide your synopsis and a cover letter containing your full contact information.

Thanks for considering LDP and Ca$h Presents.

<u>NEW RELEASES</u>

LIFE OF A SAVAGE 4 by ROMELL TUKES

CHI'RAQ GANGSTAS 4 by ROMELL TUKES

TORN BETWEEN A GANGSTER AND A GENTLEMAN by J-
BLUNT & MISS KIM

BABY, I'M WINTERTIME COLD by MEESHA

ANGEL 4 by ANTHONY FIELDS

<u>Coming Soon from Lock Down Publications/Ca$h Presents</u>
BLOOD OF A BOSS **VI**
SHADOWS OF THE GAME II
TRAP BASTARD II
By **Askari**
LOYAL TO THE GAME **IV**
By **T.J. & Jelissa**
TRUE SAVAGE **VIII**
MIDNIGHT CARTEL IV
DOPE BOY MAGIC IV
CITY OF KINGZ III
NIGHTMARE ON SILENT AVE II
THE PLUG OF LIL MEXICO II
CLASSIC CITY II
By **Chris Green**
BLAST FOR ME **III**
A SAVAGE DOPEBOY III
CUTTHROAT MAFIA III
DUFFLE BAG CARTEL VII
HEARTLESS GOON VI
By **Ghost**
A HUSTLER'S DECEIT III
KILL ZONE II
BAE BELONGS TO ME III
TIL DEATH II
By **Aryanna**
KING OF THE TRAP III
By **T.J. Edwards**
GORILLAZ IN THE BAY V
3X KRAZY III

STRAIGHT BEAST MODE III

De'Kari

KINGPIN KILLAZ IV

STREET KINGS III

PAID IN BLOOD III

CARTEL KILLAZ IV

DOPE GODS III

Hood Rich

SINS OF A HUSTLA II

ASAD

RICH $AVAGE III

By Martell Troublesome Bolden

YAYO V

Bred In The Game 2

S. Allen

THE STREETS WILL TALK II

By Yolanda Moore

SON OF A DOPE FIEND III

HEAVEN GOT A GHETTO II

SKI MASK MONEY II

By Renta

LOYALTY AIN'T PROMISED III

By Keith Williams

I'M NOTHING WITHOUT HIS LOVE II

SINS OF A THUG II

TO THE THUG I LOVED BEFORE II

IN A HUSTLER I TRUST II

By Monet Dragun

QUIET MONEY IV

EXTENDED CLIP III

THUG LIFE IV

By **Trai'Quan**

THE STREETS MADE ME IV

By **Larry D. Wright**

IF YOU CROSS ME ONCE II

ANGEL V

By **Anthony Fields**

THE STREETS WILL NEVER CLOSE IV

By K'ajji

HARD AND RUTHLESS III

KILLA KOUNTY III

By Khufu

MONEY GAME III

By Smoove Dolla

JACK BOYS VS DOPE BOYS IV

A GANGSTA'S QUR'AN V

COKE GIRLZ II

COKE BOYS II

LIFE OF A SAVAGE V

CHI'RAQ GANGSTAS V

By Romell Tukes

MURDA WAS THE CASE III

Elijah R. Freeman

THE STREETS NEVER LET GO III

By Robert Baptiste

AN UNFORESEEN LOVE IV

BABY, I'M WINTERTIME COLD II

By **Meesha**

MONEY MAFIA II

Angel 4

By **Jibril Williams**

QUEEN OF THE ZOO III

By **Black Migo**

VICIOUS LOYALTY III

By Kingpen

A GANGSTA'S PAIN III

By J-Blunt

CONFESSIONS OF A JACKBOY III

By Nicholas Lock

GRIMEY WAYS III

By Ray Vinci

KING KILLA II

By Vincent "Vitto" Holloway

BETRAYAL OF A THUG II

By Fre$h

THE MURDER QUEENS III

By Michael Gallon

THE BIRTH OF A GANGSTER III

By Delmont Player

TREAL LOVE II

By Le'Monica Jackson

FOR THE LOVE OF BLOOD II

By Jamel Mitchell

RAN OFF ON DA PLUG II

By Paper Boi Rari

HOOD CONSIGLIERE II

By Keese

PRETTY GIRLS DO NASTY THINGS II

By Nicole Goosby

PROTÉGÉ OF A LEGEND II

259

By Corey Robinson

IT'S JUST ME AND YOU II

By Ah'Million

BORN IN THE GRAVE II

By Self Made Tay

FOREVER GANGSTA III

By Adrian Dulan

GORILLAZ IN THE TRENCHES II

By SayNoMore

<u>**Available Now**</u>

RESTRAINING ORDER **I & II**

By **CA$H & Coffee**

LOVE KNOWS NO BOUNDARIES **I II & III**

By **Coffee**

RAISED AS A GOON I, II, III & IV

BRED BY THE SLUMS I, II, III

BLAST FOR ME I & II

ROTTEN TO THE CORE I II III

A BRONX TALE I, II, III

DUFFLE BAG CARTEL I II III IV V VI

HEARTLESS GOON I II III IV V

A SAVAGE DOPEBOY I II

DRUG LORDS I II III

CUTTHROAT MAFIA I II

KING OF THE TRENCHES

By **Ghost**

LAY IT DOWN **I & II**

LAST OF A DYING BREED I II

BLOOD STAINS OF A SHOTTA I & II III

By **Jamaica**

LOYAL TO THE GAME I II III

LIFE OF SIN I, II III

By **TJ & Jelissa**

BLOODY COMMAS I & II

SKI MASK CARTEL I II & III

KING OF NEW YORK I II,III IV V

RISE TO POWER I II III

COKE KINGS I II III IV V

BORN HEARTLESS I II III IV

KING OF THE TRAP I II

By **T.J. Edwards**

IF LOVING HIM IS WRONG…I & II

LOVE ME EVEN WHEN IT HURTS I II III

By **Jelissa**

WHEN THE STREETS CLAP BACK I & II III

THE HEART OF A SAVAGE I II III IV

MONEY MAFIA

LOYAL TO THE SOIL I II III

By **Jibril Williams**

A DISTINGUISHED THUG STOLE MY HEART I II & III

LOVE SHOULDN'T HURT I II III IV

RENEGADE BOYS I II III IV

Anthony Fields

PAID IN KARMA I II III

SAVAGE STORMS I II III

AN UNFORESEEN LOVE I II III

BABY, I'M WINTERTIME COLD

By **Meesha**

A GANGSTER'S CODE I &, II III

A GANGSTER'S SYN I II III

THE SAVAGE LIFE I II III

CHAINED TO THE STREETS I II III

BLOOD ON THE MONEY I II III

A GANGSTA'S PAIN I II

By J-Blunt

PUSH IT TO THE LIMIT

By **Bre' Hayes**

BLOOD OF A BOSS **I, II, III, IV, V**

SHADOWS OF THE GAME

TRAP BASTARD

By **Askari**

THE STREETS BLEED MURDER **I, II & III**

THE HEART OF A GANGSTA I II& III

By **Jerry Jackson**

CUM FOR ME I II III IV V VI VII VIII

An **LDP Erotica Collaboration**

BRIDE OF A HUSTLA **I II & II**

THE FETTI GIRLS **I, II& III**

CORRUPTED BY A GANGSTA I, II III, IV

BLINDED BY HIS LOVE

THE PRICE YOU PAY FOR LOVE I, II ,III

DOPE GIRL MAGIC I II III

By **Destiny Skai**

WHEN A GOOD GIRL GOES BAD

By **Adrienne**

THE COST OF LOYALTY I II III

By Kweli

A GANGSTER'S REVENGE **I II III & IV**

THE BOSS MAN'S DAUGHTERS I II III IV V

A SAVAGE LOVE **I & II**

BAE BELONGS TO ME I II

A HUSTLER'S DECEIT I, II, III

WHAT BAD BITCHES DO I, II, III

SOUL OF A MONSTER I II III

KILL ZONE

A DOPE BOY'S QUEEN I II III

TIL DEATH

By **Aryanna**

A KINGPIN'S AMBITON

A KINGPIN'S AMBITION **II**

I MURDER FOR THE DOUGH

By **Ambitious**

TRUE SAVAGE I II III IV V VI VII

DOPE BOY MAGIC I, II, III

MIDNIGHT CARTEL I II III

CITY OF KINGZ I II

NIGHTMARE ON SILENT AVE

THE PLUG OF LIL MEXICO II

CLASSIC CITY

By **Chris Green**

A DOPEBOY'S PRAYER

By **Eddie "Wolf" Lee**

THE KING CARTEL **I, II & III**

Anthony Fields

By **Frank Gresham**

THESE NIGGAS AIN'T LOYAL **I, II & III**

By **Nikki Tee**

GANGSTA SHYT **I II &III**

By **CATO**

THE ULTIMATE BETRAYAL

By **Phoenix**

BOSS'N UP **I , II & III**

By **Royal Nicole**

I LOVE YOU TO DEATH

By **Destiny J**

I RIDE FOR MY HITTA

I STILL RIDE FOR MY HITTA

By **Misty Holt**

LOVE & CHASIN' PAPER

By **Qay Crockett**

TO DIE IN VAIN

SINS OF A HUSTLA

By **ASAD**

BROOKLYN HUSTLAZ

By **Boogsy Morina**

BROOKLYN ON LOCK I & II

By **Sonovia**

GANGSTA CITY

By **Teddy Duke**

A DRUG KING AND HIS DIAMOND I & II III

A DOPEMAN'S RICHES

HER MAN, MINE'S TOO I, II

CASH MONEY HO'S

THE WIFEY I USED TO BE I II

PRETTY GIRLS DO NASTY THINGS

By Nicole Goosby

TRAPHOUSE KING **I II & III**

KINGPIN KILLAZ I II III

STREET KINGS I II

PAID IN BLOOD **I II**

CARTEL KILLAZ I II III

DOPE GODS I II

By **Hood Rich**

LIPSTICK KILLAH **I, II, III**

CRIME OF PASSION I II & III

FRIEND OR FOE I II III

By **Mimi**

STEADY MOBBN' **I, II, III**

THE STREETS STAINED MY SOUL I II III

By **Marcellus Allen**

WHO SHOT YA **I, II, III**

SON OF A DOPE FIEND I II

HEAVEN GOT A GHETTO

SKI MASK MONEY

Renta

GORILLAZ IN THE BAY **I II III IV**

TEARS OF A GANGSTA I II

3X KRAZY I II

STRAIGHT BEAST MODE I II

DE'KARI

TRIGGADALE I II III

MURDAROBER WAS THE CASE I II

Elijah R. Freeman

GOD BLESS THE TRAPPERS I, II, III

Angel 4

RICH $AVAGE I II

MONEY IN THE GRAVE I II III

By Martell Troublesome Bolden

FOREVER GANGSTA I II

GLOCKS ON SATIN SHEETS I II

By Adrian Dulan

TOE TAGZ I II III IV

LEVELS TO THIS SHYT I II

IT'S JUST ME AND YOU

By Ah'Million

KINGPIN DREAMS I II III

RAN OFF ON DA PLUG

By Paper Boi Rari

CONFESSIONS OF A GANGSTA I II III IV

CONFESSIONS OF A JACKBOY I II

By Nicholas Lock

I'M NOTHING WITHOUT HIS LOVE

SINS OF A THUG

TO THE THUG I LOVED BEFORE

A GANGSTA SAVED XMAS

IN A HUSTLER I TRUST

By Monet Dragun

CAUGHT UP IN THE LIFE I II III

THE STREETS NEVER LET GO I II

By Robert Baptiste

NEW TO THE GAME I II III

MONEY, MURDER & MEMORIES I II III

By **Malik D. Rice**

LIFE OF A SAVAGE I II III IV

A GANGSTA'S QUR'AN I II III IV

MURDA SEASON I II III

GANGLAND CARTEL I II III

CHI'RAQ GANGSTAS I II III IV

KILLERS ON ELM STREET I II III

JACK BOYZ N DA BRONX I II III

A DOPEBOY'S DREAM I II III

JACK BOYS VS DOPE BOYS I II III

COKE GIRLZ

COKE BOYS

By Romell Tukes

LOYALTY AIN'T PROMISED I II

By Keith Williams

QUIET MONEY I II III

THUG LIFE I II III

EXTENDED CLIP I II

A GANGSTA'S PARADISE

By **Trai'Quan**

THE STREETS MADE ME I II III

By **Larry D. Wright**

THE ULTIMATE SACRIFICE I, II, III, IV, V, VI

KHADIFI

IF YOU CROSS ME ONCE

ANGEL I II III IV

IN THE BLINK OF AN EYE

By **Anthony Fields**

THE LIFE OF A HOOD STAR

By Ca$h & Rashia Wilson

THE STREETS WILL NEVER CLOSE I II III

By K'ajji

CREAM I II III

THE STREETS WILL TALK

By Yolanda Moore

NIGHTMARES OF A HUSTLA I II III

By King Dream

CONCRETE KILLA I II III

VICIOUS LOYALTY I II

By Kingpen

HARD AND RUTHLESS I II

MOB TOWN 251

THE BILLIONAIRE BENTLEYS I II III

By Von Diesel

GHOST MOB

Stilloan Robinson

MOB TIES I II III IV V VI

SOUL OF A HUSTLER, HEART OF A KILLER

GORILLAZ IN THE TRENCHES

By SayNoMore

BODYMORE MURDERLAND I II III

THE BIRTH OF A GANGSTER I II

By Delmont Player

FOR THE LOVE OF A BOSS

By C. D. Blue

MOBBED UP I II III IV

THE BRICK MAN I II III IV

THE COCAINE PRINCESS I II III IV V

By King Rio

KILLA KOUNTY I II III

By Khufu

MONEY GAME I II

By Smoove Dolla

A GANGSTA'S KARMA I II
By FLAME
KING OF THE TRENCHES I II III
by **GHOST & TRANAY ADAMS**
QUEEN OF THE ZOO I II
By **Black Migo**
GRIMEY WAYS I II
By Ray Vinci
XMAS WITH AN ATL SHOOTER
By Ca$h & Destiny Skai
KING KILLA
By Vincent "Vitto" Holloway
BETRAYAL OF A THUG
By Fre$h
THE MURDER QUEENS I II
By Michael Gallon
TREAL LOVE
By Le'Monica Jackson
FOR THE LOVE OF BLOOD
By Jamel Mitchell
HOOD CONSIGLIERE
By Keese
PROTÉGÉ OF A LEGEND
By Corey Robinson
BORN IN THE GRAVE
By Self Made Tay
MOAN IN MY MOUTH
By XTASY
TORN BETWEEN A GANGSTER AND A GENTLEMAN
By J-BLUNT & Miss Kim

BOOKS BY LDP'S CEO, CA$H

TRUST IN NO MAN

TRUST IN NO MAN 2

TRUST IN NO MAN 3

BONDED BY BLOOD

SHORTY GOT A THUG

THUGS CRY

THUGS CRY 2

THUGS CRY 3

TRUST NO BITCH

TRUST NO BITCH 2

TRUST NO BITCH 3

TIL MY CASKET DROPS

RESTRAINING ORDER

RESTRAINING ORDER 2

IN LOVE WITH A CONVICT

LIFE OF A HOOD STAR

XMAS WITH AN ATL SHOOTER

Anthony Fields

CPSIA information can be obtained
at www.ICGtesting.com
Printed in the USA
LVHW081756021222
734478LV00006B/621

9 781958 111567